A lone mutie rushed toward them, lashing out with the jagged blade of his knife

Jak spun like a dervish, trying to dodge the attack, but the creature had the advantage of surprise. The crude knife slashed upward, and Ryan, a little to one side, saw blood spurt from the boy's arm.

Krysty stood by the open door of the gateway, and the mutie's eyes were drawn ____ ____ ____ crimson of her hair. It dived toward th____ ____ ____ ____ sidestepping neatly. Th____ ____ stumbled on the thresho____ ____ plates of the chamber.

"You're dead," Ryan s____ panga raised.

"No!" Doc shouted, grabbing Ryan by the back of his coat and dragging him out of the entrance. "It's set on chron."

The lights danced faster and faster, strobing. The walls were vibrating steadily, and more than one of the six wondered if they were in any danger.

The scream that erupted from the gateway chamber was a tearing cry of anguish, so piercing that it felt as if it were scraping the inside of their skulls. The shriek bubbled for a moment, became louder and harsher. Until it suddenly...stopped.

The chron jump was a killer.

JAMES AXLER

DEATH LANDS

Pony Soldiers

A GOLD EAGLE BOOK FROM
WORLDWIDE.

TORONTO · NEW YORK · LONDON · PARIS
AMSTERDAM · STOCKHOLM · HAMBURG
ATHENS · MILAN · TOKYO · SYDNEY

This is for Dave Thomas, who is both my best and my oldest friend. A whole quarter century and it doesn't seem a day too much. This is with my hope that he eventually finds the pot of gold at rainbow's end.

First edition May 1988

ISBN 0-373-62506-5

Printed in U.S.A.

The frontier is always with us, just a little beyond tomorrow's dawn.

—J. K. Lobkowitz 1824-1893

Prologue

THE LAND WAS A SHIMMERING bronze oven. The noonday sun sailed through a clear sky, etching shadows across the desert, edges as sharp as a razor cut. A lone hawk circled on a thermal, eyes searching the barren wastes below for any sign of life. It had seen the clumsy movements of men an hour ago, but they were of no interest. Now the bird's attention focused on a flicker of movement near the base of one of the giant saguaros that sentineled the red-gold earth.

It was a diminutive Gila monster, barely six inches long. The coral-and-black patterns dappled its stubby body as it moved slowly, legs splayed, head raised as it watched for any potential enemy.

The man beside the cactus flapped a hand at the creature, which hissed angrily and spit venomously in his direction. When the hand was again raised menacingly the lizard scuttled down a narrow arroyo toward the east, its tail snaking a peculiar pattern in the dust.

The man hawked, gobbing a ball of orange spittle to his left. He was partly in the shadow of the cactus, but the sun was scorching through his thin cotton breeches. He shuffled his feet in the soft leather moccasins. His thick black hair was greased and tied back in a bandanna of patterned cloth. His face was broad and flat, the eyes brown slits that stared out across the floor of the canyon toward the winding trail a hundred yards off. He wore a loose shirt in pale blue cotton, tucked into a wide leather belt. A hunting knife in a sheath of tanned deerskin was on the left hip. The middle finger of the right hand was missing, and the finger next to it carried a heavy ring of hand-tooled silver, which held a chunk of raw turquoise in a rough claw setting.

The man sighed, rolling his head around to ease the neck muscles. He'd been waiting for nearly three hours, ready for someone to come riding along the trail. Just to his right there was a long sliver of petrified wood, its heart rich with purple and red shards of rock. The bones of Yietso, the great giant of the legends of the Navaho. At the thought of the old enemy the man tried to spit again, but the heat had dried his mouth.

Nobody had seen any Navaho in the canyons for more years than the fingers on ten hands. This land belonged to "the people." He was eighteen years old and fiercely proud of his warrior heritage, proud of being a fighting man of the Mescalero Apaches.

His gun lay beside him, cocked so that the flat click wouldn't betray him to an enemy. It was a stolen rifle, a battered Sharps .50-caliber buffalo gun, its butt patterned with hammered brass tacks in the shapes of the moon and stars.

The name of the young Indian was Hears Little Sees Far, references to his deafness, caused by a misfired cartridge in that same gun, and his keen eyesight.

There was a small piece of jerky in the pouch at his belt, and he absently chewed at a strip of it. By lying still he was conserving his bodily fluids, holding off from needing water. His pony was tethered in a box canyon three miles east, and there was a metal canteen tied to the blanket. It was covered in canvas and stamped with the letters U.S. and the number 7 on its side.

A half hour drifted soundlessly by. The hawk gave up watching the skittering lizard, fearing the closeness of the hiding man. It angled its wings and sailed off southward, across the serrated land. There might be better pickings in the steep-sided valley where the river ran, even at the height of the New Mexico summer.

Hears Little Sees Far kept his breathing steady, conserving his energy. The word around the wickiups of his tribe was that a lone man drove his wagon along this trail once every seven days. The white man carried liquor on his wagon. Sometimes he would even have a white woman with him. The Mescalero youth had never had a white woman before, and his loins surged at the thought. His hand crept out and caressed the narrow trigger of the old buffalo rifle at his side.

"It will be good," he muttered to himself.

HE SAW THE DUST CLOUD rising in sinuous curves through the hot, windless air of the afternoon, a pale gray spiral moving toward him. As good as his sight was, the young man couldn't yet make out what was at the center of the cloud.

The dust soared higher, and he could make out a pair of ponderous oxen drawing a white-topped wagon. It was the one.

Moving with an infinite caution, the Apache drew the Sharps to him and cradled his face against the warm metal, squinting one-eyed along the sights. He drew a careful bead on the nearer of the pair of oxen, his finger settling on the trigger.

Something struck him. A smashing blow in the center of his spine, a hand's span above the leather belt. It jerked his whole body, the gun dropping from his nerveless fingers. His head was thrown back in shock, eyes staring blindly into the screaming light of the sun. His legs kicked uncontrollably, and he felt warmth around his thighs where he'd fouled himself. Vaguely, in the far-off distance, the young warrior's ears caught the rumble of a shot being fired, the sound echoing off the cliffs on the farther side of the wide valley.

"Good shot, trooper," said the tall, lean man on the ridge behind the dying Indian.

"Thank you, General," the soldier replied, rising from his crouched position, the smoking Springfield .45 carbine in his gloved right hand. It was the reliable 1873 model.

"Looks like his back's broke. Best go and finish the bastard off."

"Yes, sir." The trooper saluted and walked leisurely down the slope, drawing the Colt Navy from his belt. The rest of the troop sat on their horses, waiting quietly. All were dressed in the dusty blue uniforms of the Seventh Cavalry.

Their leader brushed at the orange dirt on his yellow-striped breeches with the back of his hand. He was a little above average height and as skinny as a lath. Everything about him was thin and tight: narrow eyes, slitted against the New Mexico sun; lips drawn like a line of ink. He had an oddly yellow complexion for a man who spent so much time out of doors, and the corner of his mouth was turned down and seamed with old scar tissue, as though from a vicious blow. Nobody ever asked him how he got the injury. Under the hat there was a cascade of tumbling yellow hair, as gold as Kansas wheat. A brass-hilted saber hung at the officer's left hip, the tip of the scabbard scraping the earth.

The afternoon was disturbed a second time as the trooper stooped by the twitching Mescalero and put the muzzle of his well-used pistol just behind the right ear, taking care not to get grease on the gun. He squeezed the trigger and stepped smartly away from the fountain of blood and brains that spurted from the Indian's skull.

"That's 'nother good Indian, General," called the grizzled sergeant, leaning from the high McClellan army saddle and spitting out a stream of tobacco juice.

"Yeah. Kill one cub don't mean you got all the family. Day's coming when we need to burn out the nest."

"Wanna bring up the dune wag for the body?" the trooper shouted.

"No, leave him be. Let him rot."

"Want me to radio Cutter on the ox cart? Let him know what went down?"

The blond officer nodded, then turned on his heel and stalked toward the rest of the detachment of soldiers. He paused from habit, checking that the Stechkin 9 mm automatic pistol with the laser nightsight was snugly in its holster. The quartz wrist chron showed seven minutes and eleven seconds before three o'clock. It had been a worthwhile hunt and kill.

The puckered lips parted in something near to a smile, but the smile never got within a country mile of the cold, slitted eyes.

Chapter One

NOT FAR FROM THE Mohawk River in what had been called, nearly a century back, New York State, the summer sky was clear, but the tops of mountains still held pockets of tired snow in the shadowed high valleys. Chem clouds in virulent shades of purple and crimson were gathering far to the north, showing the signs of grim storms to come. Low on the horizon the six friends had glimpsed the fiery starburst of a hunk of prenuke hardware finally finding its way home through the polluted upper levels of Earth's atmosphere.

It was close to six months since the friends had last stood on the high plateau, which had been scraped from the side of the hill by an earthslide. The redoubt behind them had been one of those built in the late 1990s in isolated and secret places.

The leader of the group, a rangy man in his midthirties, stood on the edge of the drop, staring down at the ropes of dark blue plaited plaslon that had enabled them to make the dangerous climb. The redoubt had been untouched since the day the world caught fire in January 2001, protected by its inaccessibility. When they'd first reached the place, it had looked as though they might never get off the mountain. But they'd made it and traveled to Virginia and done there what they'd set out to do. Now, after some bizarre adventures, they'd returned to the redoubt.

"Looks like someone's been up here, J.B.," Ryan said. "Marks of feet hereabouts."

"Wouldn't have gotten inside unless they knew the entry code."

The second speaker was J. B. Dix, the armorer of the group, a short, terse man who wore a battered fedora hat and wire-rimmed glasses. The brown shirt and gray pants were stained and worn, as were the high combat boots. There was a mini-Uzi slung across his shoulders on a webbing strap and a Steyr AUG 5.6 mm pistol on his right hip.

"Doors seem shut tight, Ryan," said the third member of the party. She was a tall girl with startlingly green eyes and even more startling red hair, red like spilled arterial blood, not like warm copper. She was only an inch short of six feet with a leanly beautiful body. She wore khaki overalls, torn across the shoulder and stained with what could have been dried blood. Her boots were dark blue leather, with stacked Western heels. They were ornamented with silver, spread-wing falcons, and the toes were chiseled points of silver metal. Her name was Krysty Wroth, and she was in her mid-twenties. Krysty was the part-mutie lover of the group's unchallenged leader, Ryan Cawdor.

Wearing the same type of clothes as J. B. Dix, Cawdor stood a couple of inches over six feet, weighing a muscular two hundred pounds. He had a mass of dark, curling hair that coiled to his nape. The most striking feature of the harsh face was the black eye patch that covered the left socket. The right side of his face was disfigured by a jagged scar that sliced from the corner of his eye to below the angle of his mouth.

The wind tugged at the long fur-trimmed gray coat that he wore over his pants and shirt. On his left hip was an eighteen-inch-long steel panga, which was balanced on the right side by a handblaster, a 9 mm SIG-Sauer P-226 pistol—twenty-five and a half ounces of efficient chilling machine. Ryan gripped a Heckler & Koch G-12 automatic rifle in his right hand, and carried a couple of spare fifty-shot mags in his coat pockets.

"We better take care when we get inside," he said. "Could be trouble. And before we get to the gateway and the mat-trans chamber we'll stock up on bullets, get some self-heats and ring-pulls of food and water. Fresh backpacks. They'll come in handy."

"Don't like self-heats. Taste like warm mud. Not so good."

They laughed at the vehemence and disgust in the voice. It came from fourteen-year-old Jak Lauren, who'd joined them less than a year ago when they were involved in bloody fighting down in Louisiana. Fully clothed and soaking wet, he weighed in at just over one hundred pounds, but he was the most lethally destructive hand-to-hand fighter Ryan Cawdor had ever seen. And he'd seen plenty.

Jak was dressed in denim jeans with a jacket made out of leather and canvas, hand-colored to camouflage it, in gray, green and brown. Under it he wore a ragged fur vest, with the sleeves hacked out. A massive .357 Magnum pistol with a six-inch barrel stuck out of a crude leather holster on his hip. Concealed on his person were several slim, leaf-bladed throwing knives.

But your first impression of Jak Lauren didn't include any of that. The first thing you noticed was the mane of pure white hair that floated across the whipcord shoulders. Then you saw the eyes, glowing deep in the sockets of wind-scoured ivory like angry rubies. The contrast with his colorless skin was startling. Jak also carried facial scars. One disfigured his narrow nose, and another gouged jaggedly over the left cheek, tugging the corner of the mouth up in a crooked, mocking, perpetual smile.

The other two members of the party were huddled in the lee of the overhanging rock shelf, by the doors into the complex. One was a tall, staggeringly beautiful blond girl, wearing a short crimson skirt and blouse under a gray fur coat. As she shifted her feet tiny silver spurs on the high heels of her red boots tinkled delicately. Her name was Lori Quint, and she was sixteen years old.

The man with his arm around her, against the rising wind, was her lover, teacher and protector. He was older. Measure it one way, and he was around 230. Put another way he might only be somewhere around thirty-two years old. He looked to be in his mid-sixties.

In fact, Dr. Theophilus Algernon Tanner had been born in South Strafford, Vermont, on February 14, 1868. On June 17, 1891, he'd married Emily Louise Chandler. They'd had two children, Rachel and Jolyon. In November of 1896 Doc Tanner had disappeared.

The scientists on Project Cerberus, operating from a redoubt in Virginia, had been carrying out experiments in time travel, a process known in the arcane trade as "trawling." They'd tried several times, including picking up a Supreme Court judge. But what arrived in the chron-trans chamber generally resembled several pounds of chopped liver. Their single success was Doc Tanner, who arrived with them, more or less in one piece, in 1998.

Having been untimely ripped from his own home and life, Doc proved exceedingly uncooperative with the gray-faced men in white lab coats. Though they tried to involve him in their work, he kept insisting on being returned to his family. In fact, he made several illegal attempts to operate the chron-trans himself. In the end he became a guinea pig for a second time.

This time the transmission took place in December 2000, only a matter of days before the holocaust that destroyed civilization throughout the planet. Doc was plunged forward into a dreadful world, nearly a hundred years on, to a frontier dirt ville called Mocsin, up near the Darks. His mind scrambled, he was taken prisoner by the local baron, Jordan Teague and became the particular toy of the sec chief, the appalling Cort Strasser.

Eventually, after the bloody shambles of a big firefight, the old man was rescued by Ryan Cawdor.

Doc's memory was still erratic, but he was generally becoming more coherent.

Ryan glanced back at him. In some odd way, Doc seemed to be getting younger. Maybe it was the influence of Lori Quint.

Tanner was the tallest of the party, topping Ryan by an inch or so, and was skinny built, wearing a stained and faded frock coat over a blue denim shirt. His shrunk shanks slotted into cracked knee boots.

Doc's face was deeply lined, his were eyes a pale blue and a fringe of long gray hair framed his skull. Despite his age, Doc's teeth were peculiarly excellent. His voice was rich and deep, compelling attention.

For some time after they first met, Ryan never saw Doc Tanner without a battered stovepipe hat that looked like it could have once belonged to Abe Lincoln. But when they were sailing down the Hudson, heading south from the redoubt toward Virginia, Doc had lost patience with the hat and wheeled it into the foaming water.

Doc's contribution to the armament of the group was twofold. He carried an elegant ebony walking stick with a silver lion's head as its handle. A twist and a pull revealed the steel rapier blade concealed inside the cane. And on his hip, in a hand-tooled Mexican rig, was a gun about as old as Doc himself. It was a double-barreled Le Mat blaster, which fired .36-caliber ammunition. A quick adjustment of the firing pin and it blasted out a single round of .63 scattergun ammunition. Doc wasn't much of a marksman, but using the shotgun barrel of the Le Mat at close range meant you didn't need to be that good.

They were six friends, moving through the scorched lands like a cleansing wind, generally leaving things a little better than they found them.

"THREE-FIVE-TWO CODE, DOC?"

"I beg your pardon, my dear Ryan? What was that you said?"

"Let her go and pay attention. Entrance code into the redoubt?"

"I would imagine that it is three and five and two, Ryan, is it not?"

"Let's try it."

The wind was rising and the chem clouds gathering to spring. Already they could make out jagged silver slashes of lightning spearing the tops of the mountains to the north. Ryan had seen storms so severe that they could kill an unprotected man, and Trader had often mentioned seeing freak weather down south that carried acid rain from hot spots—powerful enough to take the skin off a person in a couple of minutes. And kill him in five.

Ryan punched in the number code on the elevated panel, waiting for the familiar hiss of hydraulics as the powerful sec doors began to operate.

The darkness within suddenly blossomed with light as the sensors picked up movement of the doors. As soon as the gap was wide enough, Jak darted through, blaster in hand, calling for the others to follow him as soon as he was sure the main entrance region was safe and clear. Ryan came though last, feeling the sting of hail on his cheeks as the storm came shrieking in after them.

The reverse code of 2-5-3 sent the doors sliding shut once more. The noise of the wind was muffled, then ceased. Inside the redoubt there was the familiar feeling of dead, stale air and a heavy silence all around them. Ryan took a deep breath.

"Nobody here," he said.

"Mebbe, lover," Krysty replied quietly.

"You hear something?" J.B. asked, keeping the Uzi at the ready.

"Can't tell. Someone's been here recently. Within the last week or so. But the doors..."

Ryan had already checked. From the prints in the dust he could clearly make out that nobody had been in or out that way since they passed through the doors, months ago.

"Mebbe someone saw when we come out and started poking around? Thought we came from inside so could get in. Mebbe." Jak shook his head.

"Better get stocked up on ammo, then go to the dorms and sleep. Rest up. We'll go to the mat-trans gateway in the morning after we eat. How's that sound to everyone else?"

Looking around, Ryan realized how bone-weary they all looked. It had been hard times trying to return to this redoubt, far harder than he'd imagined when they left Virginia. Maybe it would be better if they took a few days in the safety of the redoubt to recharge their personal batteries.

"Beds first," Lori said, yawning.

"I believe that I might second that particular motion, Ryan," Doc added. "It's been too long since I laid these weary old bones on anything softer than granite."

"Sure thing, Doc, straight to the dorms. Eat. Sleep. We'll see how the morning looks."

The plan of the complex, just inside the main entrance, showed that the redoubt had only the single way in and out. But if Krysty's mutie senses were to be believed, and someone had gotten in, then the earthslides over the years could have exposed some distant part of the building.

It was cold inside, despite the warmth of the summer weather outside. It seemed to Ryan that more of the lights in the angles of walls and ceilings had malfunctioned. It crossed his mind—but he set the thought aside—that the gateway itself might also have stopped working.

They went along in a careful single file, Jak in the lead, followed by Ryan. Then came Krysty, followed by Doc and Lori. As usual, J.B. brought up the rear of the group.

At each interior door, or at the turning of a passage, everyone stopped, flattened against the curving walls, waiting until Jak had checked it out. One of the Trader's sayings that Ryan remembered was about caution. "Nobody ever gotten himself chilled from being careful."

Even so, the ambush was so skillfully laid that it nearly took them.

Chapter Two

THE MUTIES MUST HAVE had phenomenal hearing, sharp enough to catch the whispering sounds of Ryan and the others as they cat-footed their way along the corridors, giving them time to lay their plan and take up their hiding places.

They'd picked the spot well.

It was an open area that had probably been used by the guards of the redoubt for eating. There were several dozen plas-topped tables stacked along one wall, and a metal serving counter ran down the center, with deep recesses spaced along its length, which would have held the dishes of food.

The corridor opposite led directly to the sleeping quarters, then to the storage sections of the redoubt and finally to the mat-trans gateway.

Jak Lauren had been moaning about feeling hungry and thirsty, turning to call to Ryan. "Dry as nun's..."

If the muties had been armed with blasters they could easily have sent all six to buy the farm.

The tables went skittering over as four came bursting out from cover, and a half dozen leaped from the shadowy hollows of the serving counter. All were screaming and whooping and holding knives and spears.

In that microsecond of shock, Ryan's fighting brain was working in overdrive, appraising the situation. Calculating odds and angles. Ten against six. Lances against blasters. Surprise on their side.

None of the muties was taller than five and a half feet. They were men, with the tops of their skulls shaved clean and a shaggy fringe of hair dangling at the sides and back. All wore home-weave jerkins and pants, and sandals made from old land wag tires.

The attack was so unexpected that the muties got close to their targets without a single shot being fired.

The ones from behind the tables concentrated on Doc and Lori, rushing them, screaming in high, guttural voices. J.B. whirled, facing two more, while Krysty and Ryan spun to defend themselves against the last three muties. Jak, in the lead, was far enough ahead of the rest to be spared the initial attack.

It couldn't properly be called a firefight, as the combat was too close for blasters to play much of a part.

Only the Armorer managed to snap off any bullets, squeezing the trigger on the Uzi, hearing its lethal chatter as it ripped open the bellies and chests of the two muties that had chosen him for their prey. Both went tumbling over in a welter of blood and flailing arms and legs. Their lances and knives went clattering across the plas-tiles of the old cafeteria.

The other five of J.B.'s companions were too tangled with their enemies for him to risk using the blaster again.

Lori screamed as a knife flashed, opening her blouse and leaving a thin crimson line of blood seeping over the ribs. Doc had a moment to twist the lion's head of his ebony cane, dropping the cover and lashing out with the hissing steel. The rapier wasn't really suited to the rough-and-tumble of close combat, but the old-timer succeeded in pinking one of the muties neatly through the throat, cutting the vocal cords and silencing the yelps. He withdrew the blade and lunged again, this time beneath the upraised right arm. The point pierced through the man's heart.

Krysty kicked out at the first of her attackers, slowing down his charge, giving her a splinter of frozen time to draw the 9 mm Heckler & Koch from its holster. But the mutie cocked his arm and threw his spear at her, knocking the blaster from her hand.

Ryan drew the honed cleaver from his belt, feeling the wooden hilt match his fingers. The balance of the eighteen-inch blade was perfect for hacking in a melee like this one and he waded in, lips pulled off his teeth in a ferocious grin.

He swung it in a singing figure eight, holding off the pair of whooping muties, forcing them to retreat toward the counter. One thrust at him with the spear, and Ryan chopped the point off. The man stopped, jaw gaping at Ryan's speed and power. It was all the chance the one-eyed angel of death needed. A feint toward the face and then a devastating blow to the thigh. The panga snapped the long bone, severing the femoral artery and putting a fourth gibbering mutant down on the floor. His blood gushed out, patterning the polished metal of the serving counter.

The other man facing Ryan turned to run, realizing that the ambush had failed. But Ryan wasn't done.

In three quick steps he overtook the scuttling little figure, the blood-slick blade hefted high. He brought it hacking down to splinter the collarbone on the right side of the stubby neck, angling sideways into the throat.

Five down. Five to go.

If you face someone with a knife in a confined space and you can't get away, then you get in close. Krysty Wroth knew that and she dived at her opponent, grappling with him even before her own blaster had finished clattering on the floor.

Its flesh was moist and smelled of the taint of corruption, overlaid with a sour chemical scent that was literally sickening. Krysty gagged, fighting for breath against the nauseous stench of the mutie.

Like all great killers she fought with a cold, analytic, ruthless intensity, clearing her mind of anything but the need to survive and conquer.

Back in her home ville of Harmony, Krysty's uncle, Tyas McCann, had once said he'd heard a notorious hired killer say that when he did a good job he reached an acceptable level of ecstasy. She'd never forgotten that phrase.

The mutie suffered from multidigits. There were eleven fingers and three thumbs on the right hand and nearly as many on the left, most of them stubby, residual little pink paddles of limp flesh. When she grabbed at the man's knife hand Krysty felt a momentary wave of revulsion as she broke off several of the creature's useless fingers, feeling blood spurt over her own hand from the injuries.

It whined and tried to pull itself free, but Krysty wasn't about to let it go. She reached around for the knife she always carried, but her hands were slippery and she couldn't grasp the hilt.

"Ryan!" she yelled. "Help me!"

He was there, appearing behind the mutie's shoulder, steel blade dropping crimson, actually smoking in the cold air of the redoubt. He grabbed at the flapping coat of the mutie, tugging him away from Krysty, sending him dancing off balance. The panga hissed once, twice. The first cut lopped the mutie's right hand off the arm, blood gouting high, while the second, reversed blow ripped open the man's stomach, emptying his intestines onto the floor.

Four left.

Doc ran another of their attackers through the center of the chest, withdrawing the rapier with an almost casual elegance. The mutie clutched at the wound, slumping to the floor, dead.

"Touché," Doc said.

Three of the screeching mutants were still alive and on their feet.

Seeing that they had lost the fight, with most of their group chilled, the survivors turned away, facing only Jak. The muties were all in line with Doc and Lori, and the boy couldn't risk drawing his pistol. He stood, arms by his side, staring at the gibbering trio of muties.

Ryan had gone for his G-12, but it wasn't the time or the place for the lethal firepower of the gray automatic rifle. He could only stand and watch the four-teen-year-old boy.

"Come on, bastards," Jak said, voice sibilant in the silence. His confidence stopped the muties in their tracks, leaving them waving their spears and knives in a halfhearted threat.

"Stay where y'are, then," he added, in a normal conversational tone.

His hands weaved a deadly pattern, faster than Ryan's eye could follow, flickering from side to side. Steel danced in the slim, white fingers, spinning through the air like tiny, turning mirrors.

"Gaia!" Krysty breathed, hardly believing what she saw.

"Fireblast!" Ryan exclaimed.

Lori Quint said nothing. Doc Tanner's jaw gaped and he whistled between his teeth.

"Not bad, kid," J.B. said admiringly.

Each of the three throwing knives had found its target. The talent of the albino boy was staggering, verging on the magical. Using both left and right hands he'd thrown three different knives at three different enemies and chilled them all as effectively as a twelve-bore charge through the head.

The leader of the ambush wore a strip of green cloth tied around his head. The leaf-bladed knife thunked home in the hollow between throat and chest, sending him staggering back, sinking to his knees, eyes wide in shock. Before he hit the floor, the mutie on the left was also down, the knife protruding from the socket of his right eye, blood mingling with the clear fluid as it ran down the cheek. The last of them never moved, dying where he stood, sinking to the floor as though someone had thrown a switch and drained his life away. The knife was buried in the side of his neck, neatly clipping the artery.

Ten down.

None to go.

"IF TEN GOT IN, then a hundred could," the Armorer said when they reached the dorms. Ryan made sure the door at the farther end was closed and bolted, and he set guards, in pairs, to watch the other entrance to the long room.

"Yeah. The sooner we get out through the gateway the better," he agreed. "Thought about staying here for a few days. Better not. Let's sleep now and then get the ammo and supplies in the morning. And then get the long winter out of here."

They made up beds from the tattered mattresses and thick, dark brown blankets, still showing the stenciled letters USFNY in their corners. Most of the overhead lights were out, giving the place the cold gloom of an Arctic cavern.

Despite the discomfort and the threat of a further attack, all six warriors managed to sleep surprisingly well.

Chapter Three

SOMEONE HAD PICKED OVER the shelves of self-heats since they were last in the Mohawk redoubt. The obvious guess was the muties, though not even Jak's morning exploration had revealed a way they could have gotten into the old military complex. But there were still enough cans left for them to activate for breakfast.

Ryan found he was eating yellow soup and some sort of minced fruit. The labels had faded away some time in the past hundred years. The others had different mixes. Jak opened nine cans before he found one that wasn't a particularly unpleasant pale blue slush, warmed by the chemicals triggered by opening the ring-pull, to around twenty degrees centigrade.

They hunted down the ammo section of the redoubt. This time Ryan took even greater precautions, keeping everyone in extended recce file, to avoid a repeat of the situation in the dining hall, where they'd been ambushed while in a group. He took point himself, moving slow and careful, only beckoning up Krysty, second in line, when he was sure the section was safe. Then he moved on, while she called up Jak Lauren, then Lori, Doc and J.B., keeping a good distance between each of them.

There was no further sign of muties, but there was clear evidence that they'd penetrated deep into the rambling complex: urine stains on concrete walls and piles of human excrement scattered along the corridors.

There was also some crude graffiti. Daubs in red and black, most of them completely impossible to understand. A few were the usual porno stuff—men with gigantic penises and women with absurdly huge breasts.

"Seen double-poor swampies draw like this," Jak said.

"I regret to say that I have seen similar defacement streaked all over the heart of some of the finest and most civilized cities that this planet ever saw," Doc put in sadly.

IT WAS WITH RELIEF that Ryan filled his pockets with more of the light caseless rounds for the G-12. "Happiness is a full mag," he said to Krysty with a grin.

"Look," J.B. called, pointing to the contents of a large wooden box that he'd found under one of the benches. It was marked USFNY like everything else in the redoubt.

"What have you got?" Ryan asked.

"Equaloy. Haven't seen any in years."

Ryan had first joined the traveling guerrilla leader called the Trader around ten years ago, just a few months before the Armorer enrolled with him on War Wag One. He'd seen plenty of ammo in his time, but he couldn't recall equaloy. The name rang a bell, but he couldn't pin down where.

"How's that?"

"Aluminum bullets. Self-lube. Nylon coated. Great."

Ryan remembered. "Sure. They got a flat trajectory, don't they?"

Jak was looking in the crate. "Heard. Triple velocity."

J.B. nodded. "Right, kid."

"Don't call me—"

"Sorry, kid." The Armorer favored the boy with one of his rare smiles. "Triple's right. But when they hit someone the bullet stops quick, and all the kinetic energy keeps right on going. Blows your guts apart with the shock."

"What caliber they got?" Jak asked.

"Nine mill, .357. Nothing for Doc."

"I'm fine, thank you, Mr. Dix," the old man replied, patting the pockets of his frock coat.

It was late morning by the time they'd all stocked up on food, drink and ammunition, each member of the group taking a backpack, adjusting the straps to fit, loading them up.

Pressed by Ryan, Doc Tanner finally persuaded Lori to change her clothes. Helped by Krysty, the tall blonde went into the next section of the redoubt and discarded the satin blouse and short red skirt. She emerged wearing a vac-sealed dark blue navy-style shirt and a cotton skirt in the same color, cut to the knee.

When she came out again, Doc Tanner went and kissed her hand, stooping over it like an old-fashioned courtier, smiling at the worried expression on Lori's face.

"Cheer up, child."

"I'm not too pretty, like I am before. But I keep my boots on."

"Keep them on and welcome, my dearest child. And you still look pretty."

"Don't," she sulked.

"You look delicious, my darling little captivator, even when you wear nothing at all."

"Doc!" Krysty exclaimed, pretending to be shocked. "I'm surprised at you talking like that. I really am!"

The old man stammered, shuffling his feet. "By the three Kennedys, Miss Wroth...I'm...I swear that I had no intention of giving...of offending anyone by speaking..."

"You're blushing, you old bastard." Ryan laughed. "Good to see you can show some shame!"

The six companions finally made their cautious way through the silent corridors toward the entrance to the gateway. Since they'd been inside the redoubt they hadn't seen any sign of intruders. Ryan wondered whether the group they'd managed to chill had been the only ones who'd penetrated the defenses.

With her new clothes, Lori seemed to have taken on a new confidence. She insisted on leading the way, with Jak at her elbow. Although the girl wasn't good with words, she had an almost uncanny sense of direction, which might have been the result of being born and raised in a similar, rambling redoubt up in the bitter cold of Alaska.

At one point she cut off from the main passage and took them through a series of interconnecting rooms, all of them stripped and empty. J.B. called out that he thought they'd gone the wrong way, but she shook her head.

"No. Quickest this directions."

There was a narrow staircase, dust gathered on the treads, and she led them down, then through what seemed to have been some sort of scientific laboratory.

One section of the corridor had completely lost its lighting, and they picked their way cautiously through the blackness. Krysty whispered to Ryan that she thought she'd heard someone moving, somewhere behind and above them.

There was a door open ahead of them, where the lights were working. They walked through it and into a short passageway, with several open doors on either side. Jak stopped in front of one and darted in, coming out with something in his hand.

"What's that?" Ryan asked.

"Glove. On table in there. Got something inside." The albino bent over, his fiercely white hair obscuring the glove from their view.

"What...?" J. B. began.

"Damn!" the boy exclaimed, dropping the old gray gauntlet to the floor, where it landed with a peculiar dry whisper of sound.

"What was it, Jak?" Ryan asked.

"Inside it! Bones. Fingers. Hand. All bones."

THE GATEWAY HAD THE SAME coding as the main entrance to the redoubt. Ryan pressed the buttons and nothing happened. When he tried it again, the sec-steel double doors remained stubbornly shut.

"Fireblast! That tears up the contract, doesn't it? What do we do now? Doc, any ideas?"

The old man frowned. "It would take a load of explosives to blow them open, Ryan, and the risk of damage to the main mat-trans controls is very serious."

"Figured that." He looked up at the sign over the doors, the same sign that appeared on every gateway he'd ever seen. It bore the same black lettering, compact and neat: Entry Absolutely Forbidden to All but B12 Cleared Personnel. Mat-Trans.

"Think muties broke it?" Jak suggested, hand on the butt of his pistol.

"No sign of damage," Ryan replied, examining the clear-plas panel, with its small, illuminated numbers and letters. It seemed to be untouched.

"Moving's stopped above us," Krysty said. "Could be coming closer on this level. Lot of turns and walls. We might not hear them."

The prospects if the gateway was locked off from them were difficult to evaluate. It would mean heading back out into the inhospitable valley and taking their chances on breaking free of any muties in the mountains around them.

"Try again," Lori said.

"Why not?" Ryan carefully pressed the three digit code. The glowing yellow light behind the number two flickered and went out. He tapped it firmly, like a man checking a barometer for the next day's weather. The light steadied, so he tried the numbers once more.

"Eureka!" Doc shouted, punching a fist into the air as the doors hissed apart, revealing the main control room inside, with its chattering tape decks and banks of switches, buttons and multicolored light display.

"Better close it, lover," Krysty suggested.

But the lamp beneath the number two was intractably dark, and Ryan couldn't make the closing mechanism function at all.

"Never mind," J.B. said. "Let's get in the gateway chamber and move on out of here."

Beyond the electronics-packed room was a smaller chamber, containing only a rectangular table and a steel cupboard. Someone had carved his initials on the plas-top of the table, the letters FM. In passing, Ryan wondered what kind of person FM had been and how he'd faced up to the chilling.

Krysty looked like she was about to say something, then she shook her head. Ryan raised an eyebrow. "What's up, lover?"

"It doesn't feel right. Can't hear anything, but it just doesn't feel clean."

"Muties?"

"Got to be. But I don't know where, or how close they are."

"Then let's go in."

As they went into the actual gateway room, Ryan noticed that there was an extra set of controls by the armored glass door, with a linked console. He hadn't noticed it while on the way out of the chamber all those months ago.

"What's that, Doc?"

"What's what, my dear Ryan?" Seeing where the one-eyed man was pointing, he said, "Ah, those are chron-trans repeater panels."

"Time jump? What d'you mean 'repeater panels,' Doc?"

"Part of Project Cerberus." He laughed, totally without humor. "I should know better than most. Better than any man living, I should say. I don't believe that there were ever any other successful experiments with trawling, though there were stories of... But I dismissed them as the most arrant taradiddle."

"Can't we try it, Doc?" Jak asked.

The old man shook his head vehemently. "No, my dear young fellow. No! This is only part of the control unit. A repeater. Somewhere, very well hidden and sec-locked, will be the main console for the time-travel section of the gateway."

"Can't it be worked from here?" Krysty asked. "Do you have to set the main controls as well, Doc?"

"Yes."

"You're lying, Doc," J.B. said quietly. "I know it, and you know it."

Ryan had also picked up on the old man's hesitation and the slight change of pitch in the voice. "And I know it, Doc. Can't do that to us."

"I apologize, my friends. Yes, you can work the gateway on chron-set from here. But to do so is to tamper with the works of God."

"Fireblast, Doc!" Ryan exploded. "That's a load of crap! What do you think the mat-trans is? Isn't that against the works of your God? And how come your

God's so terrific if he lets the world blow up in his face? And—"

"Calm it, lover," Krysty soothed, touching him on the arm.

"Yeah, yeah... All right, Doc. I shouldn't have held down on the trigger like that. But what's the difference between mat-trans and chron-trans? Tell me that, Doc. Come on."

Doc looked more serious than anyone had ever seen him before. "There isn't any difference, Ryan. You're absolutely correct, my friend. Both are against the laws of nature. But there *is* a difference. The transfer of material, or of people, generally works. But to push through time isn't the same. You know that it worked for me."

"Then it can work for us, Doc," Lori said, one hand resting on the old man's sleeve.

"You don't... When I was trawled and then pushed forward, it was still at the needle end of experiments. If it came to a choice between certain death and risking the chron-trans, then I'd risk it. But only then!" His voice raised in anger. "I will not be a party to a foolish and unspeakably hazardous flirtation with what I know to be a dreadful danger. And that is all I'll say."

There was a long silence. Krysty, uneasy, glanced behind her, past the main control area and out between the open doors into the endless winding corridor.

"How d'you set it, Doc? For chron?" Ryan asked. "To override mat-trans?"

"There's the single main cutout that bypasses the ordinary controls. Then press in the vectors on the panel for when you want to go. But I don't know the coding, so even if we went, there's no knowing when we might finish up. Past or future? It would be in the lap of the gods."

"Yeah, I see that." Ryan moved across and stared intently at the chron-controls, seeing what Doc had meant.

There was a double sec lock that had to be flipped back in two separate movements, then two buttons, white and black. Beyond them was the intricate set of dials and switches marked Chron Control. Ryan flicked up the cover and pressed first the white and then the black button. The gateway chamber began to hum softly, and the circular metal plates in floor and ceiling started to glow fitfully. All six of them turned to look at it.

Suddenly a lone mutie came rushing among them, lashing out with the jagged blade of its knife.

Chapter Four

JAK SPUN LIKE A DERVISH, trying to dodge the attack, but the mutie had the enormous advantage of surprise. The crude knife lashed out and Ryan, a little to one side, saw blood spurt from the arm of the albino boy, high, close to the shoulder.

Krysty was nearest to the open door of the gateway, and the mutie's eyes were caught by the dazzling crimson of her hair. It diverted itself from Jak, diving toward the girl. But she was too quick for it, sidestepping neatly. The creature, shrieking its hatred, stumbled on the threshold and fell inside, onto the glowing metal plates of the floor.

Ryan hesitated a second, about to draw his SIG-Sauer P-226 9 mm blaster, but realized, instantly, that to fire it could destroy the gateway and leave them stranded in the redoubt. So he went instead for the panga.

As the mutie pulled himself upright, Ryan noticed that the left hand was a mass of frondlike fingers, dozens of little pink tendrils, waving like a sea anemone. The hand holding the knife appeared to have only two fingers, like the pincers of a great crab, and as hard as horn.

"You're dead," Ryan spit, starting into the chamber, panga raised.

"No!" Doc shouted, reaching out and grabbing Ryan by the back of his long coat, yanking him backward out of the entrance. "Slam the door, Lori! Quick! Slam it!"

The girl darted forward and pushed the opaque glass door so that it slammed shut, the lock clicking home.

Jak was kneeling on the floor, cursing in a low undertone, the words trickling out in a steady stream of obscenity. J.B. was at his side, using a strip of whipcord to tie off the arm above the cut, stopping the bleeding. The rest of the group were watching the walls of the gateway, which were pulsing with light, red and a deep orange. Ryan could hear a faint crackling noise, and he could taste a bitter mix of ozone and cold iron.

"Doc. It's set on chron—"

"I know, I know," the old man interrupted irritably. "We'll see, won't we?"

"The arm, Jak?" Ryan asked, half turning to look at the boy.

"Hard traveling, Ryan," the boy answered, heaving himself to his feet, flexing his fingers to make sure the wound hadn't harmed any important tendons or muscles. He seemed satisfied with the results.

The lights danced faster and faster, strobing. The walls were vibrating steadily, and Ryan wondered whether they were in any danger. The equipment was, after all, the best part of a century old. Judging from the noise and the smell, it was in some peril of a major dysfunction.

"Doc..." he began.

"No problems, Ryan. Relax. It's nearly..."

The scream drowned out his words, drowned out every other sound in the gateway room.

The six friends had, between them, seen and heard a lot of dying. But none of them had ever heard a tearing cry of such utter anguish.

It started with a low, almost puzzled note, as if something were happening to the mutie that it couldn't properly understand, but was causing pain. Pain that grew worse, blanking over the bewilderment. The scream rose and fell, sharply, like the panting breath of an exhausted runner. Oddly it seemed to be moving, both close up and distant, all at the same time.

"The same time?" Ryan said to nobody in particular.

The shriek rose a couple of octaves, so piercing it felt like it was scraping at the inside of your skull with a hooked scalpel. It bubbled for a moment as if the mutie were choking on molten molasses, louder and harsher than any voice should be able to go. Until it suddenly...stopped.

There was a time-lapse control on the chamber door, so that they had to wait before opening it to see what had happened.

While they waited, J.B. went out and kept watch on the corridor, making sure there weren't any other muties creeping up on them. Ryan checked Jak's wound. The knife had cut across the top of the right arm, missing the biceps, slicing open the flesh in a gash nearly four inches long. It looked clean, and Lori was able to bandage it with a strip of cloth torn off the bottom of her skirt.

"Good job not old skirt." Jak grinned, pushing the coils of white hair out of his crimson eyes.

"Why?"

"Not 'nough for bandage."

Doc was leaning against the walls of the gateway, head cocked to one side as if trying to listen to some barely audible whispering.

"What d'you figure happened, Doc?" Ryan asked, reaching out and touching the heavy glass, finding to his surprise that it was as cold as an Arctic sarcophagus.

"Could guess, but I won't. I saw and heard some of the Cerberus experiments, and they all went sadly awry. Time travel is so hazardous, Ryan. Yet they were on the brink of success. If the bombs hadn't darkened the skies..."

The time lock clicked loudly, indicating that the door of the gateway's inner chamber could now be opened.

The metal panels on the ceiling and floor had ceased glowing. The smell of burned meat, overlaid with sulfur, wafted through the area.

"He's gone," Krysty said, standing beside Ryan.

All that remained of the mutie was a small pool of congealing blood and some scorched rags, lying at the center of a scattering of very fine grains of silver sand.

Nothing else remained.

Nothing.

Chapter Five

THE JUMP WAS OVER.

Ryan Cawdor opened his eye, wincing at the surging swell of sickness from the mat-trans journey. The walls of the gateway chamber were pale blue, streaked with a darker gray. The colors were familiar, but his brains were scrambled and he sat still, back against the cool armored glass, taking several slow, deep breaths.

After the horror of the mutie's disappearance in the Mohawk gateway, they'd swiftly made their arrangements to leave. It had taken J.B. a couple of minutes to kick the sticky mess off the floor, wiping it away with some crumbling dried rags from the anteroom. Doc had reset the main controls from chron to mat and covered the dual sec locks again. But with the main doors open into the gateway chamber and muties penetrating the complex, it could only be a matter of time before the whole place was totally and irrevocably wrecked.

They'd all taken their places, sitting in a circle around the hexagonal chamber, most bringing knees up to chins, resting their heads on their arms. A mat-trans jump wasn't a pleasant experience.

"Everyone ready?" Ryan asked.

"Sure thing, lover."

"Damn right."

"Yes, I is."

"Affirmative."

"Indeed, Ryan, my dear fellow. I think that I can say without any fear of contradiction that I'm ready as I ever will be."

The door closed firmly, the lights began to flicker and the metal plates began to glow, ever more brightly. Ryan closed his eye tightly, swallowing hard as the now familiar feeling began to close him down. The inside of his head swirled and his stomach pitched like a war wag going over a ripple road.

But, at last, the jump was over.

The gateway was bitterly cold. Ryan could see his breath streaming out like smoke, and there was already condensation on the chilly walls of armored glass around the six-sided chamber.

"Fireblast!"

Out of long habit Ryan checked the tiny rad counter pinned inside the lapel of his long coat. It was barely into the orange, showing no hot spots in the immediate vicinity.

"Where are we?" Krysty asked, stretching her long legs in front of her. Her face was pale and her sentient hair had coiled itself protectively about her throat. "Gaia! It's freezing here! Let's go back again."

It took nearly twenty minutes before everyone was ready to leave the chamber. Doc Tanner was, as ever, the last to recover from the jangling effects of the jump. He leaned heavily on Lori, his face as white as a sheet, his hands trembling.

The room beyond the hissing hydraulic doors was the same in nearly every redoubt they'd visited, roughly five paces by three with a plastic table on one side and four shelves lining the far wall. A copper bowl was on the table.

Jak picked it up and looked inside it. "Dried blood. Something like." He put it down hard on the table, and the bowl rang out like a bell.

Ryan looked at him angrily. "Keep the... Wait."

"What?" Jak looked surprised at the snap in Ryan's voice.

"That bowl. Krysty, remember it? J.B., does it come back to you?"

The Armorer nodded. "Seen it before somewhere, but..."

Krysty pointed. "I remember that. Unless there's one somewhere else, we've jumped back to—"

"Alaska," Ryan concluded.

"My home?" Lori squeaked, eyes wide with shock. "Don't want to came home. Not see Keeper and Mother Rachel and all of they."

"They're dead, Lori," Ryan said reassuringly. "Don't worry about that. But there's not much point in coming here. The place was frozen hard for hundreds of miles around."

Ryan, J.B., Krysty and Doc had visited the part of the country that had once been called Alaska many months earlier, but their time there had been filled with cold and violence. It had been there that they first met up with Lori Quint and her murderous kin.

"I wish we could control the jump, dear Ryan, but it's out of our hands. We could, in effect, be bounced back here, or to any other gateway we've been to,'' Doc explained.

''Are we going to make another jump?'' the Armorer asked. ''Right now?''

Ryan didn't answer immediately. He knew what J.B. was getting at. The mat-trans journeys were more than tiring.

''We could stay a while.''

''No,'' Lori said, her face pale, as she turned her blue eyes imploringly to Doc. ''Please, not stay. Too many thinking from yesterdays. Please, can't we go now? Please, go?''

Bearing in mind what the girl's life must have been like before they rescued her, Ryan had to admit she had a point. The Alaska redoubt didn't exactly hold happy memories for her.

''Doc?'' he asked. ''You get hit worst on the jumps. How d'you feel about going straight off on another? Be tough.''

The place was freezing. His memory of it was of a steady sixty degrees, controlled by the comp-center of the complex. If they'd broken down, then there could have been a lot of other changes around the place. It seemed like most of the redoubts were set down in what had become double-solid mutie country. Maybe it would be better, and safer, to move on as fast as they could. While they could.

Doc cuddled Lori to him, her head resting comfortingly on his shoulder. Though he looked tired and drawn, he didn't hesitate, and his voice was strong as it ever was.

"Without doubt it would be hazardous to remain here, Ryan. My vote, for what little it might be worth, is for us to quit the establishment as soon as we possibly can."

Everyone else nodded as Ryan caught their eyes. "Sure. Come on, then. Mebbe next place'll be a touch warmer."

RYAN'S MOUTH WAS FILLED with sour, yellow bile, as bitter as wormwood. He coughed, feeling cool metal against the stubble on his cheek. His head pounded like it did after a night in a frontier gaudy bar. He whistled softly to himself.

"Must be getting old," he said, voice cracking.

"You and me both, lover." Krysty lay at his side, knees drawn up under her chin, face sallow and streaked with sweat. She tried for a smile, but it came out looking like a grimace of pain. "Hope we don't need to do this for a while."

"Depends where we've gotten to. Feels warmer than last time."

It was positively hot. Ryan glanced at the rad counter, seeing that it was well through the orange, only a few units off the beginning of the red section on the tiny dial. Krysty caught the glance.

"Hot spot?"

"Might be. It's tolerable at this level. Could be a leaking power source in the redoubt."

Doc was the third one of the group to come lurching back into consciousness, holding his head in his hands and wiping away a thread of bright blood from his nostrils.

"I fear I caught myself a knock as I slipped away from the realm corporal into the realm ethereal," he said. "Not that this looks particularly ethereal. What a bilious color to the walls."

The glass was too bright for yellow, too light for gold.

Jak announced his own return to consciousness by throwing up copiously and noisily, barely managing to avoid covering himself in vomit. He coughed and spluttered, shaking his head like a dog coming out of a lake.

"Not again for bit," he said. "Feel like got sec man's boot in balls."

J.B. sat up suddenly, eyes open. He carefully removed his spectacles from his top pocket where he'd placed them for safety during the jump.

"Ugly colors," he said. "Looks like I feel. Rad count's high."

"Hot spot?" Ryan asked.

"Can't tell. Get outside and find where we are. Feels warm."

Lori was the last of the six to recover. She took so much longer that Ryan was beginning to worry. The tall blonde had an amazingly tough constitution, but she was breathing fast and shallow, her pulse racing. More like someone with a tearing fever. When she finally stirred in Doc's arms, she looked dreadful. Her eyes were blank, like old glass.

"You okay?" Krysty asked.

"No. Feel sick. Dreamed bad. Lost and Keeper after me. I run and run, but my foots don't work and

Keeper run fastest. Feel bad, Krysty. Time month starts on jump."

Doc looked worriedly up at Krysty, who smiled reassuringly. "Don't worry, Doc. Woman's problem. I got something. When we're out of there. It'll only take us a second. She'll be fine."

"Did the jump make her menses begin, do you suppose?" he asked.

Krysty nodded. "Funnily enough, I came on during a jump. It's a shame there's no more scientists. Could bear investigation, couldn't it, Doc?"

For the second time recently the old man failed to hide a blush.

As always, there was a small, bare room immediately beyond the mat-trans chamber. Roughly fifteen feet by ten feet it was furnished only with a folding, canvas-backed chair and a table with a broken leg. Marks on the wall showed where there'd been a row of narrow shelves. There was a fine layer of red-orange dust all over the floor.

"Sure is warm," Ryan commented.

The main control area was the largest that Ryan had ever seen. The ceiling was high, crossed with strips of lights. Unusually, every single one was working perfectly. At a guess, he put the room at two hundred feet by ninety.

"This is nice!" Doc exclaimed. "My goodness, but this is *very* nice!"

"How come it looks so good, Doc?" J.B. asked, running his finger over the film of dust that shrouded a chattering console of dancing lights and jittering dials.

"The air feels very dry, John. Ah, my apologies. I had forgot you prefer to be called J.B. I was saying that the air seems dry. From what my poor, ailing memory can dredge up, I seem to recall that most of the redoubts that we've visited have been damnably damp and cold. Alaska, the Darks, the swamps and so on."

"Where are we?" Lori asked. She was recovering slowly, still hanging on to Doc's arm, though it seemed to Ryan that the girl was maybe not quite as bad as she pretended.

"Where, indeed? Where, my charming little entrancer? Near or far? I fear that your old dodderer is very far away from where he should be. Oh, so many miles. So many mornings behind. I'll bring you only boots of Spanish leather, my dear child."

He shook his head, eyes puzzled. The only consolation, thought Ryan, was that Doc didn't have as many of the wandering spells as when they first met up with him.

"Rad count's still up some," J.B. said, changing the subject. "High, but still not too high."

As they moved through the control room, Ryan asked the Armorer if he had any thoughts about where they might have ended up.

"Doc's right about dryness. Never quite got the jumps figured. At times it seems like there's a change in the season. That could just be distance. Don't know. No refs for it. If it's summer could be a lot of places. You know that, Ryan."

"Yeah. Hot and dry. Sounds like the Southwest to me. Near Mexland. River Grande. Don't know that part well. Do you?"

Never a man to waste a word, J.B. simply shook his head.

"Trader said that the coast went under during the nukings. Lower California vanished. He said the Pacific laps against the foothills of the Sierras now. At least we didn't hit a gateway under the sea."

Again Doc nodded his agreement with Ryan's words. The six of them reached the door to the rest of the complex and stopped.

The green lever that they'd seen before was in the down mode, showing that the entrance was still locked and sealed. Krysty stopped Ryan from lifting the handle. "Wait."

"What is it?"

"If it's this hot in the middle of the redoubt, chances are it'll be a whole lot warmer once we get out. Mebbe we should leave our coats here. Get 'em on the way back."

"Sure. Hang on to the packs." He took off his own long fur-trimmed coat and folded it neatly, laying it on a straw-colored plastic bench. He kept the weighted silk scarf. The others took off their warm clothing, except for Doc, who insisted on keeping the faded frock coat.

"Need something to hold a touch of heat in these cold old bones," he explained.

The lever worked easily, with the familiar feeling of some massive hydraulic pressure behind the walls. Gears engaged and the twin doors slid slowly open.

The corridor swept past them; it was wider than most, with a circular roof. Immediately Ryan felt the increase in heat. Glancing down at the rad count he noticed that it had darted into the red. J.B. spotted it at the same time.

"Shouldn't linger here," he stated.

The tiny measuring devices were slightly directional, and Ryan unclipped his from his shirt lapel, glad he'd transferred it from the long coat. He held it on the palm of his right hand, turning and pointing it both ways along the passage.

"Fair bit warmer that way." He pointed.

"Hot spots be interesting," Jak said. "Find good things near 'em."

It was true. Hot spots showed heavy nuking. That meant they were often important places from the past.

"We'll go left a ways. If it gets too hot we'll come back."

They followed Ryan's lead without question. They'd only been walking along the featureless corridor for a couple of minutes when they came across the first of the bodies.

Chapter Six

"MUST HAVE BEEN MEN here when the nukes actually hit the redoubt." J.B. cocked his head to one side as he considered the evidence in front of him.

"First time I've seen that," Ryan said. "All the other places were stripped and mostly cleared."

"There wasn't a whole lot of warning. Not when it came down to it."

Ryan had also read and heard about the last bitter days before the skies darkened. "Government knew at the end ... They knew."

"Too late, my brothers. Oh, too late by too many years." Doc looked along the corridor, to the beginnings of destruction. To the first of the scattered corpses in front of them.

Lori drew her pistol, but Doc shook his head. "No danger, dearest. They've been chilled for the better part of a century ... of a hundred years. They can do us no possible harm."

There were five. Tangled together, limbs entwined in the embrace of a violent passing. They all wore the faded, crumbling rags of uniform, but the colors had bleached out long ago. One had three golden stripes lying on the rotted cloth of an arm.

Jak went and stooped over them, touching the toe of a boot to the nearest. It quivered, dried bones rattling at the movement. One of the skulls rolled a little, empty sockets glaring at the intruders. Teeth gleamed like ivory, between lips like brown parchment.

"All leather," the albino boy called, straightening up. "Look like blown against wall. Big boom."

"The biggest, son," Doc said quietly.

The bones of the hands were like frail sticks, and strands of wispy hair clung to the skulls. As far as could be seen, none of the bodies showed any marks of bullets.

"No blasters," Krysty observed.

"Non-combs."

"How's that, J.B.?" she asked.

"Cleaners, cooks, clerks. Not fighting soldiers. Don't have pistols. There'll be shelters someplace in the redoubt. Looks like they were on their way there when the missiles hit. Shock wave. The blast threw 'em there."

"Don't look like they have bones breaked," Lori observed.

"Not like that. Shock wave. Ruptures all your internal...your guts," Ryan said. "Could also have sucked out the air and choked you. It depends. Guess we'll never know."

"They won't tell us. That's for sure," Krysty said.

The rad count was intermittent, but it was generally edging upward. Ryan had made the decision that they'd keep going for another fifteen minutes or so.

Experience showed that exposure of that length didn't generally bring rad sickness.

They moved past two more groups of dead soldiers, only one of them with a blaster. A Browning Hi-Power pistol, still holstered.

Then they found the woman.

Jak was on point, and they had reached a section of the long passage with other narrower corridors winding off. And rooms on either side. If it hadn't been for the rad heat, Ryan would have stopped and explored.

All his life he'd wondered what the madness had been that had made civilized people destroy one another, like crazies tearing out their own eyes. He felt that one day he might find a clue to what had lain at the back of it.

The letters on the half-glazed door had peeled and become almost illegible. Ryan traced them with his finger. "C PTA N S R H GUY."

"Captain Sarah Guy," Doc said.

The door stood half-open, and they could see a figure slumped over a desk. The orange dust was thicker now, laid over everything like a shroud of the finest silk.

"Time we should be moving out, Ryan," J.B. urged. "Counter's well into red."

"Five more, J.B.," Ryan replied. "Just five minutes more."

He pushed the door open and walked into the office. On the one wall was a calendar for the year 2001, with a beautiful laser pic on it of the Tetons under snow.

The days had been neatly crossed through with a purple felt marker, all the way up to January 20.

On the wall opposite was a poster that read, If You Aren't Sure, Then You Aren't Right!

There was a long, fine hair dangling from the shrunken skull of the woman, which, under the veil of dust, looked as if it might once have been blond. Her head rested on her arms. The sharp edges of the shoulder bones had pushed through the frayed material of the uniform. The finger bones were pinched around a pen, and on the desk was an unfinished letter.

"Look," J.B., said, pointing to a small brown bottle that stood uncapped and empty on the corner of the desk.

"She must have had some warning," Krysty suggested. "Could be she survived a first strike, knew she was rad dead anyway and chose the easy way out for herself. Looks that way."

"Yeah." Ryan picked up the sheet of paper and blew off the layer of fine dirt. The letter wasn't very long.

There was no preamble. No date.

So Dad was right all those years we kidded him about his doomy fears. Now it's happened. Don't know if you'll get this letter. Don't know if you're still alive. The EMP wiped out everything around here. They nuked the north end the redoubt. Lot of dead. Lot of good friends. Maybe they died fast and lucky. I know that Ginny and Donna (the one Dad said had nice tits when we came home

last fall) went in that strike. I was in the shelter.
Rads are way off the top of any scale we got, so
I'm not waiting for the blood and ulcers and all
that. I guess Gramps wouldn't approve. He always said it was a coward's way out and that
you'd end up in hell. He was wrong, Mom. This
is hell.

The writing was beginning to deteriorate as the
drugs started to take her away.

Don't feel too... dark in here. The backup lights
work throughout, so it's not this. They got nuke
power, and they'll be light for another thousand
years. Funny that is... Wish I could have seen you
all more time. Bruce said not trust leaders, and he
was really right. Too late now. It's working than
I quickly. Wanted to... Just hope Gramps was
right about us all meeting someplace. Guess it's
shame write any more. If you see...

And that was where the letter ended.

Ryan put the piece of paper on the desk, and they all
left the room in silence. Lori was last out, and she
closed the door gently behind them.

Two sets of armored titanium sec doors opened up
a hundred paces along the passage, revealing what the
long-dead Captain Sarah Guy had mentioned. Missiles had hit the complex and hit hard. There was
massive nuke damage: walls scored and seared, granite turned liquid in a microsecond, then back to rip-
pled stone; jagged streaks of charred paint, the

wooden frames of doors converted instantly to charcoal. There were no more corpses.

They did discover piles of scattered, tumbled bones that bore no resemblance to anything human, to anything that might once have been human.

And eventually, only a little farther on, they reached the end of the line. The missiles had brought down the walls and ceiling, caving in the earth above, filling the corridor with spilled rocks and dirt, bright orange-red dirt.

"Gaia!" Krysty said. "Let's get out of here. It's just a big tomb."

"Stay much longer and we'll fry along with them," J.B. said tersely, his voice betraying rare emotion. "Count's up and off the red."

Ryan led them back to the main entrance to the gateway, then continued along the corridor in the opposite direction.

At every main junction there was a wall map of the whole complex, which was color-coded level by level. The gateway was simply shown as MT Chamber. It was immediately obvious that the nuking had wiped out nine-tenths of the base, leaving only a residual section. Fortunately it included the main entrance.

"At least we know the name of the place," Doc said, pointing to the top of the clear-plas-covered guide. Printed in comp-capitals were the words Shay Canyon Redoubt.

"You know it, Doc?"

"What's that, Ryan, my dear fellow? I fear that I was allowing my mind to wander a little. What were you saying?"

"You heard of this place? Shay Canyon? Know where it is?"

The old man looked bewildered, and Ryan expected one of his gibberish responses. But he was wrong. "I'm not sure, but...the name reminds me... Back in October... No, it must have been September. Or was... September. It was definitely September. 1896 was the year."

He stopped, and everyone waited for him to continue. Finally Lori jogged him by tugging at the sleeve of his coat.

"What? Oh, yes, I was just recalling that it was most definitely 1896. Poor dear Harriet Beecher Stowe had passed on to join the choir invisible at the beginning of July that year. And only two months later I was plucked from my home and hearth by the bastards of Project Cerberus."

"Doc," Ryan growled, growing impatient, "does this have some point?"

"Of course it does. I came to the Southwest for a working vacation. I lived with the Mescalero Apaches. Local Indians. Met the Navaho and Hopi peoples and lived for some time near one of their holy places. Now—" he glowered at Ryan from beneath his beetling brows "—that was called Canyon de Chelly." He spelled the name out. "And it was pronounced *Shay* like that name there. I just wonder..."

BEFORE THEY HEADED for the main entrance of the redoubt, J.B. insisted they first visit the armory that was shown on the plan.

"Probably blown it when it was all over. Case the Reds got in after it. Still, is it worth a look, Ryan? You reckon?"

"Sure. Let's go."

It wasn't far, and they had to travel through only two more sets of armored doors. Ryan kept an eye on the rad counter, seeing to his relief that the level had dropped drastically once they got away from the scene of the actual nuking at the north end.

But J.B.'s fear was correct.

They reached a series of sec barriers, all with messages warning what would happen to anyone passing through without the proper authorization. Then, as they reached the armory, they saw the evidence of self-set sab-devices. The doors were blown open, hanging crookedly off their reinforced hinges. And inside, the once orderly shelves and sections of the weapons stores were in jumbled ruined chaos.

Ryan followed J.B. into the long hangarlike room, stepping over twisted chunks of metal or arma-plas, some of them unrecognizable, some of them barely identifiable.

The Armorer picked his way into the chamber, shaking his head sadly. "If this stuff hadn't been blown away, we could have been the barons of all Deathlands inside six months, Ryan."

"If that's what we wanted," came the laconic reply from the one-eyed man.

There were hundreds of handblasters, all smashed.

"Ninety-four SB Berettas," J.B. said, "and enough M-1911A1s to sink a war wag, M-62 machine guns, some rocket and gren launchers. Not all of these are completely destroyed, Ryan. Give me a little time and I can rig up one to work."

Ryan shook his head. "No. Too heavy to carry. Leave it be, J.B., where it lies. We aren't touching the bodies. Leave the blasters the same way, like they fell. Come on."

"What's them?" Lori asked, pointing to the left to some high shelves that housed some long, sharklike shapes.

"Dark night!" J.B. exclaimed, his fedora nearly falling off the back of his head in his sudden excitement. "Missiles!"

"Not nukes?"

"No, Ryan, probably not. But there's Dragon and Copperhead antitank rockets there. Must have been overlooked in the last shambles. Launchers. Guidance units. Those are the best, there." He indicated a row of stacked rockets, around four feet long. "They're TOW Fours."

"What'd they do?" Jak asked.

J.B. closed his eyes and recited from memory. Even though Ryan knew how encyclopedic the little man's knowledge of weapons was, he was still impressed.

"TOW Four. Stands for Tube-launched, Optically tracked, Wire-guided missile. Originally replaced the 106 mm recoilless rifle. Got six wings that come out in flight. Uses a Hercules motor. Range around three miles. Flight velocity of 675 mph. Carries a fifteen-pound explosive warhead."

"How d'you aim it?" Ryan asked, looking at the greased tubes, still gleaming behind their locked doors after nearly one hundred useless years.

"Optical sensors in nose. Controls go down twin wires. Helium pressure actuators. Nightsight and laserscope. Penetrate any armor anyone had ever seen in those days. Beautiful. Real beautiful. Who'd have thought I'd ever see one."

Ryan couldn't ever remember hearing the Armorer so enthusiastic about anything.

Doc coughed and began to move back toward the corridor. "Can we get out of this death shop, Ryan? I find this—" he gestured at the broken metal all around "—saddens and sickens me."

"They're okay if you use 'em right, Doc," J.B. protested.

"There is no right, John Dix. Can you not see this? With the dealing of death there can only be wrong. Wrong!"

"That could be," Ryan admitted, "but I know that if I'm against a chiller with a stick, then I'd welcome a bigger stick."

The cut on Jak's arm was hurting him and they stopped off when they passed what had been a doctor's office, on the way to the entrance. J.B. cleaned and rebandaged the wound, which seemed to be healing fairly well.

The surgeon was still in his office. From the sprawled position of the leathery corpse, he must have been leaning back in his swivel chair when he put the muzzle of the Smith & Wesson between his teeth. The impact had blown him over, legs resting on the overturned seat. Lori stared down into the splintered exit hole in the top of the skull with a morbid fascination.

"Empty," she said.

"Would be, by now," Doc replied.

There was nothing to stay for. The grim Shay Canyon Redoubt with its flavor of ancient death was deeply depressing for the six friends. Their backpacks already held all the self-heats they needed, as well as some emergency water supplies. J.B. found some aqua-pure tabs and handed them out. Everyone had sufficient ammo for their blasters.

There was nothing to stay for.

As they neared the main entrance doors to the redoubt, they could see a tattered poster tacked to the wall. It showed a hillside covered with fighting men, most on horseback, many with hats made from feathers. They were attacking a smaller group of people, who looked like sec men in dark blue uniforms. They were in a defensive ring, battling against overwhelming odds and at their center was a tall man with flowing yellow hair.

"Seventh Cavalry fighting against the Sioux," Doc said knowledgeably. "Battle of the Little Big Horn. The Indians massacred the whites, and served them right."

The caption on the poster said simply, Custer Died for Our Sins.

Underneath, in spray-can crimson, faded to a pale pink, someone had added a line: Whose sins are we dying for?

"THREE . . . FIVE . . . TWO . . ." Ryan punched the open code into the control panel at the side of the massive armored sec doors, and after a fractional delay they began to slide back.

It had felt warm before. Now they were all struck by a smothering wave of bright heat and dazzling sunlight.

The twisted waste of red and orange desert stretched limitlessly before them.

Chapter Seven

"NEW MEXICO. OR ARIZONA. Near as I can make it.
Close to Utah and Colorado as well. Sextant isn't that
good, and the maps are kind of old."

Apart from rough local sketch plans, Ryan knew
that no proper maps, covering any appreciable area
had been drawn since the United States of America
ceased. And became the Deathlands.

The hot desert air was heavy with the scent of sagebrush, mesquite and creosote. The sky seemed higher,
the horizons farther, in that place of shimmering heat.
There were vicious streaks of chem clouds, thirty miles
or more off to the east, vivid purple against the glowing pink sky.

The doors of the redoubt opened onto a plateau,
with the remains of a narrow blacktop winding toward the valley beneath. Remote-control vid-cameras
ranged the area, protruding from the jagged rocky
overhang like the stops on a mission-hall harmo-
nium. The complex was so well hidden by the mountain soaring above it that Ryan guessed it would be
virtually impossible to detect from the flatter desert
below.

Now that they were outside, the pointer on the rad
counter was flickering on the line between scarlet and

pale orange. It was obvious that the region had once been a ferocious hot spot, which might, Ryan guessed, account for the fact that nobody seemed to have tried to break into Shay Canyon Redoubt.

"Was this always desert like this, Doc?" Krysty asked, shading her green eyes against the lancing sun.

"No. The way I recall it, far north as this was more a kind of dry grasslands. Near to the prairies. It seems as though the nukings and the long winters must have tipped the ecological and meteorological balance of the land's structure." He saw puzzlement on most of the faces around him. "It got hotter and dryer, so the grass died off and the sands came north from Mexico. If we're near to Canyon de Chelly, as it seems... That was always desert land, but you could cultivate it."

"What with, Doc?" Krysty asked.

"I recall the Navaho had peach orchards, until brave Kit Carson came riding in and grubbed them all up."

"Which way shall go?" Jak asked. "Seems like lots of nothing every which way."

Ryan scanned the horizon. The terrain looked like he'd once imagined the hot spots of Deathlands must have looked shortly after the dust and smoke cleared. A land that was twisted and tortured, rock scraping skyward at every angle. Red dominated, and orange, shaded down through pink into gray. It was difficult to judge distances properly in the clear air, but it looked like the jagged mountains to the north could be a good fifty miles off.

Jak's question was a fair one. Which way should they go? Which way could they go? They all looked much the same.

"Anyone for going back inside and trying another jump tomorrow?"

Nobody answered.

"Anyone got any idea of any special direction for us to go?"

Again nobody spoke.

"How about west, along the valley toward those low hills? You all agree?"

Only the faint whistling of the light breeze broke the silence.

Ryan laughed. "Well, you don't disagree, so we'll go down and west. J.B., you like to lead off for a change? I'll cover the rear."

It was late afternoon by the time they climbed down to the rim of the escarpment. There was no sign of any ville as far as the eyes could see. Apart from some unidentifiable birds circling above a clump of stunted trees ten miles to the north, there was no life to be seen. The shifting sand around their feet showed all manner of tracks: the swirling trail of sidewinders, weaving their way, the skittering marks of rodents and, once, the huge pad marks of a big cat. Jak paced the distance between the paws, whistling at his calculations that the puma could be more than twelve feet long.

As they neared the bottom of the old blacktop Krysty hesitated, peering toward the west. The others all stopped, waiting to hear what she'd been able to see.

"A column of dust. Could be whipped up by the wind. We called 'em dust devils back home in Harmony. Then again..." She paused.

"Then again it might be wags? Men? Horses? Could be anything," Ryan said.

"Could be. It's far off, lover, moving over behind a low mesa. Now...now it's gone."

The last two hundred yards of the blacktop had totally vanished, disappeared as though it had never been. There had been a landslide and what looked like a series of flash floods, washing away at the land over the decades, changing the topography, hiding the road. There was a trail at the bottom of the valley, but from it there was no trace of the redoubt. Just a blank side of a mountain, scraped red-raw by the harsh weather.

"No wonder nobody has gotten up there," J.B. said. "Just hope we can find the place when we leave."

"Rock there shapes like the head of an old man with a big hat," Lori said, pointing just off the trail, near a dry riverbed. They all saw the frost-riven boulder that she'd pointed at.

Doc Tanner laughed. "Damned if it doesn't look somewhat like me, my dainty little cherub of passion and devotion."

"No!" she said crossly, stamping her foot. "I said like an *old* man, Doc. Not like you."

"Lotta horse tracks," J.B. said, kneeling at a fork in the trail.

"Shod or unshod?" Ryan asked.

"Both. What kind of animals do your Indian friends ride, Doc?"

"By the three Kennedys, John Dix! We are talking about events that took place about two hundred years ago. Then, the warriors of the tribes rode ponies. Unshod. Around here were many different small tribes. Chiricahua and Mescalero Apaches, as well as the Hopi and Navaho. But if any had survived the long winters, then who knows?"

"Could any have lived through?"

Doc rubbed at the stubble that silvered his chin. "I guess so, Krysty. They lived in mountain and valley fastnesses, often far away from any places of white men. Away from what might have been important strategic targets in the holocaust of 2001. So they could have lived."

"Well, someone around here's been riding horses, and there's narrow wheel tracks as well," J.B. returned.

"Wags?" Ryan asked.

Jak also stopped to look, his long white hair falling forward to veil his pallid face. "Not wags," he said. "Wheels too thin."

"Look more like prairie schooners to me, though these tired old eyes aren't as sharp as they used to be."

"What're they?" Lori asked.

"Wooden wags, with big high wheels to get through the rivers and the soft sand. With canvas tops. They left their ruts clear across the country from east to west. Moved the frontiers, they did."

Ryan didn't like the way the trail showed signs of such heavy use. The country was so bare that they'd stand out like a legless mutie at a gaudy house dance.

"Mebbe we should find a camp for the night," he suggested.

"Could do with water. Place like this isn't likely to have much. Head for those trees. It's the only spot of green for miles."

The Armorer was right. In such an arid waste, the sun baking down from dawn to dusk, a man would lose around a pint of precious bodily liquid every hour. And the sun would cook out the sweat, so he didn't even realize the way he was dehydrating. Not until he found himself on hands and knees wondering why the earth kept moving away from him.

Mariposa lilies dotted the floor of the valley, interspersed with spiky clusters of yucca. A large gopher snake writhed in front of Jak Lauren, making the boy reach for his Magnum. He only checked his shot at a warning word from Ryan.

"Noise like that'll carry for miles."

"Sure."

IT HADN'T LOOKED THAT FAR to reach the grove of small cottonwoods, yet they walked steadily for more than three hours before they came close enough to distinguish individual trees, to see the glittering silver bark and the large lacquered leaves shifting in the light, hot breeze.

"Indians used to make drums out of the trunks of the cottonwood," Doc said.

"There might be water," Krysty suggested. "I can sort of taste it. Mebbe deep down. Don't know."

The sun was slithering down behind the tops of the mountains to the far west, casting elongated shadows across the jagged landscape. The chem clouds that had threatened a storm had disappeared, and the sky was clear from edge to edge.

Doc looked close to exhaustion, leaning heavily on Lori. But as they reached the head of a draw that wound in toward the trees, he straightened and began to sing in a steady, melodious voice.

"Bringing in the sheaves, bringing in the sheaves,
We shall be rejoicing, bringing in the sheaves."

Ryan turned and half smiled at Krysty. The six companions had been through some bitter times, times of infinite peril. They'd survived them, and they were still together. Krysty returned his smile.

Doc, meanwhile, had moved from one frontier hymn to another:

"We will gather at the river,
The beautiful, the beautiful, the river,
We will gather at the river,
That flows by the throne of God."

"Doc?"

"What is it, my snowy bird of passage?"

"Way back your days...old days...was there God in old days?"

Doc Tanner paused in midstride, looking intently at the boy's face, making sure that he wasn't being teased.

"You aren't joshing me?"

"What does...?"

"Never mind. Was there God in my olden days? I'll tell you, that if there was, he kept himself well hidden, Jak."

J.B. collected some wood for a fire from a tangled deadfall across the draw, a hundred yards or so below the cottonwoods. It was all bone-dry and burned with a clear gold light and little smoke. Ryan had the uneasy, prickling feel at his nape that someone had been watching them ever since they left the hidden redoubt. Someone, or something.

"No chance of any fresh food around here, is there?" Krysty asked.

Ryan shook his head, lying back on a bed of soft sand and staring into the flames of the crackling fire. "Guess not, lover. When we get into the hills there'll probably be deer. Higher and there'll be bear and goat. Too dry for any fishing. Mebbe I can catch you a snake or two, if that's your fancy."

"No thanks."

There had been no water. Lori had taken a jagged length off a branch and started to dig near the center of the grove of trees. She got down to around three and a half feet, reaching earth that was less dry. But it wasn't damp enough to try to siphon any water from its bottom.

Once Ryan thought he heard the far-off cry of an animal, sounding like a coyote. Krysty and Jak heard it, as well.

"Definitely a coyote," the girl said. "Heard them around Harmony."

"Or man sounding like coyote," the young boy suggested.

THEY ALL HEARD THE COUGHING roar of a mountain lion, tearing the darkness apart with its sudden power and violence. They reached for their blasters, but the sound wasn't repeated.

It was around eleven o'clock, the light full gone. A sliver of moon had appeared briefly, then vanished behind a bank of low cloud. The fire was burning low, all of the wood finished. Jak stood up and stretched.

"Get more branches," he said.

"Yeah. We'll keep a watch. Don't want that cougar creeping up on us when it's dark. Want me to come with you?"

"No, Ryan. Be fine. Get from deadfall. Lots there, huh, J.B.?"

"Yeah. Watch the ground. It's rough. Lotta scrub and dry stuff. Take care. You could easy turn your ankle on it."

"Sure." A wave of the hand and he was gone, ghosting away among the silent trunks of the cottonwoods. Ryan watched him, seeing the silver sheen of the albino's hair, floating like a beacon in the darkness.

"Go after him, lover," Krysty whispered, touching Ryan's arm.

"Why?"

"Because . . . Go on."

Ryan knew better than to waste time pressing her for a reply. The mutated blood in Krysty's veins had given her strange skills and talents. And if she felt unease, then there might be some reason for it.

He uncoiled from the sand and padded silently after Jak.

The scent of the mesquite was even stronger and Ryan paused, kneeling and rubbing his hands through the dust, which still carried the heat of the day, and dried his skin. He stood and adjusted the SIG-Sauer blaster in its holster. He followed the boy, out from the cottonwoods, down the dry creekbed, toward the deadfall of jumbled branches. He heard Jak a little ahead of him, picking his way over a scattering of dead brush.

Ryan was just about to call out a warning that he was approaching the lad, knowing that Jak's razor-honed reflexes might lead to his attacking him before knowing it was a friend, when he heard a gasp and the thudding sound of a body falling and landing hard. There was a faint crackling among the bushes, and then nothing.

"Jak," he called softly.

He strained his hearing for a reply, but the night was still. "Jak? You okay?"

Was that a groan? A low, mumbling kind of a moan from ahead of him?

"Jak? Where are you?"

"Down bastard hole, Ryan. Left riverbed. Went past big rock, big as me. Stepped on brush and went in."

"You hurt?" The boy's voice had seemed tense with pain.

"It's trap, Ryan. Sharp spike branches in pit here."

Stepping as if walking on eggshells, Ryan picked his way forward, seeing the large boulder looming ahead of him. He strained his good eye and could make out the dark shape of the pit trap. "Jak. How deep?"

"Six feet. Mebbe. Broke chest bones, Ryan. Can't stand...can't..." The voice faded away.

Ryan decided immediately that he needed a light from the fire and as fast as possible. He turned around and stared into the glowing emerald eyes of an enormous mutie cougar, which stood less than ten feet away from him.

Chapter Eight

TWENTY-FIVE OUNCES of precisely engineered steel; seven and three-quarter inches long; barrel length just under four and a half inches; fifteen rounds of 9 mm ammunition. The P-226 leaped into Ryan's fist before he'd even consciously thought that he'd better draw it from the hip. It fitted there like an extension of his arm.

In the dim light it wasn't possible to see the exact size of the animal. Its tawny skin seemed to glow faintly. It was around sixteen feet from its jaws, with the glistening saber-teeth, to the squat, bunched muscles at the end of its back and had to weigh in at around seven hundred pounds of mean.

"Back off, bastard," Ryan hissed. Over the years in the Deathlands he'd encountered any number of muties, animals and humans, and some that lay somewhere between. A lot of them would respond to the threat of an armed man.

The mountain lion hunkered down on its haunches, long tail flicking angrily from side to side. Ryan's eye, away from the bright embers of the fire, was becoming more accustomed to the darkness of the creekbed. He kept staring at the unblinking green eyes of the huge creature.

"Get out of here," he said, actually taking a cautious half step toward the animal. "Come on. I got an ace on the line with you." The barrel of the SIG-Sauer was steady on the puma's jaws, the best target with the best margin for a close hit if the big cat moved suddenly in any direction.

Its mouth opened with an infinite slowness, and Ryan could taste the hunting scent of the big meat eater's breath. Ryan had never seen a carnivore of such a size. Its lethal, curling tusks sprouted from the upper jaw, twisting and pointing forward and up. If it came for him the pistol wouldn't stop the attack. It might kill the animal but it was too close not to be able to rip out Ryan's belly before it was chilled.

If it would turn then he could shoot it, knowing it wouldn't then be able to twist and power itself at him. He waved the gun, getting a deep-throated, rumbling growl in return. The tail stopped twitching, and he could see the powerful muscles along its back tensing ready for a spring. Ryan got himself braced to shoot for the head and dive sideways at the same time, hoping it wouldn't come to that.

The mutie cougar erupted toward him.

The broad trigger was firm and Ryan squeezed it twice, feeling the buck of the gun. The built-in baffle silencer that had been developed during the late 1990s muted the sound of the blaster. It also meant there was virtually no muzzle-flash from the heavy pistol in the blackness.

Ryan had no way at all of knowing where the bullets had hit the animal. He knew with an absolute certainty that he couldn't have missed at such close range.

The creature's leap brushed against him, even as he dived to his left, rolling, coming up with the gun ready. He'd felt claws actually tangle in his long dark hair, ripping out a chunk by the bloody roots.

In the darkness, near the brink of the pit, he could dimly make out the thrashing shape of the cougar, hearing its snarling, spitting rage. It crossed his mind that if it fell in the trap on top of the injured Jak Lauren, then the boy would surely buy the farm.

The sailing moon appeared briefly from behind its blanket of cloud, scattering a waxen light over the New Mexico land and showing the fiery sheen of the animal's eyes as it stared intently at Ryan. It was crouched, ready to spring again. Black in the moonlight, Ryan could see blood pouring from a gaping wound in its throat, slightly to the right, toward the shoulder. There was no sign of a second wound.

It wasn't the time to risk a poor shot. Ryan steadied his right wrist with his left hand, extending the P-226 like the finger of the avenging angel, and leveled it at the broad, thrusting head of the mountain lion.

He snapped off five quick shots, spaced one-third of a second apart to allow for any recoil.

In the moonlight he saw the skull of the puma explode into shards of splintered bone, and brain, blood and tissue erupted in a fine mist. The cougar fought its way to its feet, staggering, destroyed, then the lines went down and it toppled sideways, claws scraping on the bare rock.

"Fireblast," Ryan said softly. Behind him he could hear the sound of feet running toward him, voices calling his name. To recover from the violent tension, he stayed kneeling, fishing out ammunition from his pants pocket. He reloaded the pistol.

"Ryan! You okay? Ryan!"

"I'm here, lover. Watch your step. Jak's gone into a trap and broken some ribs."

"What was the shooting?" J.B. asked, hard on Krysty's heels.

"Mutie lion snuck up on me. I chilled it. Could be a pair, so watch the brush."

"The lion still rules the barranca," Doc said, obscure as ever.

"Where's the pit?" Lori asked.

"Just ahead, by that big boulder. Fuck it! Moon's going in again. Lori, go get a burning branch. Doc, go with her. We'll need light to get the kid out."

"Don't call me 'kid,' you old one-eyed bastard."

The voice, feeble and shaken, came floating up from the hole in the ground. Ryan grinned at the others. "At least the runt ain't dead."

Jak was alive, but he was in poor shape. It took the careful efforts of the other five, working as a team, to get him out of the hole. The flames from the makeshift torches showed how close he'd come to a brutal ending.

The pit was around six feet deep, with sharpened spikes of wood, thick as a baby's arm, set around the bottom. Being skinny and small, Jak had slithered in between the stakes, his chest catching a glancing blow on one of them. As Ryan lifted him out, passing the boy's light body up to J.B., Jak winced and then went suddenly limp. Peeling off the ragged vest, Krysty probed carefully, getting a cry of pain when she touched him on the left side.

"One, mebbe two broken ribs. Could have something damaged inside. Stomach. Liver. I'm not a doctor." She looked across at Doc Tanner.

"Nor am I, my dear. Science at Harvard and then philosophy at Oxford, England. Not a jot nor a tittle of medicine."

"Maybe we should rest him up. Or get him back to the redoubt," Krysty suggested.

"His face is whitest than white," Lori said, sitting in the dirt by the side of the semiconscious boy, holding his small hand in hers.

"Got any painies, J.B.?" Ryan asked. "You used to have some."

"Sure. Back on the war wags. All gone. I haven't seen any since way before Mocsin. Best let him sleep. See how he is in the morning."

"Sure." Ryan looked around. "After that big mutie cat, I guess we double up. I'll take until two. Krysty, take until four with J.B., and Doc and Lori through until dawn. At any sign of anything...anything, then wake everyone up. And keep an eye on Jak."

But the boy slept fitfully through the night, until Lori gently shook Ryan awake.

"First light," she whispered.

Ryan stretched. Sleeping out in the open, without even a horse blanket for cover, was second nature to him. And to the others. You got used to it—used to waking stiff, muscles cramping, often with your clothes sodden from overnight dew.

And always cold.

The sand beneath him was still dry, but the boulders and the trunks of the cottonwoods glistened with water. The sun was barely over the eastern rim of the hills, showing pink, with a halo spread around it like a great circular rainbow.

"How's Jak?"

"Just awaked," she said.

"How are his bones?"

Krysty shook her head, the long scarlet locks tumbling about her shoulders, their color heightened by the rising sun.

"Not so good."

"Fevered?"

"Yeah. Being he's albino, you can't tell if he's flushed or not. But his skin's dry as sand and he feels like he's burning up. Says his chest hurts. You can hear him draw breath."

Ryan stood, tightening the laces on his combat boots, rubbing at the thickening stubble on his chin. "What kind of noise?" he asked.

"Hear for yourself, lover. Come on."

Doc was pushing a couple of self-heats in among the smoldering embers of their fire, trying to get them beyond tepid warmth. Lori stood, shoulders hunched, peering into the mist that lay in the hollows of the land way off to the north, shrouding the peaks of the rounded mesas.

J.B. squatted beside Jak. The boy's face was as white as ever, but his red eyes caught Ryan's approach and he tried to sit up. The Armorer gently pushed him back down again, glancing up at Ryan.

"Kid's not so good," he said.

"Don't call..." Jak began not even managing to finish the sentence. He lay down, eyes closing. Ryan noticed that the young lad's fingers were twisting and knotting on his chest, as if they were possessed of a life of their own.

He knelt down, feeling the coolness of the earth on his hands. Doc was muttering angrily, and Ryan called him to be quiet. "I'm trying to listen to Jak's breathing," he said.

"My apologies. But these confabulated, sockdologizing tins refuse to warm up. I swear they are doing it to perversely annoy me. But I shall be quiet, Ryan, of course I shall. I thought that his respiration was less than healthy."

Ryan thought it sounded a whole lot less than healthy.

The movements of the chest were shallow and rapid, and sounded like a failing engine. As the sunlight grew stronger Ryan noticed to his alarm that Jak's natural pallor was becoming tinged with a pastel blue around the lips and below the fluttering eyes.

And even as he watched, the breathing was becoming slower.

Chapter Nine

"HE'S DYING."

"No. No, Ryan."

"Lori, I'm real sorry about this, but you can look at him. There's some kind of damage to his guts."

"Help him."

Doc took her arm. "I fear that what our leader says is all too true, my dearest child. No doubt a reputable surgeon could pluck the boy from the jaws of Hades. None of us possesses sufficient skill in the arts of medicine."

"We can all save he. All of us." Lori was almost in tears.

"I fear not," Doc said.

"What if we got him back to the gateway?" Krysty suggested.

"Broken ribs," J.B. said. "And something worse broke inside him. There's drugs and all that but we don't..."

"When we rode the war wags with Trader there was a medic around. Kathy on War Wag One. Me and...we just don't have that kind of skill at saving lives."

"Just killing," Krysty said bitterly, turning away from Ryan and walking through the grove of shimmering cottonwoods, toward the dried riverbed.

He followed her, catching up near the tangled deadfall. She turned around and held up a hand. "I know, lover. I shouldn't have said it. I *know* that. But to see a boy of fourteen dying in front of us... It's not right, Ryan."

"Nobody ever said it had to be right, Krysty. You know that."

"Sure. Doesn't mean I have to like it, though. So, what do we do?"

"Rig a travois. Use branches from the cottonwoods. We'll haul Jak down to the trail. Looked well-traveled. We wait and hope someone comes along. Someone who can help him."

"If nobody comes?"

"I guess he'll be dead by sunset."

It didn't take long to build a crude stretcher that two of them could drag along, its ends bouncing over the rough ground. Doc said that he'd seen things like it when he'd visited with the Apaches as a young man. But then they'd used ponies to pull the travois.

"Sure wish we'd got us a horse, Doc," J.B. said. "Or even a half dozen of 'em."

Jak had become feverish, throwing his head from side to side, the long white hair tangling, already stained with orange dust. Ryan tied him to the travois to prevent him rolling off. As he secured a length of cord around the boy's chest, Jak's eyes snapped open.

"Watch gators, Pa!" he called, his voice cracked and frail.

"Stay easy, Jak," Ryan said quietly, not sure if his words penetrated the burning maze of the boy's brain.

The ruby eyes came back from some limitless distance, focusing briefly on Ryan's face.

"If don't make it...been good. All you. Good." Then the fire swept in and his head slumped. His eyes closed and he was still.

"Has he gone?" Krysty asked, at Ryan's shoulder. "He looks..."

"No. Still breathing, but it's shallow and real fast. He's baking up."

IT WAS A LITTLE AFTER ten o'clock in the morning when they finally reached the trail and laid the travois in the shade of a giant saguaro. There was a low butte a half mile to the north, commanding a view all across the wide valley.

"I'm going up there for a recce," said Ryan, "see if there's any sign of life. Keep watch down here. I'll be back in a half hour."

Bushes of milky locoweed dotted the desert, scattered in clumps among the cactus. Ryan walked briskly away from his friends, boots crunching through the soft sand. A scorpion scuttled from the heavy approach of the man, tail curved menacingly over its back.

In his heart, Ryan felt that Jak was almost certainly doomed. Sure, miracles happened.

But they didn't happen very often.

It was difficult to tell with the albino, but Ryan suspected that the boy was hemorrhaging from some internal injury. In the heat of New Mexico, even in the shadows, he would be burning up. They'd given him all the water they could spare during the morning, but it was just impossible to get his temperature down near normal.

He eased the G-12 across his shoulders. The ground was already rising ahead of him as he reached the bottom of the butte. Though he hadn't mentioned his fears to the rest of the group, Ryan was only too aware that the owners of the horses that had pitted the trail might not be too friendly.

Like so many elements of life in the Deathlands, you could only cross the bridge when you came right up to it.

Ryan ran his fingers through his hair, wincing at the amount of grit that matted it. Sweat was trickling down inside the patch over his left eye and he eased it away, tentatively rubbing at the puckered socket. The salt in perspiration always made his eye sore.

As far as he could see in any direction, there didn't seem to be any sign of life. There wasn't even a bird circling in the delicate blue of the sky. He thought he could hear, very faintly, the distant rumble of thunder, as some chem storm boiled up.

His wrist chron showed it was just short of eleven o'clock. He decided to rest there for a few minutes, maybe wait until noon. Then he would rejoin the others, and they could wait together for death to claim the fourteen-year-old boy.

The numbers crept around toward twelve, and he waited along.

He heard a sharp buzzing and flapped his hand at a sleek, striped bee that was hovering near the back of his neck. Ryan had heard tales from the south of the Deathlands of swarms of fierce killer bees that would attack cattle and people, and sting them to death. He stood, brushing dirt from his pants, and looked around to see if the bee was the harbinger of a deadly swarm.

But the sky was clear and untouched. It was very close to midday and he sighed. Things didn't look good for Jak.

The sun hung directly overhead, reducing his shadow to a tiny circle of sharp darkness that puddled his boots. The temperature felt like it was way over a hundred. It looked like nobody was going to travel the trail that day. Ryan took a last look around. He hesitated, shading his eye with his hand. Over to the northwest, just visible behind a crooked-backed mesa, he could see a small pillar of swirling orange and gray dust.

It was moving steadily to the spot where the others were resting. Ryan watched it for a few seconds longer, making sure that it wasn't one of the natural dust devils, whipped up by the erratic wind. But it continued unabated. He turned and began to jog slowly down the face of the butte, to rejoin the others.

"They're about five miles off. Couldn't see any other trail, so they have to pass this way."

"We wait here?" J.B. asked, glancing doubtfully around them. "Not much good for defense."

Ryan sucked in hot air between his front teeth, whistled it out again. "Guess you're right. If we move back there—" he pointed to a slope of gently rising land, under the ridge of one of the infinite number of mesas "—we can find some cover."

"Will that not leave our rear a trifle exposed?" Doc said.

Ryan nodded. "Yeah, but that trail's ahead of us. If they try to circle, then we can see them good and clear—as long as we don't get anyone else coming up behind us."

Working together like the team they'd become, the five friends managed to haul the travois across the dried-up bed of the creek, wrestling it up the farther slope, onto flatter ground. They eventually found a level place behind a ridge of frost-broken boulders beneath the mesa.

Lori stayed with the delirious boy while the other four found good places to defend among the rocks. The trail came within a hundred paces or so of where they waited.

The dust cloud was larger, unmistakable, and Ryan called to Krysty to see if her keen sight could make out any more.

"Men on horses. Gray clothes, I think. Could be thirty or so. It's hard to tell. Looks like they're riding in pairs."

"Sec men?"

"Can't tell."

"Whites or Indians?" Doc shouted.

"Can't see."

"Blasters?" hissed J.B., who'd taken up position on the end of the line.

"Gaia!" Krysty called. "I know my sight's better than most, but I can't count the damned fleas on a pig at twenty miles. They're still too far off for me to make out."

In the stillness that followed they could all hear Jak's little voice, babbling jagged, broken phrases. Moments from his past. From his imagination. Moments from nowhere.

"Baron Tourment gripping...swampies closing on me with teeth bloodied . . . Slain waxwing's shadow in eyes... Let's lick breasts sweet and sweet and... Seen into night . . . Father!"

"Want Lori to try to keep him quiet, Ryan?" Doc asked.

"No. We're not worried about hiding. We want them to see us. Let the kid rave all he wants to. Mebbe help him some."

Gradually the horsemen, in double column, drew closer. They were all wearing uniforms of light gray and were mostly mounted on bay steeds. Ryan could see the sun dancing off shining metal, indicating that they were all armed. He couldn't rid himself of the nagging feeling that there was something wrong. They rode too tight together, and it looked as if they wore similar uniforms. And that meant sec men.

And sec men meant trouble.

"Don't all show yourselves," Ryan called to his companions. "Keep undercover and keep 'em covered. Wait for my word. If there's any threat, then pour it in them. Keep careful."

Ryan waited until the men, twenty-seven of them in all, were level with their hiding place, on the narrow trail.

"Hey!" he shouted, standing behind the boulders, waving his hands above his head. The SIG-Sauer was unholstered and the Heckler & Koch rested at his feet, ready for use.

His sudden appearance had a dramatic effect on the mounted patrol.

There was a shouted command from a tall rider at the front and the column wheeled, straggling a little, stringing out along the side of the trail. It halted at another command.

Ryan stood still, the others remaining hidden and silent. He held his hands out wide in the universal gesture, showing that he held no weapons and meant no harm. Over the years, Ryan had also often come to recognize the gesture as that of someone about to spring an ambush.

The line of men watched him. Ryan ran his eye along them, noting a variety of things: they all wore the same uniform, dusty and gray, with what looked like a golden stripe down the sides of their pants; most wore slouch hats, all had boots; some had swords slung at their hips, others holstered pistols; nearly all of them had long blasters hidden in buckets on the side of the saddle, but he couldn't make out what type they were. The leader was much taller than most, riding a well-muscled black stallion.

"Hi, there," Ryan shouted from his vantage point, knowing from the position of the sun that the patrol of sec men—for that's what they had to be—couldn't see him clearly. "Got a man sick here. Can you help?"

The leader had a thickset man behind him, with three stripes faintly visible on his upper arm. Behind

him came a single rider, holding a guidon that fluttered at the tip of a spear. The rest of the men were
strung out at the rear.

With his eyes locked on Ryan Cawdor, the leader
took off one of a pair of leather gauntlets and began
to brush at the dust on his clothes. The rest of the column followed his example, the men disappearing behind a quivering wraith of reddish-gray. The cloud
cleared away slowly, and Ryan and his concealed
companions could see the sec men properly for the
first time.

The uniforms weren't gray. They were dark blue,
with a stripe of yellow down the side of the breeches.
The saddles were a peculiar, high, old-fashioned kind
of design. Ryan could only see the hilts of the long,
curved sabers, but they looked like brass. It wasn't
possible to make out any of the blasters that the sec
men carried.

The leader took off his hat very slowly and deliberately, revealing a tumbling mane of golden hair as
long and lush as Lori's blond tresses. The face was
thin, with a yellow mustache, the eyes narrow. It
seemed to Ryan that there was something wrong with
the thin-lipped mouth. It looked skewed, as though
from some old wound.

And it looked oddly familiar.

But his eye was then caught as the wind unfurled the
flag atop the lance, held by the young galloper. It was
dark blue, and it carried only a large golden number:
seven.

"By the three Kennedys!" Doc exclaimed, close by
Ryan on one side. "We've chron-jumped by mistake.

This is 1875. That's Autie Custer and the Seventh Cavalry!''

Ryan had read about General Custer and his blue-coat pony soldiers. Forty miles a day on beans and hay had been one of their slogans. Custer had been the brightest and best young officer in the country, and he'd ridden to his death in some dreadful ambush in the nineteenth century.

To his right Ryan glimpsed J.B., his angular jaw dropped in amazement.

"Is it a chron-jump, lover?" Krysty whispered from the other side.

"I don't know," Ryan began.

At a signal from the yellow-haired officer, the shooting began.

Chapter Ten

RYAN DIVED SIDEWAYS to save his life, his brain a jagged maze of swirling confusion.

Had they stumbled on some distant ville where the baron used a military force of sec men, armed and uniformed like something out of a Remington painting or a Brady daguerrotype?

Or was Doc right? Had they accidentally triggered the gateway into operating on a chron-jump system?

Which century were they in? The nineteenth or the twenty-second?

Doesn't much matter, he thought, as he landed in a rolling dive behind the barrier of the boulders. Splinters of rock stung his face and neck as a bullet missed him by less than a hand's span. By the time he'd come up from the somersault, he had the G-12 and was crouching behind cover, ready to join the firefight.

"Let them have it?" J.B. shouted from his right side.

"Yeah. Hold 'em off." Ryan raised his voice so that all four could hear him. "Don't let them get close, but watch the ammo."

Ryan had been in firefights where thousands of rounds had been blasted off in a couple of minutes of bloody action. That was when you had the supply wags at your back. Now, they were friendless in a strange and hostile land, more hostile than he'd imagined at first. All they carried was all they had. That and no more.

"What blasters are they using?" he yelled to J.B., ducking instinctively at the weight of lead hissing around them.

The Armorer's knowledge of firearms was legendary, his ear for a make or model of blaster almost infallibly accurate.

"Can't believe it, Ryan. Sounds like they got Springfield carbines, 1873 models, .45 caliber. But there can't be that many left working in all Deathlands."

Ryan knew the guns, single-shot center-fire weapons with a long, slow trigger pull. In the back country you sometimes came across one, generally rebored and rebuilt, held together with rusting baling wire, the butt long rotted. For all of the sec men attacking them to be armed with the same type of blaster was stretching coincidence to such an extent that he began to think Doc was right. They must have chron-jumped.

It was a weirdly exciting idea, but one that had to be set on the back burner. Survival came first.

"Hold fire!" came the shrill yell from the leader of the sec men.

Ryan risked a glance around his boulder, seeing that the blue-uniformed sec men had spread out in an efficient skirmishing line, each man picking his own cover from the range of hollows and scattered rocks. The officer was just visible near the center of the men, holding up his drawn saber, the sunlight glittering brightly from the blade.

Ryan picked the momentary silence to try again. "We got a man wounded. Don't mean no harm! Why d'you blast us?"

For fifty heartbeats there was no reply. Then he heard the harsh voice of the skinny blond sec officer. "If you speak the truth, then all of you come out, hands high, blasters in the dirt."

Doc's voice hissed from Ryan's flank. "Not a chron-jump. They didn't call guns 'blasters' in Custer's day. There's something rather suspicious here, Ryan. I advise some caution."

The warning wasn't necessary. There was something about the tall, lean man that rang a distant bell in Ryan's memory. And the memory was tainted with a dark shadow.

At least it was good news that they hadn't traveled centuries back in time. Yet why were these men all clothed in such outdated uniforms? Dressed as the old Seventh Cavalry, which had been wiped away by Crazy Horse and the Sioux up on the Little Big Horn?

Ryan wasn't a doomie or a senser, but the prickling of the short hairs at his nape gave its own warning.

"Come out and show yourself!" the sec officer shouted.

"Don't, lover," Krysty whispered. "Something's real bad here."

"First, you come here and talk some about it," Ryan replied to the hidden man.

"Ma didn't raise me to lay my neck under the ax, stranger. Come out now, or we come and take you. Better my way."

"You say!"

"Mister, I don't have the time to wait here in the sun while you fart around with me. You got ten seconds to come out." A pause. "How many you got yonder?"

"Enough," Ryan called. "With enough blasters to make you pay a price."

"You say!" mocked the yellow-haired man. Ryan could still see the last foot or so of the sword's blade, protruding behind the boulder. A rising wind blew a veil of dust between the two sides.

Behind him, Ryan heard Jak moaning in pain.

"Ten seconds, stranger. What you got to lose? One way or another, we get you."

"I know the voice," Krysty hissed. "Can't place it though."

"And I," Doc added. "I associate it with past wickedness, but I fear that the memory is blurred. Like so many."

"Five seconds!"

Ryan leveled the smooth muzzle of the G-12, holding his breath as he drew a careful bead. The laser-enhanced scopesight gave him a perfect view of his target, though it shimmered a little in the desert heat.

"Two seconds, stranger. You show yourself and you don't get harmed. You got the general's word on that."

"You first . . . General."

"For a man with just two seconds left to live, you got a lotta gall, stranger. Show yourself to me. Seems like I might know you from somewhere."

Ryan didn't reply, concentrating his attention on a difficult shot, the caseless rifle steady on the rounded edge of the boulder. The range wasn't anything to the G-12, but the target was almost impossibly small.

"Ready, troopers? Harknett, take five men and go left, along the draw, come around behind him. Bulmer, do the same to the right. Go on my word." The orders carried clearly to the five friends as they waited, hidden from the sec men.

"Wait," Ryan breathed, finger tightening on the trigger of the blaster.

"That's it, stranger," screamed the man in blue.

The sound of the gun, suppressed by a system of baffles, was no louder than a spinster's genteel cough in the middle of a Sunday sermon on the sin of sloth.

The recoil pushed against Ryan's shoulder with an insistent nudge. Straining his ears, he heard the sound of success. The thin ringing noise of steel on steel, then the piercing whine of the bullet as it ricocheted into the air. There was a yell of inarticulate anger and through the sight Ryan could see the blond man shaking his jarred wrist. The saber had been sent spinning from his fingers and now lay a half dozen paces beyond the ridge of stones.

"Put the ace right on the line." J.B. grinned. "Should stir some shit down there for the sec men."

"Yeah," Ryan said with a wolfish grin that puckered the scar on his cheek.

They all heard the order to fire, and ducked against the crescendo of bullets that sang and spit around them. But they were safe in the dip. Ryan knew that if the sec men managed to get around back of them, on the top of the ridge behind, then their time would be counted down in seconds.

"Die, you bastard!" came the scream from behind the swirling cloud of powder smoke.

The carbines were single shot, and there was a momentary but appreciable delay in the volleys. Ryan sensed the rhythm, waiting for the moment to squint around the right-hand side of the covering rocks, trying to find a target for the G-12. His friends were doing the same, but only he and the Armorer possessed blasters capable of causing problems for the distant sec men.

"Wait for them to try moving," he called. "Some'll go left, and some right. J.B., you take any going to the left."

"Sure."

The golden-haired officer didn't waste any time. Obviously angered and shaken by having his sword shot clean out of his hand, they heard him snapping orders to his patrol. Moments later, screened by another burst of fire from the carbines, the sec men made their move.

"Now," Ryan said, showing himself for a moment, the Heckler & Koch now set on triple burst. He squeezed the trigger three times. The innovative blaster had a built-in dispersal factor, to allow for any normal variability of aim. Of the six men scurrying along, partly hidden by the dead ground, Ryan saw four go down, the other two diving flat for the minimal cover. Out of the corner of his eye he saw that J.B.'s racketing mini-Uzi had knocked down three of the half dozen sec men trying to circle them on the left.

The double burst of lethal fire had the temporary effect of silencing the remainder of the hidden sec men. From where they waited, Ryan and the others could hear a man screaming, gut shot, kicking up a whirling cloud of orange dust.

"That'll give them something to think on," Krysty said.

"Just be more careful when they creep at us," J.B. replied, taking a quick look around the protective rocks. "They're sitting tight. Didn't know how many there was of us." He paused. "But now they know better."

The silence from the sec men lasted several minutes. Ryan had a chance at a snap shot at the long-haired leader of their attackers as he scuttled across to join the rest of his men, obviously to plan their next moves without bellowing out orders that could be heard from higher up the hill.

Though the lay of the first deck of cards favored the defenders, Ryan had seen enough firefights to be pessimistically aware of how slim their chances were. The sec men were only armed with the single-shot carbines, but they seemed well drilled and disciplined. And there were still at least twenty of them alive, against the five friends. What was more relevant was that only the G-12 was really suited to distance shooting. The Uzi would take its toll if they were rushed.

The handblasters of Doc, Krysty and Lori wouldn't be of much use out in the open like this.

If the blond officer played the rest of the hand with adequate skill, then the troopers could surround them and get to the high ground and pick them off one by one.

It didn't look good.

WHOEVER WAS IN CHARGE of the sec men knew his job. He made sure that Ryan and the others didn't get a chance to relax or to grow confident in their position. Every half minute or so there'd be a ragged volley of shots, closely aimed, keeping heads down, leaving a bitter layer of dust in the baking air.

Ryan slithered back down to see how Jak was. Lori was still kneeling beside him, fanning with her hand to try to keep the horde of midges from settling in his open mouth and on the crusted, staring pink eyes. The boy had finally sunk into a coma, but his body still twitched and jerked and he was looking, open-eyed, into some unimaginable distance. Every now and again he blinked and his lips moved as if he were speaking, but no audible sound emerged.

"Can't you help him, Ryan?"

"Tried. Those bastards aren't feeling much like giving any help."

"Can I try?"

"That way you die as well as the kid. No."

"What do we doing? Just waiting?"

"Yeah. If they rush us, we can take a whole lot of them to get the ice."

"Ryan!" The voice was J.B.'s, urgent, calling him to the firing line.

"What?"

"Look." He pointed to their right, and then up the left. "Dust. They got men around the side."

"Fireblast!" He turned and looked behind them, up the hill to the skeletal row of boulders marking the ridge. "If I'd known they'd start blasting us, I'd have gone there. Too damned late now."

"Best we go out and try and take them?" the Armorer suggested.

Ryan shook his head doubtfully. "Can't. Can't leave Doc and the girls. Sec men'd overrun them in ten seconds."

"Can't stay here. Pick us off, easy as spotting blood on a snowfield."

"When one is caught between a rock and a hard place then one must pick the lesser of the twin evils," Doc said.

"Yeah. Best we do it now. You and me, J.B., dodge down, toward them. Pour it in. Doc and Krysty come after. Lori stays with Jak. There's still a chance for them."

Krysty glanced behind them, up the slope, staring. Ryan's eye was caught, and he, too, looked. Then Doc and finally J.B.

The ridge had been bare fifteen seconds earlier. Now it held a line of mounted men. Dark, in colorful clothes, all holding rifles.

"Apache Indians," Doc whispered with an almost religious awe.

"The hard place just got harder," Ryan said.

Chapter Eleven

THE SOLDIERS SAW the Indians at the same moment that Ryan and his friends did. There was a shout of recognition, and the carbines spit lead at the newcomers. Several of the sec men showed themselves, and Ryan and J.B. took advantage of their carelessness to cut down three more.

But the Apaches still showed no sign of wanting to enter the fight on either side. Ryan kept low, hearing bullets slice through the air above him. The horsemen were about five hundred yards behind them, sitting impassively. Ryan could make out that they were dark and stocky, and wore headbands of colored cotton.

At a yell of command from the sec officer, the shooting stopped.

"It's all wrong," Doc moaned. "The way it's always been, the Seventh Cavalry comes riding over the hill and rescues us poor whites from the demon Indians. And by the three Kennedys, there's General Custer, looking like he rides well right here and now. And that's all wrong, too."

One of the Apaches heeled his pony a couple of steps forward. The bright sunlight glittered on something at his belt, such as an ax or a broad-bladed knife. The cavalry and the Indians kept their positions, with

Ryan and his companions the meat in the hostile sandwich.

"We could do some chilling with them sitting tight together on the ridge," J.B. suggested. "Get the retaliation in first."

"Mebbe they're not against us. Seems like the sec men don't see them as friends."

Doc looked at Krysty, nodding at her words. His rheumy eyes blinked like a stone-warmed lizard's and the dust stirred in the deep creases around his beaked nose.

"I've an idea, Ryan," he said. "I trust there is no objection to my... what did they call it? Ah, yes. To my running it up the flagpole and seeing if the cat brings it in." He hesitated. "Or something rather like that."

"Go for it, Doc."

"You're certain, Ryan?"

"My best shot's heading down the hill with all blasters busy. That or sucking the .38. And that ain't my style."

Doc stood, showing himself above the ring of protective stones.

"Get down!" Ryan shouted, seeing the old man fold at the knees like an ungainly heron, just before a scattering of bullets splintered close by him.

"My goodness," the old man said, as mildly as if he'd been refused a second lump of sugar in his cup of coffee.

"Can't you do it from there?" Krysty asked.

"I believe so." Doc wriggled around so that he faced up the hill, toward the patient statues of the silent Apaches. Doc cleared his throat, then called up in a guttural, harsh voice, the words echoing across the flank of the mesa.

The leader of the Indians leaned forward along the pony's neck, as if he couldn't believe what he was hearing. The rest of the line of warriors all began to chatter excitedly to one another.

"What'd you say, Doc?" Krysty asked. "Sure put the wolf in the sheep pen."

"Remember that my grasp of Apache was never more than somewhat rudimentary, friends," Doc replied. "I may have made a suggestion of the utmost obscenity concerning the sexual proclivities of the chieftain's mother."

"But?" J.B. prompted.

"But I hope that what I called out was a traditional appeal and offer of help. 'My enemies are your enemies. So shall they be, as long as the sun rides the sky and the grass grows.' "

Ryan looked at the Apaches. "Sure hope it works, Doc. You got them fired up."

As suddenly as they'd appeared, at a signal from their leader, the mounted warriors turned their ponies and disappeared over the line of the ridge... And reappeared in a double, whooping line, heeling their small, nimble-footed ponies down the rock-tumbled slope, passing close by Ryan and his friends, who leaped away from the flying hail of pebbles and whirling dust.

"They got about every kind of damned blaster I ever heard of," J.B. shouted above the bedlam of their passing. "Remingtons, Winchesters, Gallaghers, Springfields, Spencers, Burnsides and Sharps."

"Saw a coupla M-16s in there," Ryan called. "Most patched and mended."

It was an unusual luxury for Ryan Cawdor and the others to be able to sit back in relative safety and watch a firefight going on below them.

The Apaches were masters of their animals and the cruel terrain, weaving and darting in close to the sec men, who suddenly found themselves the besieged instead of the besiegers. The Indians hung around the necks of their mounts, snapping off shots at the hidden cavalrymen. There were puffs of powder smoke drifting across the serrated land.

"Man on horseback doesn't shoot straight," J.B. said.

"Also hard to knock down," Ryan added. "Could it be a hot spot standoff? Not enough power on either side to take the other."

In less than five minutes his guess was proved to be right.

Two of the Indians went down, in each case their animals being shot by the carbines. Both Apaches got up and jogged away unharmed, vaulting easily behind their comrades. From where they watched it wasn't possible for Ryan and the others to see if the sec men were taking any casualties. There was a passing temptation for Ryan to lead the four of them down and try to force the sec men out with their superior blasters. But it seemed a whole lot more sensible to stay where they were and await developments. It certainly looked as if Doc's appeal to the Apaches had worked.

So far.

"They're pulling out," Krysty said. "Guy with the pretty yellow hair just shouted for them to pull back to their horses."

With her sharp hearing, the redheaded girl was right. While they watched the indeterminate battle petering out below them, the Apaches broke off the engagement, allowing the sec men to withdraw in good order. Ryan stood to watch them, and he saw the leader of the white men turn in his high saddle and stare back at him. There was the flash of sunlight off a spyglass and then the patrol and its leader vanished in a cloud of dust, heading away along the trail toward the north.

"Now all we have to do is make our peace with the Apaches," Doc said, standing and stretching his creaking knees, brushing his coat clean of dirt.

"Yeah, that's all." Ryan grinned.

Before the Apaches could come back up the slope, Ryan led the others to where Lori was waiting with Jak. The albino boy was visibly sinking toward the long quiet of death. His breathing was so shallow that his chest barely moved at all, and the ruby eyes were closed.

The teenage girl looked up, face pale with fear. "Muties gone? They ride on and then I hear blasters. Are we saving?"

Doc stooped and kissed her on top of the head with a touching, infinite gentleness. "Don't worry, my dearest child. They aren't muties. Leastways, I don't believe that they are. They all looked just as they did when I visited with the Mescalero Apaches a few years...a few hundred...two hundred...five hundred miles away from home.''

"Here they are," J.B. said laconically, holding the Uzi casually in his right hand. Ryan held the G-12 against his hip, his finger on the trigger, watching as the stocky horsemen came whooping up the slope, then becoming silent at a command from their leader.

Now that they were closer Ryan could see what had been glittering at the belt of the Apache war chief. It was a peculiar dagger, with a broad, triangular blade that gleamed with the sheen of gold. The hilt was studded with uncut stones of different colors. Even from a distance the weapon had the unmistakable patina of age and genuine quality.

The Apache reined in his horse a few paces from the small group, looking down intently at the unconscious boy. Ryan had seen Indians before; because of their way of life at the time of the long winters, some of the tribes had survived better than the people of many large cities. They made great trackers and hunters, and still held their communities in the more distant parts of the Deathlands.

"Who speaks our tongue?" the warrior said in broken English.

Doc Tanner cautiously raised his hand, showing his oddly perfect teeth in a smile as every single one of the Apaches stared at him. "I must confess that it was I who addressed you."

"Anglos do not know the words of the people," the Indian insisted, face impassive.

"I was among your people, close by here in the Canyon de Chelly, many, many years past."

"You are muties."

It was a statement and not a question, with an assumption that could mean a swift and sudden passing in many regions of the country.

Ryan took a step forward. "We thank you for your help. We aren't muties. None of us."

"The woman's hair." He pointed at Krysty. "And the hair of dead boy."

"We're not muties," Ryan insisted.

The expression on the face of the war chief made it obvious that he didn't believe the words of the tall white man.

"The tongue of the Anglo is the tongue of the desert rattler," he said. "Not to be trusted by the people."

The two groups looked at each other for several stretched seconds. One of the Apaches pointed with a long spear at the unconscious figure of Jak. He said something to the leader.

"What'd he say, Doc?" Ryan asked.

"I'm sorry, Ryan, but I fear that my grasp of their language was never outstandingly good. The dialect of the Mescalero is far from simple to try to comprehend."

"He says that the boy with hair like snow is near the long sleep without waking."

"We know that," Krysty said.

"The Yellowhair and his running dogs have done this thing?"

"Is it Autie Custer?" Doc asked in English.

"Custer died more than two hundred years past," the Apache replied, looking at Doc Turner with the kind of pitying expression you reserved for a leg-broke horse.

"I know that... But it's the Seventh Cavalry. I saw the guidon. And his hair and—"

"There is a story like the road down from a mountaintop, winding and slow and with many twists to it. Such is the story of the Yellowhair and the pony soldiers who ride with him."

"I'd kind of like to hear the story," Ryan said. "You got someplace we could take the kid?"

The Indian swung down off the bright blanket that took the place of a saddle for the Mescalero. He knelt by Jak, studying him with dark eyes. "He will be with the spirits before the sun has slept below the far mountains."

"Then we'll bury him," J.B. said.

"We have a shaman who has the sight and the hands. He could—"

"What's a shaman, Doc?" Ryan asked.

"Kind of halfway house between a doctor, a priest and a faith healer."

"The boy is losing the fight. He has fallen?"

"Yeah. Into a trap for a mutie cougar, way back." Ryan pointed in the vague direction of the redoubt, not wanting to give away too much.

"The lion of the mountains?"

"Dead."

The Apache stood, nodding, as though that answer had confirmed his decisions. "The travois you have built will be pulled by our horses. You will all come with us." He turned to his men, then faced Ryan Cawdor. "You are the enemies of Yellowhair?"

"He sure isn't a friend."

"Good. But if you betray us . . ."

"Sure, Chief . . . We don't know your name."

"We do not know your names. There will a time for that when we reach our rancheria."

Ryan glanced at Doc Tanner for an explanation of the new word. "It means a kind of camp. Often up high. In the canyons."

"Can this shaman save Jak?" Ryan asked quietly, while the Apache leader swung himself on his pony, calling orders to his warriors.

"Can you, Ryan?" the old man replied.

AS THEY LEFT THE SCENE of the abortive firefight, Ryan glanced over his shoulder, seeing that the spiraling dust cloud from the patrol of sec men was still moving steadily toward the north, where dark purple clouds were gathering. The cavalrymen had taken their dead and wounded with them, bodies tied ankle to wrist over the saddles.

Jak's head lolled helplessly to one side as the makeshift litter bounced slowly along, drawn between two ponies. His long white hair seemed dulled and lifeless.

Ryan and the others walked along by the Apaches, toward the line of red cliffs that marked the side of one of the long mesas.

Over the years he'd seen several old vids of what were called "westies," mainly about firefights between the soldiers and different tribes of Indians.

Now, unbelievably, he was living in one of those vids.

Chapter Twelve

THE RANCHERIA OF THE subtribe of the Mescalero
Apaches was in a box canyon, nearly a two-hour ride
from where they'd encountered the six whites.

If Ryan and his friends had managed to get hold of
a detailed map of that part of New Mexico, printed
way before the holocaust, they'd have found it was
named Drowned Squaw Canyon.

The jaws of the canyon were less than a dozen feet
across, barely wide enough for a pair of horsemen to
ride in side by side, and it lay at the farther end of a
wilderness of coulees and dry riverbeds that wound
and twisted in an almost impenetrable maze. Even
from fifty paces away, it didn't look to Ryan as if there
were any way into the canyon.

The trail continued for a hundred yards or so, between two-hundred-foot walls of sheer crimson rock,
gradually widening until it opened into an area about
six hundred paces across. At the farther end, under the
lip of a wall of seamless stone, was a pool of deep,
clear water.

There were small fires burning among fifty or sixty
low huts, which Doc told them were called wickiups.
As they walked into the canyon with the horsemen,
women and small children came running from the

huts, excitedly calling out to one another at the sight of the white strangers. The leader waved them back with his rifle, shouting out orders as he dismounted.

"Do you want food?" he asked Ryan.

"Yes, and water. But first the boy must be treated. You said—"

"Our shaman is called Man Whose Eyes See More. I have asked an old woman to go and wake him. The whitehead will rest there, by the fire."

While they waited for the shaman, Ryan led the other four around the camp of the Mescalero Apaches.

At their leader's orders the Indians kept away from the visitors, but three of the older women, faces wrinkled, eyes almost buried in the folds, brought them earthenware bowls of green chili stew, with chunks of mutton floating in it. They also gave them corn on the cob, blue corn bread and spicy yerba tea.

Ryan hadn't realized how hungry he'd been after the action of the firefight, and he devoured two bowls of the hot stew.

The sun had disappeared behind the cliffs to the west of the canyon, making the air feel cool and shadowed. They sat down near Jak, outside the turf-topped hut. The boy was now on the very brink of death. His breathing was so subdued that it was no longer possible to see respiration. J.B. had knelt beside him, holding a small mirror to the bloodless lips, bringing only the faintest mist to the polished metal.

"Where's their—" Krysty began, stopping as the buckskin curtain across the mouth of the nearest wickiup opened.

It was Man Whose Eyes See More.

He was so skinny that it looked like he'd have to run around in a rainstorm to get himself wet. Most of the Apaches were close to the five-foot-six mark, but the shaman was scraping at seven feet tall, weighing barely 120 pounds.

Man Whose Eyes See More was dressed in an elegant pair of seersucker pants of ancient cut that were missing one leg below the knee. His top half was clad in a striped cotton shirt with a white collar and a brocade waistcoat with mother-of-pearl buttons. There was a flaming scarlet cravat knotted casually around his scrawny neck, which was held in place with a silver stickpin with an empty claw setting. A pale cerise kerchief dangled from the vest pocket. His feet were bare and a whole lot less than clean.

He looked slowly along the line of white men and women, utterly impassive. He stepped in closer to Ryan and reached out, laying a hand across his forehead, gazing deep into the single eye.

"The anger for your brother is ended," he said quietly.

"Yeah. You could say that."

The shaman also paused in front of Doc Tanner, his face crinkling in bewilderment. "You are of time and not of time. Dead and not dead. Living and not living. Old and not old."

"Hungry and not hungry. Angry and more angry. Cut the quack's tricks and look at the kid there," Doc replied.

"The Gan, the spirits of the mountain, will not permit too much hurry. Only Ysun, the giver of all life, can help your friend. I shall pray to White Painted Woman and she will help. If she wants to help."

"What if she doesn't?" J.B. asked, struggling to muffle a chili-spiced belch.

"She will...or she will not. That is the way now, as it was before the time of the great fires in the sky and before that. At the times of our forefathers, who lived in peace beneath the tall cliffs. Before the dry time came."

"The kid's near dead," J.B. said with a dangerous calm, hand dropping to the butt of the holstered Steyr pistol. "Less talk, friend."

"You talk threat to me, Anglo," the shaman said, with a superior smile. "I lift my hand and all of you are dust."

"I pull this trigger, wizard, and your guts spill around your ankles. Get to it."

Man Whose Eyes See More nodded slowly. "There is much fire within you. Much anger. Much that is bitter and sour. But I shall do what I can. I do not feel there is bad in any of you." He stared intently again at Ryan as he spoke.

Two of the old men ushered the five friends away from Jak. Ryan glanced over his shoulder, seeing that the tall shaman was sitting cross-legged, fumbling at a small leather bag slung around his neck by a narrow thong.

The chief, golden knife at his hip, saw them coming and waved for them to sit around the crackling fire outside his own wickiup.

"Leave Man Whose Eyes See More. He has the great power. Our people have not had such a true shaman for many generations. If he does not heal your companion, then he is past all help."

It didn't seem like much consolation.

The afternoon slipped gently into evening. The fires began to glow more brightly as the pools of shadow deepened and spread. The women of the rancheria went about the business of making the last meal of the day. Drowned Squaw Canyon filled with the scent of roasting chili and iron pots of stew bubbled. Children ran around like stocky models of their parents, the girls in long fringed dresses and the boys in cotton pants and bright shirts. Doc Tanner leaned back, puffing contentedly at a pipe given to him by one of the older warriors.

"Upon my soul, but I believed when we saw General Custer leading out the Seventh Cavalry across the dusty landscape that we had inadvertently managed a chron-jump. It was so like the old pictures. Whatever happened to the faces in the old photographs? Boys, hell they were men that stood... What was I saying?"

"Chron-jumps, Doc," Lori prompted, lying with her head in his lap, ignoring the disapproving looks and clucking tongues of the older women, who tossed their braided hair as they padded fatly by.

"Chron... Was I?" His face brightened. "Indeed I was. Merciful heavens, but I fear that my brain has not yet returned to its former grandeur. I would like one day to meet dear Mr. Cort Strasser and repay a little of the debt."

The thought of the psychotically sadistic sec boss of Mocsin, up in the Darks, cast a momentary chill over the group. But he was long gone and far away.

"And besides, the bastard's dead," Krysty said, her fiery hair tied back in a ponytail.

"Hope so," said Ryan. "Go on, Doc."

"I was wondering as I looked around here...that precious little has changed since I was here back in 1896. Precious little. It was but six short years after the pitiful and shameful episode of Wounded Knee. I was...but that is another tale, my friends. Crazy Horse was dead those twenty years. Sitting Bull had joined his ancestors six years earlier. Little Billy Bonney asked his last question fifteen years before."

Ryan was beginning to think that Doc was going to ramble his way through every famous person the old West had ever known. But the warrior stopped him, leaning forward, the massive knife seeming to tug at its sheath on his hip.

"You talk of being here so long ago. No man lives to be that great age. Why do you tell these lies to us?"

Doc spit words at him in Apache, making the chieftain sit up, face darkening.

"Keep it friendly, Doc," Ryan urged. "What did you say to him?"

The Mescalero answered himself. "He tells me that my father would open his own belly with shame that his son showed such little respect."

"Doc Tanner here tells the truth. It'd take too long to explain how or why, but if he says he was hereabouts a coupla hundred years ago, then you better believe that he was."

"He talks of dead names. But not of the Apaches. What of them?"

"Never knew Cochise. He died when I was only a skinny kid of seven or eight. He wasn't a Mescalero, was he, Chief?"

"No. Chiricahua."

"I met Geronimo twice. Mid-nineties, around Fort Sill, Oklahoma. Poor old devil was drunk most days. Surely must have been a devil of a man when he was younger."

"Mimbreno, not Mescalero," the Indian said, obviously fighting to contain his disbelief at this absurd litany of tall tales.

"I know that, sir," Doc responded. "He told me his real name. I would guess you don't know that. Geronimo was a white man's name. Spanish for Jerome."

"What was his name of the people?"

"His Apache name was Gokliya. He said it meant a man who sleeps a lot."

"Something like that," the chief replied. "You met...I can..."

"Shouldn't we go to see how Jak is?" Ryan suggested, to break the uneasy tension of the moment.

"The shaman might not appreciate being interrupted," Doc said.

"It is best to leave him. The painting with sand takes a long hour. And then the Healing Way is not easy for him. It is tiring. We can go at dawn."

"That's a time off," J.B. observed.

"We could talk some," Ryan said. "Tell us about General Yellowhair."

The Apache nodded. "It is well. Listen, then...."

Chapter Thirteen

THE LAST SCATTERED PATCHES of light drifted into smaller corners, shrinking, eventually giving in to the encroaching night. The dry wood crackled smokelessly on the cooking fires, filling the canyon with an unforgettable aromatic scent. Ryan was aware of the rancheria settling down all around him, ready for the darkness. A half dozen little children were scolded away from the deep pool where they'd been noisily throwing stones.

As quiet descended, they could all hear, occasionally, the rhythmic chanting of the shaman as he worked over the motionless figure of the boy. Ryan couldn't make out anything that sounded like words. There was a single syllable, stretched, then a pause, followed by two syllables, repeated over and over again.

Krysty had asked if she could go to see how Jak was recovering. Or not. But the chief firmly refused. "Man Whose Eyes See More will save him. But when he talks to the spirits it is better that he talks alone. If he does not send word by the dawning that your friend is well, then...then he will be at one with the sky and the earth."

"You got some pretty ways of saying 'dead,' don't you?" J.B. muttered.

Finally the tall Apache decided that the time had come for them to talk. It was obvious that he would much have preferred that the two women left them, but he fetched up short of actually telling them to leave. More bowls of food were brought, with warm, fresh-baked corn bread.

And a crock of cooled liquor. That J.B. recognized as pulque, made from the agave plant. Lori sipped at her earthenware beaker, then coughed and spluttered. "I'm tasting on fire," she said, tears streaming down her cheeks. Her distress brought the first smile that any of them had seen to the mouth of the Mescalero war chief.

Doc wasn't amused. "Let's hear your story," he said.

"Yes. It is time."

First came the introductions. As guests, the Anglos introduced themselves.

"Ryan Cawdor, from the Smokies."

"Krysty Wroth, from the ville of Harmony."

"J. B. Dix."

"Dr. Theophilus Tanner from South Strafford, Vermont. Doctor of Science, Harvard. And Doctor of Philosophy at the University of Oxford, England." He shook his head. "Not that I suspect that any of that is now worth doodlysquat." He stood up, knees cracking, and bowed low to the watching Apache chief.

"Lori Quint. I'm awfully pleased to meet you, sir," she said, the words cautious and hesitant, as if she feared they might spin in her mouth and choke her.

"I am called Cuchillo Oro. I am the chief of the Mescalero people in this place. A part of the nation of the people, the Apache."

"Knife of gold," Doc said. "I must confess that I have been admiring that dagger you wear. Sixteenth-century cinqueda, I believe."

The warrior drew it from the soft leather sheath, offering it, hilt first, to the old man. "My name comes from a great fighter from three thousand moons past. He was called Cuchillo Oro and this knife belonged to him. Now it is mine. The golden knife. And the name of Cuchillo Oro."

Doc passed it on to Ryan, who whistled at the weight of the knife. The blade was unusually broad at the hilt, tapering down to a needle point. Apart from the golden sheen, dark in the firelight, the steel was without decoration. The hilt was studded with rough, uncut gemstones, polished to a smooth patina by centuries of use. Ryan passed it to the Armorer, who ran his thumb along both edges of the blade, hissing at the black line of blood that appeared, etched on his hard skin. "Sharp enough." J.B. tossed it in the air, spinning it a couple of times, grinning like a kid as the hilt smacked satisfyingly into the palm of his hand. "Great balance. Man could pay good jack for a blade like this one. Any time you ever decide to pass it on...?"

Cuchillo Oro took it back before either of the women could touch it. "This is more than a knife. It is a part of the heritage of my people, a heritage that goes back many, many years. When the Anasazi hunted and farmed the tops of the mesas. Before the dry years came and sent us into the canyons. Listen, Anglos, and I shall tell you of the people, and of the affliction of General Yellowhair that has come upon us. Then, you will know...."

Cuchillo Oro spoke for a long time with scarcely any interruption. In the darkness they heard the monotonous sound of the shaman's chanting, but it seemed to fade until it was a part of the background, as natural as the melancholy hooting of a screech owl, circling above the sky-scraping cliffs of Drowned Squaw Canyon. Or the far-off howling of coyotes, crying for the serene, sailing moon. And above it all they heard the ghosts, called the night wind, whispering among the ice-riven boulders that lined the mesas.

First the war chief told them something of the history of his people.

Long before the Anglos came to the Americas, thirsty for power and gold, the people were there, controlling the land and guarding it. Cuchillo spoke of the fights against the encroachment of the whites, and the bitter slaughters on both sides. Doc Tanner nodded sagely at this part of the story, listening to the listing of the old names and the old fights.

"Kit Carson was a hero to your men and young boys, but he ravaged and destroyed all that he could not begin to understand. Canyon de Chelly is close by here, and it was a place of wonder. Of houses old when the sun was young. Animals and rows of trees bearing tender peaches. Carson came, smiling behind his cloak of bloody treachery and... it was done."

The name of General George Armstrong Custer came into the tale, and the Seventh Cavalry. The chief spoke of the buffalo soldiers, the black regiments of the Ninth and Tenth Cavalry, fighting all across the Indian frontier, long before it became the Deathlands.

Montana, New Mexico, Arizona, Dakota, Kansas, Nebraska, Texas—where there were Indians, blocking the progress of the white men, then the cavalry was also there.

The combination of tribes at the Little Big Horn had given the Indians their biggest single victory, a victory that marked the high point of the waters. It left the handsome and popular General Custer dead among the coulees above the winding river. "Dead forever," Cuchillo Oro said. "But now he stalks the land again."

For a hundred years the fortunes of the Indians declined. Too many of them were herded and guarded on reservations, often on the poorest land. Disease and drink took their dreadful toll, and the old ways almost vanished.

"But not quite," Cuchillo said quietly.

The ghost dances kept going. High above the deserts the rituals and old magics did not die. Many of the whites thought them so feeble that the freeways had killed them. Down in the southwest the Hopi and Navaho, the Mescalero and San Carlos, the Jicarilla, the White Mountain and Chiricahua...all clung to the vestiges of their ancient cultures, waiting until they could once more become strong.

"We thought the time had come."

"When, Cuchillo Oro?" Ryan asked. "When the missiles destroyed all the cities of the Anglos and left them weak and you more powerful?"

"*Ai*, such was the time."

For some minutes the warrior allowed his talk to slip again into the past, prompted by the use of his own name. Doc had mentioned the famous leaders of the people, Cochise and Geronimo. The original bearer of the golden cinqueda, Cuchillo Oro, had been an almost legendary fighting man, waging bloody war against his particular enemy, Captain Cyrus Pinner, his feud spilling to include virtually any white man. Cuchillo Oro had been, like the shootist known as "Edge," a man who walked alone.

Like Edge, and Herne the Hunter and other notorious Westerners, Cuchillo Oro had eventually vanished from the pages of history, into the swirling mists of folk legend.

"But where do you come from, Ryan Cawdor?" the Apache suddenly asked.

"Round and about. Been north and east lately. I figured it was time to come this way."

"Horses or wags?"

"Both. Lost them all. You were telling us about how Yellowhair appeared here."

Cuchillo Oro went on, the firelight playing off the planes of his face.

Ryan guessed he was in his early thirties, six feet tall, well muscled. He had dark eyes and high cheekbones, a firm jaw and good teeth that gleamed when he smiled. Which wasn't often. His thick, dark hair was held by a wide headband of emerald-green cloth, knotted at the back. Apart from the golden knife, he wore a Browning Hi-Power 9 mm pistol, double action.

A couple of years before the long winters began, in 1998, the United States government embarked on an ambitious project, less than fifty miles from the sacred lands of the Canyon de Chelly.

With state backing from both Arizona and New Mexico, and opposition from many liberal organizations, it was decided to establish and fund a new museum for the United States cavalry. Originally it was to be close to the site of the old Fort Apache, near the San Carlos reservation, but that was aborted by a strong environmental lobby on ecological grounds. The final site, burrowed into the side of an excavated mesa, was opposed mainly by the local Indians.

Who were overruled.

The museum was built with an almost indecent haste, opening only twelve months to the day after the first chunk of the sacred mesa had been blasted away. It was filled with all manner of artifacts, both genuine and facsimile: uniforms, diaries, weapons, photographs, dioramas, flags, Indian art and videos.

With a nearby gift shop doing a fine business in scented candles, wind chimes and compact discs of "Songs of the Cavalry," leading off with "Garryowen." There was also an album of inspirational readings by the late and great Duke Wayne. The grand opening, graced by the vice president himself, was boycotted by any representative of the Indian nations.

The speech that got most headlines was made by an aged descendant of Autie Custer himself. It was filled with references to heroism and courage, adversity and the American way of life.

"It did not speak of the people," Cuchillo Oro said with a grim smile. "But the days were coming closer. The thunderheads gathered to the east and to the west. We waited, as we have always waited."

College students and some of the growing ranks of the young unemployed were hired to wear the re-created uniforms and ride doped horses, and to carry some of the hundred or more Springfield carbines built especially by a firearms expert.

They galloped, whooped and fought out some of the most significant battles of the Indian Wars, from 1860 to 1890. A few local Indians took the chance of getting some drinking money by hiring on as Sioux or Apache or whatever the script demanded from them.

The one fight they avoided showing was, naturally enough, the Little Big Horn. But they did have a long blond wig for someone to wear when they were doing the grand parade of cavalry heroes. You couldn't leave Custer out of that.

"Then the sky became black. The father of my father's father saw it. The rocks melted and the desert became as glass. And the dead ... Oh, my brothers, there were so many dead."

"Nobody will ever know the full score of the megacull," Doc said. "But in the late nineties I worked a while with M.I.T. up in..." He saw the question on the faces around him. "Massachusetts Institute of Technology. Experts there calculated that if only one percent of the Russians' missiles got through it would take our economy several decades to get anywhere back to what might be termed normal. If it ever did get back. And they also concluded that—based on the same one percent—millions upon millions would starve in the first few months. *Just* one percent of the missiles. Nobody could know what happened back then, but it was surely more than one percent.''

The museum hadn't been all that far away from some missile silos, and the area had been nuked with small, low-yield rockets, creating intense local damage but not too much spillover. The hot spots cooled fast out in the desert. Shock waves from Armageddon brought down the wall of the mesa, burying the United States Cavalry Museum. And so it remained for nearly a hundred years.

"Many of the people survived the first days of the attack. Our homes were often in remote canyons like this, well shielded from the great waves of power and the burning winds. The cities died. We went back. Back to the ways of the old people. They were changed little, you understand. The long winters were not easy. There were bad times. The cold months of three and four years after the sky blackened. The Navaho caught a sickness and their spirits did not save them.''

"You know why?'' Krysty asked.

"They had been close to the cities and the Anglo dead. Places where spirits of darkness dwelled. They were touched, and they did not try the old ways. They were always in a hurry. They forgot that the cures that bring back the harmony and balance can take many days. They did not take that time. And in those two times of cold, the Navaho were almost destroyed."

"What about us?"

The Apache looked at the tall blond girl, brow furrowing in bewilderment. "What of you?"

Lori tried again. "Pink people like us? Is there many around here?"

"She means, Cuchillo Oro, were there any Anglos in these parts?"

Doc Tanner's explanation was enough. "Yes. Few and poor. Double poor. But we had no firefights with them. Not for many scores of moons."

The Apaches, as their neighboring tribes declined, had taken over most of the hunting lands for a couple of hundred miles around. Secure in their healthy mountain fortresses, they had flourished, carrying on living in the old ways, hunting by their own knowledge as they always had.

They had spread their shadow clear across to the Canyon de Chelly. During the span of those Mescalero alive during the brief time of the last world war, all was peace. A peace that lasted, according to Cuchillo Oro, until recent years.

"First one and then two. Then a hand and then two hands. Anglos with blasters. Swift and evil men and women. They came from the north and the east, some from Mexland."

Ryan asked what had happened to these renegade whites when they came straying onto the lands of the Mescalero. Cuchillo Oro slowly drew the great golden knife and mimed drawing it across his own throat. One of the squaws had just brightened the fire with dried wood, and the flames shone off the mirror of the broad blade.

The war chief talked then of a time when the land had moved. He had only been a young man, barely in his teens. But he recalled the way that the earth had danced beneath his buckskin boots. The seismic disturbances had gone on for some months, and were occasionally severe. The Apaches had called it the time when all men walked as if drunk.

It had been a particularly bad shock that once again moved the earthslide that had covered up the United States Cavalry Museum, opening up the low roof of the single-story building as neatly as if it had just been built.

But the Apaches hadn't known about this until some weeks later. There had been a group of renegade Anglos, traveling together on beat-up wags, moving slowly across the country. There were too many of them for the Apaches to take on in a direct firefight, but they monitored their progress. Cuchillo's father, Pony Rides Far, had ordered the young men of the Mescalero to keep clear of the whites. He did not want a confrontation that might risk anyone leading the armed killers back to Drowned Squaw Canyon.

The whites had enlarged the museum, building themselves a crude replica of one of the old cavalry forts, near a bend in the river a quarter mile away from the tumbled mesa. For some years there had been a balance between the two groups. The Apaches lacked the firepower to hit the fort and the museum.

"It was a mistake by my father," said Cuchillo Oro. "Man Whose Eyes See More urged him to attack the Anglos as soon as they came into our hunting lands. But Pony Rides Far wanted peace. For that wish my father died. They caught him when his horse fell and he... I will not talk of his passing. But they will be paid. One day, they will be paid."

Equally the whites could find no way of taking on the Apaches in their box canyon. Twice they'd come out against the Mescalero, and twice they'd been beaten back with heavy losses. Cuchillo thought that one day they would come again.

Because there had been a change.

After the uneasy years of quasi peace, the Anglos had suddenly found a new leader. The man they now called General Yellowhair.

"Where'd he come from?" Ryan asked, leaning forward. "I've gotten the idea I've seen that bastard before. Someplace. Some time. But I can't be sure."

"No man knows. Some say he was found in a box of glass within the mesa, sitting astride his black stallion. Frozen in time. And they woke him and he rides again for the pony soldiers."

"Bullshit!" Doc snorted. "Truth to tell there was a moment when I wondered if we'd chron-jumped, seeing Autie Custer there, all yellow hair streaming in the wind. Like he'd just left Reno and Benteen and Miles and Keogh and the rest and come like a grinning demon from Hades."

Ryan had never heard any of the names that Doc was mentioning, but he figured they had to be linked with this strange General Custer.

"But I knew then he wasn't. There is something phonier than a three-dollar bill about him. You mark my words, friends."

Cuchillo could shed no light at all on the problem. All he knew was that things had become immeasurably worse since the appearance of the General. That was what his men called him. No other name. Just "the General." And he'd brought cunning and an iron discipline to what had been a bloody-minded rabble of mercies and hired killers.

Now they all wore uniforms. Had parades. Discipline tougher than it had been even in the days of the original Seventh Cavalry, when there were more deserters than fleas on a dog.

"We have fought with them in a dozen short firefights. Each time we have been beaten. They have taken prisoners from our young men. Several. And then there is nothing. We see and hear nothing. They are taken and never return. It is as if the spirits have devoured them."

It was a fairly familiar story around the Deathlands. Not with the unique flavoring of the Cavalry Museum and the mysterious stranger with the blond hair. But the tale of a local balance being upended by the arrival of a gang of guerrilla butchers. Often that was the way local barons arose, taking power with the blaster. And holding it by maintaining the balance of terror on their side.

"What are you going to do?" J.B. asked, picking up a burning length of wood and using its glowing end to relight the pipe he'd been smoking.

The Apache shook his head. "We have talked much of it. There have been councils with the old men. Our shaman has asked the spirits for help. But there is little hope. They are stronger than us. Unless there is some aid, we shall have to leave this place. It will be stained with blood."

"Could be a way to beat the sec men," Ryan said thoughtfully.

"How?" the chief asked, which for some unaccountable reason made Doc start to snigger, turning it clumsily into an undignified coughing fit.

"I don't know, Cuchillo Oro," Ryan replied. "Don't know enough about them. Or you. But the Trader used to say that you could always find a way."

"Right," J.B. agreed. "Over, under, around or through. There's always a way."

THE MOON DRIFTED STEADILY across the top of the cliffs, showing the time to be approaching midnight. Ryan's wrist chron flicked on at 1:17. The fire was sinking. For at least a half hour there had been no sound from the part of the camp where the Apache shaman was battling to save the life of the boy.

Lori had fallen asleep on Doc's lap, sucking her thumb like a little girl. J.B. had dozed, then jerked awake, grinning sheepishly at Ryan. Krysty sat, elbows on knees, staring into the softly tumbling embers of the fire. Ryan was sitting quietly with his arm around her, occasionally asking Cuchillo Oro a question about the strength of the sec men. Where did they ride on patrol? How many at a time? Did they have any grens? Guards around their fortress?

He returned again and again to their leader.

"I can tell you no more, Ryan Cawdor," the Mescalero eventually said. "It is late. Our sister the moon will soon be at her slumbers and her brother will stir himself for a new day."

"Yeah. I'm ready for bed myself. You say we can have that hut there?" He pointed to a low-roofed shack to the left of the canyon.

"Yes. You have seen many fights, Ryan Cawdor?"

"Too many."

"Most against Anglos?"

"Anglos. Blacks. Women. Muties. Animals. You name it, and I guess I've fought it."

The Apache pressed him, and Ryan's secret suspicions were confirmed. "But you know the way of chilling men like these pony soldiers?"

"Some."

"And your blasters...they are better. Better than what we have and better than the Springfield carbines of the dog-faces?"

"Cuchillo, you want us to throw in with you against Yellowhair and fifty or more sec men? If that's what you want, then let's have it out on the table so we can all see it."

"There are three of you...if I count the old man."

"Five, mister," Krysty said.

"But only J.B. and me got blasters that'd be much use."

Cuchillo Oro rose to his feet. "The people do not beg for help, Ryan Cawdor."

"I don't expect you to beg. I'll talk to the others about it first thing in the morning and let you know what we decide."

"This land is..."

"Your land," Ryan finished. "Heard that before, Cuchillo Oro. I told you. I'll let you know. Right now I'll go look at the kid and see if—"

"There is no need. Ysun, life-giver, aided me in my work."

Man Whose Eyes See More stood behind them, naked above the waist, eyes hidden behind an antique pair of mirrored sunglasses. He looked drained and frail.

"Jak?" Krysty asked.

The shaman gave a half smile. "He will live."

Chapter Fourteen

"BASTARD TIRED, RYAN. Feel like been long journey. Tired."

Dawn had tiptoed over the crest of the towering cliffs at the head of the canyon, above the pool of calm water, spilling down in a cascade of golden-pink light. Ryan had snatched three hours' sleep, waking early and crawling from under the pile of musty blankets, leaving Krysty, J.B., Lori and Doc still dozing.

The shaman was lying on a disgustingly dirty old mattress at the side of the bed where Jak was resting, out in the open air. Man Whose Eyes See More was reading a cracked and faded old book with a torn cover. Ryan could just make out that it was called *Backflash*. It seemed to be a kind of future fic book— back in the days when people thought that there would be a future.

Jak looked up, eyes creaking open, showing the pale pink coloring. The shaman ignored them both.

"Bastard tired," the young boy repeated.

The shaman had brushed through the long white hair, removing the tangles and burrs, cleaning out the orange dust. Jak, because of his albino coloring, never looked anything that remotely approached healthy.

Now he looked more like a bathed corpse, resting on its funeral bier.

The skin, taut across the sharp cheekbones, was almost transparent, but the thin smile was still Jak Lauren.

"Ready kick ass, huh?" he said.

"If you feel as bad as you look," Ryan joked, "then you should have been nailed in the long wooden box a week ago."

"Thought gone, Ryan."

"Thought so, too, son." He looked at the shaman. "How d'you do it?"

"What?"

"Bring him back."

Man Whose Eyes See More nodded. "It's true that he was already walking with the spirits, but he wished to return to this world."

The camp was still silent. Most small settlements like this would have had a number of stark-rib mongrels, scavenging and fighting for scraps. There wasn't an animal in the canyon, except for the string of ponies tethered near the water. The sun was creeping higher, and Ryan could begin to make out the texture of the sheared rocks above the pool. Part of his fighting instincts was always to make sure he knew all the ways out of anywhere. As far as he could see, Drowned Squaw Canyon didn't leave a man much choice. The cliff seemed to rise almost vertically, with no obvious holds for a climber.

The Apache watched him from behind the silver, reflective lenses. "No man ever made it."

"The rocks?"

"Yeah. There's old Mescalero stories about a time we were attacked by a bunch of Cheyenne, looking for new hunting lands. They tried a trick and set fire to the canyon floor. There was a young man, called Wings on Feet, who was supposed to have gotten up there and hauled up the whole tribe. Then they looped around the Cheyenne—or it could have been Comanche—and drove them into their own trap."

"You believe that?" Ryan asked.

There was the hint of a smile. "I believe in the old magic, Ryan Cawdor. I have the power. I can see. I can heal. I've seen things you wouldn't believe."

Ryan shook his head, brushing dust off the knees of his pants. "I've seen you bring the boy back from the wrong side of a chilling. I believe you."

"He has broken ribs. And there was...was another thing wrong with him. That is now well. He must rest for three or four days. I have strapped his ribs for him."

"Feels tighter'n jump in chamber. But doesn't pain."

Ryan grinned down at the pale boy. "Good to see you, Jak. Take it real easy now."

"Ryan."

"What?"

"When... Heard firefight. Who? Not them here? Who?"

"Sec men, Jak. But it's kind of a long story. Get Man Whose Eyes See More to tell you."

He nodded to the shaman and patted Jak on the shoulder.

"Ask women for food," the Apache said. "Will your women not make it?"

"Wouldn't like to ask them. I'll get something later." He took a couple of steps and then turned back to face the shaman. "Oh, there's one other thing."

"I know, Ryan Cawdor. 'Thanks' is not a word that sets easy on your mouth. But I see it in your heart. And that is enough."

The others were awake, eager for news of the boy. Cuchillo Oro appeared as Ryan was telling them the good news.

"But he will not be well to ride for some days. You must stay here."

Ryan and the others had talked about the words of the Apache war chief before they all went to sleep. Though J.B. wasn't sure how they'd do it, he agreed with Ryan that they should try to help the Indians against the sec men. "I'd help a froth-mouth wolf against a sec man," he'd said, grinning.

Both women had also given their agreement to offering aid to Cuchillo Oro and the Mescalero.

Only Doc Tanner had hesitated. "I fear that I must appear rather a pantywaist, friends. Yet I am no Caspar Milquetoast. But I ask everyone here present to give their thoughts to what we are here for. We travel and arrive through the gateway, not knowing where we'll end up. We are like the desert wind that blows across the land."

Krysty had spoken then. "Sure. But the wind cleanses and purges. Drives out sickness, Doc. That's what we do. Or try to do. We get somewhere and there's wrong...we do what we can. Don't you see that?''

The old man had finally nodded his agreement. ''You sounded like an old-time river-crossing preacher. Indeed you did. But I suppose we must all try and stand up for what's right. Very well, I agree.''

RYAN TOLD THE WARRIOR with the golden knife of their decision.

Cuchillo Oro sat, cross-legged, hugging a battered Winchester rifle. He said nothing for a long minute, staring at the ground. Finally he looked up at Ryan.

''You do this because our shaman saved the life of the boy?''

''That's part of it. Seems like the General and those renegade chillers of his would be better off if someone stopped their breathing. But I don't know yet how we can do it.''

''Won't be quick, won't be easy and there'll be a lot of dying.'' J.B. flicked at his eyes, batting away a stubborn insect. ''You got to know that. It costs, Cuchillo Oro.''

''My people have paid that price for fifty generations.''

Chapter Fifteen

"WE GOT TO KNOW MORE about them if we're going to have a chance of chilling them," J.B. said, sitting around the blazing fire. The others were with him, including the pallid Jak Lauren, who was propped up on a straw mattress, red eyes following the council of war.

Cuchillo Oro was on the far side of the circle, flanked by a half dozen of his oldest and most experienced warriors. The shaman, Man Whose Eyes See More, squatted immediately behind his chief.

The day had meandered by for Ryan and his comrades. Every couple of hours the shaman would prepare various infusions of herbs to speed the boy's healing—red alder and green hellebore with a sliced corm of a jack-in-the-pulpit.

"That plant always reminds me of Georgia," Doc said.

"What's Georgia?" Lori asked.

The old man assumed his baffled expression. "I'm damned if I know, my dear. Georgia...Georgia...on my mind, perhaps. I'm so sorry...."

The ensuing unguent, when the shaman poured it from the small copper cauldron, was thick and oily, and had a dreadful smell.

"Fireblast!" Ryan gagged. "Smells like a swamp-ie's outhouse! That's triple-gross."

"It is a handful of crushed seeds from a secret herb that makes the smell," said Man Whose Eyes See More, carefully ladling out a cup of the liquid to take over to the boy.

"Sure must be good stuff," Krysty said, wrinkling her nose in disgust.

The Mescalero wise man smiled, actually cracked his cheeks and laughed. "It smells. That is all it adds to the medicine."

"Then why...?" asked Ryan.

"If a medicine tastes of honey and sweetness, then the man does not believe it does good. To become well means you must suffer."

THE WORD HAD GONE SWIFTLY around the Apache camp in the box canyon that the Anglo strangers were going to fight with the people against Yellowhair.

Everywhere they went they found smiles. Directed by one of the young women, Krysty discovered that she was being followed. Even when she went behind a small grove of mesquite bushes to relieve herself a gaggle of girls, watching her every move, stooped to try to see how she was made. They giggled when she shook a furious fist at them.

"Gaia!" she exclaimed when she rejoined Ryan and the others. "Be good to have some privacy when you want to take a leak!"

Her long hair, tied in a ponytail, swished from side to side in time with her anger. The Apache shaman noticed, and his mouth gaped in wonderment.

In the middle of the day, the whites were all brought food, though it was again obvious that the women resented serving Lori and Krysty.

They began with a spiced soup that had small pieces of gristly meat floating in it. All of them tried it, though Doc only sipped suspiciously at his brown bowl.

"Good," J.B. pronounced. "What was in it?"

Cuchillo Oro and the inner council of the tribe were eating with them. His dark eyes were veiled as he glanced around at the five Anglos. Jak was still resting under the care of Man Whose Eyes See More.

"It is a rarity."

"Why?" Ryan asked, suddenly sharing Doc's wariness about the soup.

"The women take many hours to collect enough of the grubs from the yellow jackets to heat and then boil up."

"Oh, dark night!" the Armorer exclaimed, taking off his beloved fedora and laying it carefully to one side.

"Why d'you do that?" Lori asked, her own face a couple of shades paler than normal.

"When I throw up I don't want it falling in my puke," J.B. replied grimly.

The second course was a whole lot safer—green pumpkin stew and chili fritters, served with corn bread. Ryan whistled at the strength of the peppers. "Don't the people eat anything that hasn't got chilies in it, Cuchillo Oro?" he asked.

"Yes, of course." He paused. "But not often."

To keep cool in the heat of the day they all drank deeply from pitchers of mesquite bean juice, savoring the piquant flavor.

"Better," Ryan said. "Lots better."

Cuchillo picked shreds of the stew from between his teeth with the needle tip of the great golden knife.

"Now that we have eaten we must talk. Talk now of war."

"Yes," Ryan agreed, feeling a buildup of gas and wondering whether it would be good or bad manners to let it out. It was probably better to keep it in.

"Will your women stay to talk of war?" asked the oldest of the Apache council, a grizzled veteran, lacking a hand at the end of his left arm. He was called Fights Two Lions, Ryan recollected. He hadn't asked the Apache which of the two lions had taken his hand.

Doc answered the question, lapsing into the tongue of the Mescalero, bring a snort from the old men around the embers of the fire—a snort that could have been either anger or amusement.

"What did you say, Doc?" Krysty asked.

"That you did not just talk of war, that you also were both skilled in the making of war. And if any doubted it then they might find...well..."

"What, heart of my heart?" Lori asked, touching him on the back of his hand.

"Well...that they might find their winkle was missing from its usual location, next time they woke up."

Ryan still didn't know whether the Mescalero elders had been angry or amused.

But none of them again raised the issue of whether Krysty and Lori should be there with them.

Ryan launched in, outlining the discussion he'd had with the others. Strategically he'd mainly spoken with J.B.

"We have to know everything there is to know about these sec men. The pony soldiers, as you call them, and their leader. We must see their fort and this museum. See them on patrol. Test them a little. See how they react. Only then can we work out what must be done to beat them."

"So easy, white eyes!" mocked another of the elders, a man with a face deeply scarred by smallpox, whose name Ryan didn't know. "We have done this. This and more. We know their power. Know their camp. We have... we have tested them a little, as you say. And we do not know how to beat them. But you...the great Anglo with one eye can see more than all the people!"

The rest of the Mescalero nodded, but Ryan noticed that Cuchillo Oro made no move, either to agree or to disagree.

Ryan stood up, glaring at the pocked man. He allowed his hand to fall to the butt of his handgun, the threat obvious.

"The Mescalero mock that I have one eye. But are the Mescalero blind children that they can see nothing?" He was vaguely surprised to hear himself speaking like an old westie vid.

"We are..." the Apache began, but Ryan pointed an accusing finger at him, pushing him into silence.

"The Mescalero say how they have looked, tested and fought, and...they still do not know how to win." His voice became openly incredulous. "Then the Mescalero should leave their home and go. Go before the pony soldiers decide to come and beat you, take your women. Enslave your children. If you say you do not know how to win, then I say that we will tell you."

His voice rang with confidence. The scarred warrior said nothing, mouth turned down in annoyance, eyes looking past the white man toward the pool that filled the farther end of the canyon.

Cuchillo Oro spoke, addressing the Apache first.

"Soft, my brother. All men know that Stones in Face is the bravest of the warriors. And the Anglo has come here as our guest and says he will be our friend, that he will fight with us against Yellowhair. It is true that we people need such help. To say not is to speak like a crazie. So, we will talk together and fight together. And then, my brothers, it will be a good day to die."

Ryan hoped he meant for the collection of renegades and mercies who now rode together under the banner of the Seventh Cavalry.

It took most of the afternoon, but an agreement was eventually thrashed out. Twice they broke off the talking so that both sides, Anglo and Apache, could go their own way and discuss what was to be done. It was in the softly fading light of early evening when Ryan Cawdor finally stood up, followed by the other whites.

"That's it. Day after tomorrow. Dawn. You and six of your best warriors, me and the Armorer, here, mounted on your strongest ponies."

Cuchillo also stood, reaching out to clasp Ryan's hand. "We shall go to Many Deer Canyon and watch for the pony soldiers."

The Mescalero were familiar with the patterns of the patrols from the cavalry fort, but there was no way they could raise sufficient strength to do more than mount a dangerous hit-and-run sortie against the sec men. Which was all that Ryan and J.B. wanted them to do. They needed the chance to observe the sec men in action, to judge if there was any obvious weakness in their discipline.

During their first run-in against the General, Ryan had been too busy worrying about saving their skins to consider any points of tactics.

"Are there many deer in Many Deer Canyon?" Krysty asked.

Stones in Face answered her. "In the time of the fathers of our fathers of our fathers of our fathers there were deer. So many that a man might stand all day and watch them pass him by and never see an ending of their numbers. Now... Now, Fire Hair Woman, there are none."

"If that's my name, what are the names of the rest of us?" she asked.

Cuchillo replied. "The names of our people come from how they look or what they do. Only a chief can give such names."

"Me?" Lori said.

"Keeps Night Warm," the war chief replied.

"I don't... Keeps what warm?" The burst of laughter from everyone made the girl blush with a sudden realization. "You mean like with fucking. Sorry, Doc, I mean making of love."

"I think that's a real nice name, dearest," Doc reassured her. "I shudder to thing what kind of malicious nomenclature you have contrived for me, Cuchillo Oro. Tell me."

"Your name, you mean? I have talked with Man Whose Eyes See More and he tells me that he believes you are old mutie. Not in body, but in mind. He sees something in you, Doc Tanner, that is not as in other men. So you cannot have name as others do. I call you Doc. That and no more."

"Could be worse, I guess. How about John Barrymore Dix? And Ryan? And there's the young boy as well. What about them?"

"Young warrior is called Eyes of Wolf," Cuchillo replied.

"And me?" J.B. asked, giving Doc Tanner a dirty look for blurting out his disliked given names.

"Man Whose Weapons Strike Fear into Hearts of All Enemy."

"Fireblast!" Ryan exclaimed. "By the time you shout that out, the firefight's started and finished."

Cuchillo joined the laughter. "It is the way of my people. There was famous warrior called Young Man Whose Enemies Are Even Afraid of His Horses. But in books it was made into Young Man Afraid of His Horses. That is not the same. We call J. B. Dix by name of Weapons Strike Fear."

"Better," the Armorer said.

"How about Ryan?" Krysty asked. "What d'you call him, Cuchillo Oro?"

"His name is hard. One Eye Chills," the Mescalero replied. "Is a good name?"

Ryan nodded. "Sounds fine to me, Golden Knife. Now, seems like supper's near due. Then we should bed down early. We'll be off at dawn to see what we can find out about those pony soldiers of yours."

After another filling meal, well spiced with red and green chilies, the group went back to their hut, set against the massive stone walls of the canyon.

They had lamps with wicks that guttered in bowls of oil, smelling strongly, giving off a soft, golden light. At Krysty's request, the Indian women had brought in blankets and pinned them together across the low roof beams of the hut, giving the illusion of separate small rooms. She and Ryan took the one nearest the door. Doc and Lori had the next one, and J.B. shared the third one with the recuperating Jak, who'd been brought to join the others, with the reluctant agreement of the tall shaman.

To his delight and amazement, while wandering around the village, Doc had found an old solar-powered ceedee player from before the long winters. It had been kept by an old man who knew nothing of what it was or how it worked. It had been handed down from father to son, as an artifact from the dead days. Doc had asked if he could borrow it and, reluctantly, it had been handed over. He sat with the small black and silver box on his lap, peering into the top. It had been easy to remove the case, and he'd found that a single wire had become disconnected.

"Eureka!" he exclaimed. "Battery works. Not much of a charge left after a hundred years, but it still functions."

"All you need is..."

"Love," Doc cackled, baring his gleaming teeth at Ryan. "Upon my soul, but this is marvelous, my dear friend. You see, there is a compact disc within. Still there from that moment when...when all music died."

"Will play, Doc?" Jak asked feebly. "Seen some of them that worked. Try. Go on, Doc. Try. For me. Please. Try."

They gathered around this strange surviving piece of prenuking technology. Doc pressed the round button marked with the symbol for "play." A faint light glowed deep within the player, and they could all hear a tiny hissing sound.

And the music flowed out.

It was a melancholic, swelling sound, the solemn strings pouring into the long room, silencing Ryan and all his companions. Despite the age of the machine and the disk, the music was fresh and pure, untainted. Krysty was standing next to her man, and she reached out and took his hand. Ryan squeezed her fingers, closing his good eye, feeling a glimmer of what life might have been like before the holocaust turned America into the Deathlands.

Doc folded Lori in his arms. The dim light of the lamps was strong enough to show the glint of tears among the stubble on his deeply lined cheeks.

None of them had any idea of how long the music lasted. The sounds of the Mescalero camp outside the walls of baked clay drifted from them until the whole world was the music. When it ended, the machine whirred briefly and then gave a sharp, terminal-sounding click.

"Guess that's it," J.B. said, breaking the stillness in the room. "Don't figure that'll be playing for us anymore."

"Least we heard it the once." Krysty sighed. "Gaia! It was so beautiful. What was it called?"

There was a trumpeting sound as Doc pulled out his swallow's eye kerchief and blew his nose with unusual vigor.

"Why, 'pon my soul, I had forgotten that such sounds had ever, ever existed."

"What was it, Doc?" Krysty repeated.

"The *Adagio in G Minor*, by the Venetian, Tommaso Albinoni. So beautiful."

Most evenings the group would sit around, rapping about the day gone, or about the days to come. With a potential firefight the following morning, there could have been much to say. But the age-old music seemed to affect everyone in the same way. Jak muttered he was feeling real tired and was going to get some sleep. J.B. mumbled in turn about having to strip and field-clean his blasters, get them ready for the next day. Doc and Lori made no excuse, simply wandering off behind their section of blankets, arm in arm.

"Leaves you and me, lover," Krysty said quietly. "Mebbe time to hit the straw?"

"Could be. Yeah, it could just be."

To Ryan and his contemporaries the idea that the sexual act could best be performed in conditions of privacy, behind locked doors and preferably in the dark, would have seemed absurd. In the Deathlands, privacy was a privilege reserved for the very rich or the very powerful. And the two things normally went together. Of the hundreds of times that Ryan had done it, only a handful had been in anything approaching seclusion.

Tonight was no exception. Indeed, it was better, far better, than most times.

The light was dim and the blankets pressed in around them, giving the lovers the illusion of being on their own. All they had to do was shut out all the other sounds around them. Jak moaning in his sleep from the combination of pain from his injuries and drugs the shaman had given them. J.B. whispering as he took apart both of his blasters. The soft clicking of oiled metal and the unmistakable noise of springs being tested.

From Doc and Lori's end of the room, there was only the rustling of straw and an occasional giggle from the girl.

"I love you, Ryan," Krysty whispered. "Don't say anything back. I just wanted you to know that being with you and loving is all I want. The only times I'm happy is when I'm with you."

He kissed her on the side of her neck, feeling the pulsing flow from her heart. His hand slid inside her shirt, cupping the firm breast. She'd peeled off the khaki overalls, and he only kept on his brown shirt.

It was a relief to feel secure enough in Drowned Squaw Canyon to be able to go to bed and take off clothes and boots. But Ryan made sure his blasters were to hand near the cotton pillow.

She pressed against him and he could taste the sheen of excitement on her skin. Safe in the secluded canyon, Ryan knew this coupling would be sweet...so very sweet.

Chapter Sixteen

RYAN AND J.B. STOOD by their ponies, waiting for the half dozen Apache warriors to join them. The pallid glow in the sky above the lip of the canyon heralded the false dawn. Doc and Lori were still sleeping when Ryan and J.B. rose and got dressed, strapping on their weapons. Jak was awake, calling out good luck to them. Krysty woke as soon as Ryan stirred, hastily pulling on her overalls to stand with him as he left.

Cuchillo Oro was the first of the Indians to appear, heeling his pony across the dry, packed earth. He held up a hand to greet them.

"*Haiee*, my brothers. Let today be a good day to die."

"Wish you wouldn't say that," Ryan grumbled. "I'm not figuring on dying. Not yet."

"You make many jests, One Eye Chills." Cuchillo grinned.

"I do? And I'd kind of like it better if you stuck to calling me Ryan Cawdor, Chief. If that sits all right with you."

"And I'm J. B. Dix. I appreciate the honor of being Weapons Strike Fear and all that, but I answer better to my own name."

A girl, as slender as a fawn, with liquid brown eyes, came and stood by Cuchillo Oro. She wore a dress of deerskin that was embroidered with hundreds of colored beads in a swirling pattern of suns and arrows. Ryan had noticed her watching Jak Lauren several times during the past day.

"This is my only daughter," the war chief said, reaching from the saddle to pat the girl proudly on the shoulder. "She is called Steps Lightly Moon."

The girl hid her face behind her hand, peeking at the two white men. Then she spun on her heel and ran quickly away, darting between the rugged boulders with the speed of a dragonfly.

"She's very beautiful, Cuchillo Oro," Ryan said, the Armorer nodding his agreement.

"She wishes to talk with Eyes of Wolf."

"With Jak?" Ryan exclaimed. "Well . . . let her go talk. The kid's still doped up to his ears, but I'm sure he'd appreciate a pretty little thing like that to talk to."

"My daughter wishes to do more than talk with the white-head. She is foolish, and her skull rattles with ideas. She would marry with him."

Ryan didn't quite know what to say to that. "Marry? I don't . . . What'd you think about it, Chief?"

"They can talk. I have told her. But only if one of your women is there."

Ryan didn't bother pointing out again to Cuchillo Oro that neither Krysty nor Lori would much appreciate the idea of belonging to anyone.

The rest of the war party arrived, all hard-faced warriors in their late twenties or early thirties armed with a variety of old rifles.

"We ride," Cuchillo said, leading the way along the narrowing trail toward the entrance to the box canyon. Ryan winked at Krysty and swung up on the back of his horse. As a concession to the two Anglos, the Apaches had provided them with worn Western saddles.

"Take care, lover," Krysty said. She patted J.B.'s animal on the flank as it walked past her. "Good luck, J.B. Bring us back a sec man for the pot, you hear me?"

THEY CANTERED ALONG in the lee of a tall mesa. On top Ryan could just make out the tumbled ruins of pueblos, old before the first white man appeared on the continent.

The sun was beginning to shine above the rim of the range of low hills away to the east. Ryan found such perfect weather unusual. The sky was an unsullied blue, with only the hint of a scattering of fluffy clouds at the edge of seeing, to the distant north. The chief led the way, with Ryan and J.B. in his dust. The rest of the Mescalero brought up the rear.

A couple of miles from Drowned Squaw Canyon, on a back trail, they passed the ruins of an old adobe church. Its roof had tumbled in, whitened stumps of rafters showing against the crumbling walls. One window on the western flank of the building remained intact, a cross carved within it. The oak doors swung to and fro on the massive iron hinges, creaking in the soft breeze. Most of the graves had long since disappeared, but one stone, with a winged angel on top of it, remained. Ryan heeled his horse past so that he could try to decipher the faded wind-scoured inscription.

"Frederico Garcia Nolan," was the name. The dates were no longer legible. Using the angled shadows of the rising sun, Ryan was just able to make out a line beneath. "Loving the land, he now sleeps at peace beneath it. Stranger, ride by."

He glanced around, looking out across the dramatic land with its sculpted buttes and mesas. "Could be worse places to end up," he said.

"A man should not lie beneath the dirt," Cuchillo Oro replied. "Out in the open, under the sky and sun and moon. That is the ending for a warrior."

"It's a matter of opinion, Chief," Ryan said, pushing his horse into a fast walk.

STONES IN FACE RODE in front of the war party, scouting the trail with extreme caution. Cuchillo had told Ryan that there was little danger of being ambushed by the Seventh Cavalry as they always went out in regular patrols. Also, they didn't know the region as the Mescalero did, with its winding trails, its looming mesas and its snaking dry riverbeds.

"Only danger is to ride blind-eyed into a camp of the pony soldiers," he said. "They do not come often so far from their rancheria that they need to spend a night away. They leave, as we did, at the dawning. But if they come to Many Deer Canyon, we shall be there before them."

They guided their animals up a gentle slope, rising steadily toward a ridge of higher ground, then looping west, diving down into the cool deeps of a narrow canyon. Finally, following the hand signals of Stones in Face, they reached a natural bowllike plateau ringed with boulders. It commanded a view across a wide valley, with stunted trees lining the bed of a meandering stream and thick mesquite bushes. At its farther end there was a sharp-edged notch, barely ten feet across, that led through to the main trail.

"This is Many Deer Canyon," the chief said. "The dog-faces will come through the gap and camp while they drink coffee and smoke by the water. That is always their way."

"But they might not come today?" J.B. asked, swinging stiffly down from the saddle, wincing at the soreness in his thighs and lower back.

"They might not come," another of the warriors answered.

"And they might not come tomorrow," Ryan said. "Or the next day."

Cuchillo crouched by the edge of the plateau, staring out. "Only the spirits know these things. But, look, Ryan Cawdor. See the dust that rises there. I told you, my brother. It will be a good day for us to die."

Of the eight men who stood upon the ridge watching the lazy spiral of reddish dust, it would not be a good day for dying for two of them.

The Armorer had brought his miniature binoculars with him, foldouts with image intensifiers. He steadied them against the top of one of the rocks, trying to focus on the oncoming patrol.

"Too much damned dust," he said. "Can't see 'em properly. Means we can't fight them."

The warrior named Long Knife sneered at that. "Anglos fear their own running dogs."

"Now what the big fire's that supposed to mean!" Ryan exclaimed.

"It means that we have fought for the history..." He hesitated. "That is the right word? History?"

"Yeah. Go on."

"The people have fought always. It is the will of Cuchillo Oro that you help us. How? By saying you cannot see!" He muttered something in his own tongue, spitting in the dirt, the saliva immediately soaking into the dust and vanishing.

"What did he say, Cuchillo?" Ryan asked.

"Nothing. Long Knife lets his words run faster than his brain."

"I say that I will fight the pony soldiers, and you stay and be safe and cook and sew beads with the other women," the warrior retorted, hand gripping the hilt of his saber so hard that his knuckles showed white through the bronze skin.

"Man once said that talk was cheap...but the price of action is colossal," Ryan replied, deliberately insulting Long Knife by calmly turning his back on him, knowing that J.B. was in a position to chill the Apache if he tried to coldcock him from behind.

"They are closer," another of the Mescalero interrupted, crouching out of sight, peering between two of the boulders.

J.B. joined him, again easing the focusing screw on the glasses. "Yeah. Got 'em now. There's around a dozen, with another out front. Don't seem too worried about any attack. They're cantering along like they were going to a friendly barn raising.''

Ryan glanced across at his old comrade. ''Barn raising, J.B.? Fireblast! What do you know about raising a damned barn?''

The Armorer looked sheepish. ''Heard them say that on westie vids, Ryan. Don't know for sure what it means, but it sounded right.''

Long Knife wouldn't let the argument go. He stood so close to Ryan that the white man could smell his sweat. He turned his face to stare into Ryan's single eye.

''You believe I fear you?''

''No, Long Knife. I don't think you're frightened of me at all.''

''You think I fear the pony soldiers.''

''Oh, by the long winter! We're all here for the same reason, you stupe bastard!''

It was the response that the Apache wanted. He took two shuffling steps away, drawing the dull steel blade from the makeshift sheath. He waved it in the air, threatening Ryan with it. ''You will accept this in your stinking flesh and you will die, white-eye devil.''

Ryan watched him, calm and controlled. ''If I draw this handgun, you'll be on your back looking up at the sun, Long Knife. And the sec men'll hear it and all of this is for nothing.''

Cuchillo didn't interfere, watching as the two men faced each other. For several long heartbeats neither moved. Finally the chief spoke.

"If you wish to fight the Anglo, Long Knife, then do so. Then we can return to the rancheria, for the hunt will be over."

The warrior's eyes flicked to his chief. "You take the side of the Anglo against your own brother! How can this be?"

The hand fell to the hilt of the golden knife. "I am leader here. It is you and it is me, my brother. We must not fight each other."

"They're stopping by the stream," J.B. said, seemingly ignoring the conflict. "Unsaddling, so they're resting up for an hour or so."

"Now what do we do?" Stones in Face asked.

Ryan stared down at the tiny, antlike figures. The horses had been tied in the shade of the trees, while the men relaxed, some of them filling canteens at the edge of the stream. The leader was clearly not the yellow-haired General but a tall, burly man with gingerish hair that was thinning around the top. As Ryan watched him, the man took the bright golden kerchief from his neck and wiped sweat from his forehead.

Two sentries were posted, one walking slowly toward them, the other trailing his Springfield carbine as he picked his way back toward the narrow notch at the mouth of Many Deer Canyon.

The discipline was evident, and Ryan whistled softly. It wasn't going to be easy to take such an organized force of sec men. He glanced around, looking at the weapons that the Mescalero had brought with them.

There was an 1841 muzzle-loading Mississippi rifle in the hands of a tall warrior whose name Ryan didn't know. A Winchester carbine at the side of Stones in Face. Another warrior hefted a sawed-off 12-gauge percussion scattergun that J.B. had spotted as a twentieth-century replica of a much older English blaster.

Cuchillo himself had a long Sharps buffalo gun. The .50-caliber weapon was one that Ryan had used a couple of times in his life, and he admired the accuracy of the gun. It was bound around with silver wire, holding a split stock together, and a pattern of tiny brass nails had been hammered into the butt.

As well as his saber, Long Knife was carrying a—

"Fireblast!" Ryan exclaimed, jumping to his feet as he saw the Mescalero warrior vault lightly onto the back of his pony. He kicked it in the slats to force it into an instant gallop, down the winding trail that eventually led to the floor of the wide canyon. Toward the sec men.

Cuchillo Oro called out to the disappearing figure, but the sound of the pony's hooves on the rocky path drowned out any hope of Long Knife hearing him. The chief turned grimly to Ryan.

"I am sorry for my brother," he said. "But he must do what he must."

"I heard that before," Ryan said.

"Best get out of here," J.B. called. "Soon as the sec men see him the crap'll hit the windshield for us all."

There wasn't time.

Long Knife came out of the mouth of the trail onto the bottom of Many Deer Canyon like a gren out of a launcher, whooping and firing his old Remington pistol in the morning air. He held the reins of the pony in his mouth, the saber whirling in a circle of singing death in his left hand.

It was like seeing a nest of insects disturbed by heavy feet. The two guards came running back to rejoin the rest of the sec men. Orders were yelled out, voices thin and reedy to the listeners on the top of the plateau far above.

One of the warriors spun around, darting toward the tethered ponies, ignoring a shout from Cuchillo Oro. He leaped on the animal's back, whipping it away down the same trail.

"It is Corn Planter," Cuchillo said sadly. "He shares a father with Long Knife. His duty is to save him if he can."

There were snowy puffs of powder smoke from the grove of trees, and they could hear the flat cracks of the Springfields. None of the troopers had noticed that the lone Indian galloping toward them had companions on the bluff above.

The trees were nearly a half mile away from where Ryan watched. J.B. shook his head in answer to the glance. "Too far. Can't reach with anything I got. You could hit 'em with the G-12. Mebbe put a couple down. Once they see us up here they could circle around, and we'd be in big trouble."

Ryan agreed with the Armorer. Outnumbered, they could easily be trapped up there. The sec men only had to send a galloper back to their fort and bring another twenty or so reinforcements. And that would mean all of them getting to buy the farm.

Now they could also see Corn Planter, better mounted, closing the gap fast on his half brother. But the sec men were getting the range, recovering from the shock of being charged by a single horseman. Puffs of dust, torn apart by the breeze, speckled the earth near the pony.

It was only a matter of time.

Cuchillo Oro watched the tragic scenario as it unfolded below them, standing at Ryan's shoulder, fingering the hilt of the golden cinqueda. "He is with his fathers," he said quietly.

One of the warriors took his rifle and prepared to fire down at the hidden sec men, but the war chief checked him. "No, brother. There is no reason for adding more deaths."

Stones in Face called out in despair as they all saw Long Knife's pony stumble and fall, throwing the warrior clean over its neck. He landed clumsily, staggering to his feet, now holding only the saber.

"Move," Ryan urged under his breath, knowing it was too late. They saw the first bullet hit home, somewhere near the shoulder, spinning the Mescalero around, the sword pitching from his fist to land point first in the earth. A second shot hit him in the guts, doubling him over like a man poisoned. A third shot killed him clean. Ryan had taken the glasses from J.B. and focused them in time to see the bullet drive upwards through the lower cheek, past the rear of the right eye, exiting through the top of the skull. It punched out a chunk of bone, releasing a spray of blood and brains, gray-pink in the sunlight. The body slumped in the dirt.

On top of the mesa the watchers could hear the ragged cheer of exultation from the sec men.

Nobody would ever know what went through the raging mind of Corn Planter, seeing his half brother butchered in front of his eyes. He was still a couple of hundred yards away, with a reasonable chance of reining in his pony and galloping for the cover of the rocks behind him.

Instead he shrilled a piercing war cry, flattening himself on his animal's neck, urging it on faster toward the stunted trees by the water's side.

The carbines rang out once more.

"They're not great shots," J.B. commented. "Should have had him over by now."

A ball from one of the carbines struck the pony between the eyes, felling it like a thunderbolt, the legs splayed as it slid down on its belly, throwing Corn Planter to the left. He fell onto a heap of jagged rocks, rolling twice, before lying still. Ryan could see that the warrior's right arm protruded at an obscene angle, and one leg seemed doubled beneath him.

"Done," Ryan said.

What had started out as a simple recce patrol had gone woefully awry. One dead, one as good as dead and the rest of them perched up high like stranded eagles with the vultures below likely to spot them and come after them at any moment.

"He is not dead," Stones in Face said, his voice harsh, as though torn from him.

"As good as," Ryan said.

"We must try to save him," the warrior said. "Honor calls to us."

"Honor's a fucking empty word. If anyone else moves I'll blow them away. Two gone . . . for nothing. Or, if you like, for your bastard honor."

Ryan gripped the G-12 as if it was the flaming sword of an avenging angel. He was furiously angry, the brilliant red rage possessing him. Part of him almost wanted the Apaches to call his bluff so he could spread them all over the mesa's top. The long scar across his cheek pulsed, and his eye raked the Mescalero like a rabid laser.

Nobody moved. Cuchillo shook his head. "There are times when all that is left is honor, brother. But you are right. More killing is pointless. We must get down from here, back to the trail. Once we are there we can break for safety. The pony soldiers will never catch us."

The insensate rage faded away as quickly as it had flared up. Ryan breathed slowly, calming himself, surprised at the anger. When he'd been a younger man it had been much worse, barely controllable. His memory still retained the image of the nineteen-year-old Ryan Cawdor in a gaudy house near where Albuquerque had once been. A pimp had made the mistake of trying to roll him, cutting the whore with a straight razor when Ryan dodged. Ryan had ripped half the face clear off the streaked bone of the skull.

A torn eyeball had flown across the stuffy little room, barely missing the screaming mouth of the bloodied girl.

"Sure," Ryan said to the Apache. "Let's go."

He risked a last quick glance over the lip of the cliff, seeing that the sec men were flocking like vermin to the unconscious figure of Corn Planter.

Ryan turned away and followed the others to where the ponies were tied.

When they reached the bottom of the snaking pathway, Cuchillo reined in his pony. "I must stay to see this thing to its ending. I am his chief. I must share the time of his passing from the earth. The rest of you go back to the rancheria and I will follow."

The remaining Mescalero began to move off, but Ryan and J.B. stayed where they were. The Apache chieftain looked at them.

"Why do you stay, brothers? This is no business of yours."

"Came out to find what we could about these blue-coat bastards," Ryan said quietly. "Might as well stick around."

"It is good. Let us head away from the river, there." He pointed to a draw that ran at right angles across Many Deer Canyon.

The doomed day's final horrific scenes were about to begin.

Chapter Seventeen

THE TWO DEAD HORSES LAY where they'd fallen. A buzzard was circling curiously, deterred from coming closer by the presence of the noisy group of sec men near the trees. The body of Long Knife had been moved, and the three watchers couldn't see any sign of Corn Planter.

It had taken a great deal of time to reach their hiding place, and the day was wearing on. The sun was already dipping below the brink of the canyon walls, the shadows making it difficult to see what the cavalry was doing by the narrow river. Ryan and the others could hear shouting and laughter.

Once there was a scream, quickly silenced.

"They into torture?" J.B. asked.

"My father's spirit would answer that," Cuchillo Oro replied. He stared at the Armorer, but J.B. met the look.

"I guess that means they do."

The Apache nodded. "They use fire and knives. When I saw what remained of my father I fell to my knees and wept like a foolish woman. So little was left of what had been a tall, strong and proud man."

"I've seen bad, Cuchillo Oro."

"I believe you, Weapons Strike Fear. But to see your father...like a hacked, twisted log, burned and blackened..."

The words faded away into the stillness.

"They're moving," Ryan said, breaking the silence.

The sec men had saddled up, and now the burly figure with ginger hair led them out of the clump of trees, cantering toward the neck of the canyon.

"Look," J.B. said, pointing at something that dangled from the lower branches of one of the trees.

"Long Knife," Cuchillo said. "His pain is done."

"And that looks like Corn Planter," Ryan said.

It was a grim sight. Hauled along behind the last horse by a rope bound around his wrists, the naked body of Corn Planter bounced and tossed over the rough ground. Even from where they watched, the dark smears of blood along the trail were clearly visible. The Apache was gagged but from the way the body jerked, it was obvious that the wretched warrior still lived.

The dust from the horses concealed the man's suffering for a moment, the patrol nearing the opening to the main trail.

As they filed through the notch, the last of the sec men paused a moment, taking off his slouch hat and waving it in a triumphant gesture of bravado.

"No," Cuchillo Oro grated. He hefted the Sharps rifle and shot a bullet clear through the sec man's head, kicking him off the back of his horse.

Ryan would have been a whole lot happier if the chief hadn't pulled the trigger. At least they were fairly safe where they were, halfway along the canyon, with a clear line of withdrawal to the other end of the valley. The cavalry was on the wrong side of the neck to come at them in any strength. In some ways, Ryan almost hoped they'd try for it. With J.B.'s Uzi and his own G-12, the sec men would have a hard time of it.

"One is paid," the Mescalero said, calmly reloading the long gun.

"Nice shot, Chief," J.B. said. "Good clean kill."

A figure appeared, silhouetted in the pinched opening, a carbine in its hands. Ryan nearly risked a shot, but held his fire.

"Better go," he said. "No point in sitting here and waiting. Can they get around behind us?"

"No. The canyon runs many miles, and there are no side trails. A man on foot could get above us, but the pony soldiers do not do these things. It would take many hours, until past night, for them to circle us. We have time."

Whoever was in charge of the patrol made his decision quickly. There was a burst of shooting from the notch, making Ryan and the other two men duck down. By the time they glanced out again, the body of the sec man had been dragged into safety.

"Might as well go, Cuchillo," Ryan said. "Nothing now to hang around for."

But it still wasn't done.

JERKING ACROSS A FEW INCHES at a time, the crude wooden framework almost filled the gap. With the glasses Ryan could easily make out that it was built from broken branches, probably washed out on the trail by a flash flood in Many Deer Canyon. It was about eight feet high and nearly the same width.

The naked body of Corn Planter was spread-eagled across it, stretched into a human letter X, head sunk on its breast.

"Dead?" Cuchillo asked.

"No," Ryan replied, slowly lowering the glasses. "No, he's still alive."

The high-power binoculars showed more than he wanted to see.

The Apache's whole body was a mass of oozing cuts and grazes from being dragged behind the horses, and much of the skin had been stripped away. The glasses revealed the jagged stump of white bone, protruding through the flesh of the broken arm. The face was puffed and swollen, teeth missing from the sagging jaw. It looked from the unnatural angles that many of the fingers had been bent back and snapped.

Corn Planter seemed locked deep into unconsciousness, mercifully unaware of the cruel and shameful indignities offered him.

Cuchillo reached out for the binoculars, but Ryan shook his head. "Better not. You know what's out there. No reason to see it close."

"Smoke," J.B. said. "They've gotten a fire going."

"It is not for cooking food," Cuchillo muttered, laying the Sharps down at his side.

He was right.

Even without the binoculars they could make out that piles of kindling were being pushed around the bottom of the bondage frame. The smoke was thin and almost white, showing how dry the wood was. The heat finally brought Corn Planter back to consciousness. They saw the head suddenly toss upward, the mouth opening in a scream of shock and agony. It was a tearing, jagged cry that scraped at the nerves.

"His eyes are gone," J.B. observed.

An arm came from the left, holding a long torch, an orange flame dancing merrily at its end. Ryan considered a shot, but the billowing smoke made it an impossible target.

"Is he...?" Cuchillo began.

The Armorer had lifted the binoculars once more. "No," he said. "Still alive."

The Apache chief had his head buried in his hands, rocking from side to side, chanting to himself. Ryan had seen and taken enough. He reached across Cuchillo Oro and took the heavy buffalo rifle. He checked the double action of the trigger and glanced down at the sights, testing the light wind from left to right.

The range was well below a quarter mile.

The torch was moving slowly up the Apache's scarred body, toward his face. Ryan leveled the gun, holding his breath, bringing the sights onto the target. His finger was light on the trigger, the wire-bound stock pressed snugly into his shoulder.

The Sharps kicked back and his vision was blinded by the burst of smoke. At his side, Cuchillo jumped, as though the bullet had struck him. He looked out across Many Deer Canyon.

Understanding.

The corpse of Corn Planter slumped in its bonds, a small dark hole drilled an inch above the breastbone.

Bright blood trickled from the wound—surprisingly little blood for a fatal wound.

"Your gun, Chief," Ryan said, handing him the smoking rifle.

"I could not do it . . . I thank you, brother. You set his spirit free."

"Hope so, Cuchillo."

There was again a scattering of shots from beyond the smoldering fire, but none of the bullets came anywhere near the crouching men. J.B. jerked a thumb over his shoulder, toward the far end of Many Deer Canyon.

"Mebbe we oughta move, Ryan."

"Be nice to find some way of leveling the score against those bastards."

"You killed one of them. That does not happen often," Cuchillo Oro said, reloading the heavy weapon.

"They killed two of us," Ryan retorted. "I guess that we probably have just about as many fighting men as they do. We got a camp we can hold against them. They got this fort they can hold against you. They got better weapons. Discipline. And you said last night that they got a mess of self-heats out back of the museum."

"Yes. There is what is called a small redoubt hidden under the mesa. And they have deep water that stays all year."

The firing died away, and the canyon was silent once more. Ryan glanced up at the darkening sky. It would be dusk in a couple of hours. With a dozen armed men out there, it would be a good idea to get moving as soon as possible.

"I would wish to remove the body of Long Knife," Cuchillo said quietly.

"Not now. You think they aren't going to be looking for that? Send a couple of your young men tomorrow or the next day, Chief. Long Knife's dead. A couple of days won't hurt him none. If we try now the sec men can bring their tally up to five for the day. Is that what you want?"

"No. But it is another cut in the coup stick against the Anglos."

A bullet smacked into the top of the boulder, close by Ryan's head, showering them all with knifing splinters of rock. As he ducked again, Ryan felt something beneath his fingers. The dry crackle of old paper, partly buried in the fine sand. He dug it out, unfolded it and read the faded lettering: Ma's Cinnamon Rolls. Have the Nicest and You'll Have a Nice Day.

He could catch the taint of scorched flesh from the corpse of Corn Planter.

"Yeah."

Chapter Eighteen

"FIGHT *WITH* BASTARDS and you have to fight *like* bastards!"

Ryan was beginning to lose patience. They had returned safely to Drowned Squaw Canyon, free from pursuit by the sec men. Cuchillo Oro had spoken little, riding his pony with his head down, locked into his own thoughts. J.B. and Ryan had talked tactics, finally agreeing that they needed some sort of showpiece victory. It might only be a skirmish that left the final battle as blurred as before, but it would show Yellowhair and his cavalry renegades that they meant business. And it would encourage the Mescalero for any future conflict.

Now, the next morning, Ryan was finding it very hard going. He felt like he was flicking cherry pits at a lump of dough. His ideas stuck there, and nothing happened.

The Armorer had been looking at a torn and crumpled map of the area, trying to scout a possible location for a confrontation. One that would leave the odds firmly and safely on their side.

But the Apache didn't like it. Didn't like it at all.

The oldest man of the tribe, who was nearly blind and who spoke very poor English, eventually strug-

gled to put their side of the argument. His name was
Many Winters.

"Bad is here. Yellowhair and pony soldiers are bad.
Do bad things. Wish to chill all people here at rancheria. We fight. Always fight. But with honor. Anglos
do not know honor. If the spirits say we win, then we
win well. Not bad like Yellowhair. But you come and
say beat bad with bad. We say beat bad with good. It
is only truth way."

Ryan had stood and shouted, "Fight with bastards
and . . ."

He saw that the faces of the elders of the tribe were
looking at him with hooded eyes, blank, overlaid with
contempt. For a moment he saw the futility of it.

"Fine. That bakes the biscuit, friends. We came
here and you helped us. Saved Jak's life. And we
thank you for it. Fireblast! Course we thank you. And
you got troubles. Bad ones. Fuck honor, Many Winters! The sec men have no honor. They rape and kill
and torture. Life means less than a rat's fart to any of
them."

Man Whose Eyes See More unfolded himself ele-
gantly from the far side of the council. He wore a
white shirt with a ripple of lace down its front, over
dark blue chinos. The mirrored sunglasses flashed as
he looked at Ryan, who saw a tiny, stretched double
image of himself reflected in the twin lenses.

"You tell us that Yellowhair is evil and has no
honor. We know these things, Ryan Cawdor. And you
tell us this plan to win a small victory."

"Better small victories than defeats. Any defeats,"
J.B. interrupted.

The shaman shook his head slowly. "You see as children, through a mist. Your ways of fighting are no different from those of the pony soldiers. Winning is not all."

"Winning's the only thing," Krysty said, face flushing with her own building anger.

None of the Mescalero even looked at her. Man Whose Eyes See More went on as if nobody had spoken. "It is better that the people leave their home. Better than to fight on bellies."

Doc Tanner also stood up, waving his hands like an agitated windmill. His voice was strong and clear, his mind, for once, seeming completely free from the time-jump muddle.

"I've heard enough. In my time I have been fortunate enough to spend a little time among the people. I admire you, Cuchillo Oro, and everything you believe in. When it comes to religion, the Christians could learn plenty of lessons from the Apache. But times they are changing, my brothers."

"Honor—"

"Who has honor?" Doc bellowed, his voice echoing the length and breadth of the canyon, drawing the attention of every man, woman and child there. "I'll tell you who has persnickety honor! He who died Wednesday. Honor is a shield to bear home a slain warrior. It is a rag to wipe the tears of the widow. Does Long Knife have honor? Does Corn Planter have honor? Oh, my dear friends . . . give me leave a moment. . . . If honor is to die, then go, and ride against the pony soldiers. Death is cheap. Death with honor is easy." He paused for dramatic effect. "It is living that is hard."

In one of the wickiups, everyone could hear the frail sound of a baby crying. Other than that, the canyon was quiet. Doc looked around him, catching Ryan's eye. The old man's hands were trembling.

The shaman still stood, his enormous height making everyone look up at him. He turned to Cuchillo, who nodded for him to reply.

"You and your companions are all touched with death. I can taste it on you. It sits at your shoulder like the shadow of a man carrying a scythe."

Nobody answered him. The crying of the baby was suddenly stopped as a young woman ran to comfort it.

"It cannot be right to lie and cheat in order to beat Yellowhair," the shaman continued.

The reply came, unexpectedly, from Jak Lauren. The boy, growing stronger by the hour, was already well enough to leave his bed for a few minutes at a time. He'd joined the council, leaning against the stump of a small tree. Ryan had noticed that Steps Lightly Moon, the teenage daughter of Cuchillo, had appeared at the edge of the council of warriors, sitting as close as she could to the white-haired boy.

"You don't know what you're talking about," Jak said. "I'm only fourteen, but I know more about the world than an old woman like you." He pointed at Many Winters. "I've seen killings. More than any you."

"The cub thinks he may teach—" one of the veteran warriors began, but Jak startled him by laughing scornfully.

"It's not cubs an' bears an' that crap. It's sec men an' blasters an' blood. You want to break an' run like girls. Do it! Get the fuck out. Let 'em piss all on you. But if want fight an' win . . . do it our way."

The boy sat back, eyes closing, looking once more on the brink of exhaustion. The shaman made his way around the group and knelt beside Jak, holding his wrist in his long, thin fingers.

It was Cuchillo, finally, who answered for his people.

"We have heard the words from the Anglos. From the old and from . . . the young." He almost smiled. "Words that were not good to our ears. I have listened hard and thought long. And I believe that some truth has been spoken this day. It might be that we are too set in the old ways." Seeing half of the senior warriors around the council ready to argue, he held up his hand for silence. "No, brothers. This is our home. To run would not show honor. It would show we are like dry branches. Old and strong, but ready to crack and to break at the first cruel wind. We shall try the ways of the Anglos."

The plan that Ryan had worked out with J.B. was simple, involving an offer of peace talks that would enable them to ambush the sec men. It was treacherous and it was clever.

Ryan had explained it to Krysty before the council of war.

"We'll send word to Yellowhair that we want to talk. Try to sort out a way of living peaceably together. We'll meet at the ghost town fifteen miles to the west in the foothills. They'll expect a trap, but we'll hit them first on the way toward the meeting place. It should work.''

THERE WERE SEVERAL TRAILS into the ghost town, which had been a mining center during a brief boom period in the latter part of the nineteenth century. Called Sometime Never it had housed three and a half thousand miners at its peak. Two years later there was no sign of the mother lode, and the population of Sometime Never had shrunk to twenty-three.

By 1911 it was down to four.

In the mid 1970s there was a burst of interest in the old lost towns of the Southwest, and Sometime Never boomed briefly again. The dirt road was graded and a few shops opened, selling stones, pots and glass. A couple of eateries, an art gallery and a store specializing in genuine reproduction patchwork quilts did well for a few heady years.

It wasn't the last World War that did in Sometime Never. There'd been an earthslide that made driving up the road difficult, but the nail that sealed the coffin was the establishment of a gay commune. The big AIDS scare of the early nineties brought a visit to the town, very late one Friday night in mid-December. A couple of dozen good ol' boys, juiced to the cortex, arrived in mud-smeared pickups, several with pump-action shotguns. The idea was to throw a scare into the disease-spreading wimps up on the hill.

It all got a little out of hand.

The rednecks didn't know that the gays had an armory of M-16s, in anticipation of just such an attack.

Eventually the body count reached the respectable total of fifteen, split eleven to four in favor of the commune.

Armageddon passed almost unnoticed in Sometime Never.

By 2001 there was only one inhabitant left, and he wasn't even three cents in the dollar. He'd built a small shrine in his garden to a country singer called Dwight Yoakam, who he claimed was a prophet and whose songs contained hidden clues to the coming of a new master.

The old man heard the distant sounds of rumbling explosions and saw the skies darkening all around him. But he took it as a sign of the eternal's wrath with him and he tried to play his Dwight Yoakam albums more often and louder. But there was no electricity coming up the line to his shack. The EMP had knocked out all generators and power-operated installations across the land.

It was winter, and cold at night up in the hills of New Mexico. The old man offered to fast in order to purge himself of whatever sins of omission or commission he might have been guilty of.

The fast went very well and in just under five days he was dead.

THE NEXT DAY RYAN took Krysty and the others with him to the ghost town. Jak was, amazingly, well enough to come with them, riding on an amiable swaybacked mule. Cuchillo didn't accompany them, being occupied with the funeral arrangements for Corn Planter and Long Knife. But his daughter came as guide, keeping herself as close to Jak as was possible.

Steps Lightly Moon was so busy chattering to Jak that she nearly missed the turnoff to the deserted ghost town.

All of them stopped at a burst of crackling explosions from the far side of the wide valley. The purple chem clouds had been gathering ominously for an hour or more and had finally begun to spill their load over the mountains. Great jagged bolts of lightning burst along the orange flanks, exploding with the bitter iron taste of ozone. It was possible to see the rain teeming from the roots of the clouds, dulling the view. Thunder rolled and rumbled all around them, making any conversation difficult.

Ryan stood in the stirrups, licking his lips, tasting the storm on his breath, figuring the prevailing wind would carry it away from them.

"It will not come this way," Steps Lightly Moon said.

"I know it," Ryan replied.

"The village of spirits is not far from here."

"We call ghost town." Jak grinned.

"I do not have a cunning with the words of the Anglos."

"Talk better'n me," the boy replied.

The Apache girl flushed at the compliment, letting her fingers tangle in the pony's mane as she rode along the rising trail.

It was Ryan's intention to check out the township from every direction. He hoped to cover all the trails in, find somewhere that would tell them how the cavalry would come cantering in. If the sec men were led by General Yellowhair, then his death would be a powerful bonus. It was clear that the serious trouble with the renegades only dated from the arrival of the mysterious stranger, the tall lean man with the hollow eyes. Yet again Ryan heard the far-off susurration of memory's bell. But the identity wouldn't come at his bidding. There was no doubt that the Mescalero saw the General as the physical embodiment of evil, and that his corpse would give them a greater will to fight against the whites.

TWO ROTTING PIECES of wood supported the remains of a painted board, hanging only by a couple of rusted nails. Lori swung out of her saddle, picking her way carefully over the rutted ground in her brilliant crimson boots with the teetering heels. The miniature silver bells on the razored spurs tinkled sweetly at every step.

"What does it say, oh moon of my delight that knows no wane?" Doc asked, spitting with a delicate aim at a tiny, skittering lizard that darted away from the shadow of the horses.

The girl bent down, following the peeling letters with a long finger.

"Can't read it," she called.

"Let me, my dove of innocence." Doc clambered out of the high saddle.

He peered at the board, wrinkling his eyes. "I must confess that it is more than somewhat difficult. It's probably the most nugatory piece of... Ah, now I see it. Well, well. A fine example of twentieth-century folksiness."

"What's it say, Doc?" Krysty asked.

"Any Stranger's a Dead Stranger. Clear enough. Sometime Never must have been the xenophobia capital of the world."

They tethered their animals outside a single-story building that still bore stenciled lettering on the adobe facade: Visitor Center.

The remains of the ghost town straggled up a narrow gulch, with scattered mesquite bushes and red-tipped spears of ocotillo. Jak reached for his big cannon of a pistol at a flurry of movement among the scrub.

Out came the skinniest cat that any of them had ever seen, arching its back and mewing plaintively.

"Come, kitty," the boy said, kneeling down, wincing at a stab of pain from his ribs. The Mescalero girl was at his side before he could even begin to straighten up.

"Take care, Eyes of Wolf. You know our shaman warned to step with the light until the healing way is done."

"I'm sorry, Steps Lightly Moon," he said, pursing his lips and looking like a kid caught with his hand inside the cookie jar.

Ryan and Krysty exchanged glances and grins.

The scrawny gray cat, tail poised over it like a periscope, stepped toward the boy with a strange air of unctuous pride.

"We ate cats back home," Jak said, holding out his hand to the advancing feline.

"Been places in Deathlands where the cats would've eaten you," J.B. said, poker-faced as ever.

Just as Jak was about to pet the lean cat, its face became a mask of malevolent hatred and it hissed at him, claws raking at his eyes. The albino threw himself back just in time. Steps Lightly Moon had her knife out, poised to throw, but the cat got away clean into the bushes.

"Friendly little ville," Jak said, trying for a grin. Not quite making it.

Chapter Nineteen

THE STEEP-SIDED VALLEY WAS a blaze of color. Tiny yellow flowers of honey mesquite, in dazzling golden banks, smudged around the base of the tumbled buildings. The pale blue of bristly gilia bloomed in a delicate patch along the sides of the dry washes lining the main valley of Sometime Never. Flame-red desert mallow mingled with clumps of Indian paintbrush wherever the eyes settled.

The scent that lay over everything was that of the ubiquitous yellow creosote bush. Krysty shook her head in wonderment. "Gaia! It's one of the most beautiful places I've ever seen, Ryan. There were quiet valleys a few miles from Harmony, and an abandoned reservoir with cool places, but this is triple-lovely. You can't blame that old hermit the Apaches spoke about who used to live here and tried to stop anyone ever coming up."

Steps Lightly Moon was just behind them, waiting for Jak to catch up. She heard what the fire-haired woman had said.

"The people do not come here. The spirits are not friendly. Over the years there have been disappearances. Some who went and never returned. There are many deep holes in the hills around."

"Mine shafts," Doc said. "Old workings riddle the land hereabouts. I guess the little girl's speaking the truth. Looks like the townspeople just slipped out for a while and never came back."

It was agreed that they'd recce in pairs. J.B. went along with Jak, Steps Lightly Moon dogging them at every step. Doc and Lori wandered hand in hand, like the lovers they were. Ryan and Krysty began to explore the sun-bleached buildings on both sides of the main street, taking care where they stepped. Most of the timbers had either rotted or been attacked by hordes of insects.

Sometime Never was a comparatively rare small ville in those late days of the twenty-first century. The nuking hadn't touched the remote valley, and the depredations of the weather hadn't been too severe. The Southwest of the Deathlands didn't suffer from the screaming gales of two hundred miles an hour and the pitiless acid rain that vomited down from the deeps of violent chem storms.

Everywhere the rough-built shacks showed signs of the long-lost days before the skies burned. As Ryan and Krysty walked up the hill, preceded by the skinny cat, they kept pausing to look at some new chimera from the past.

Triple Scoop Rocky Road Only $2.50. The sign swung off a porch from one hook. The rest of the building had slipped wearily into a narrow ravine at its back.

Rocks, Cristalls, Candels and All Kindsa Rare Qrios. Ryan pushed the door open, the hinges creaking their protest. A small copper bell tinkled a merry greeting—before the spring broke and it fell silent.

"Anyone home?" Krysty called, her voice dulled by the inches-thick layer of fine red dust that covered everything.

The air in the shack was overwhelmingly hot and stuffy, with an odd lifeless quality to it. Ryan guessed that the last person who'd pushed open the door and rung the little bell had done so nearly a hundred years ago.

The shelves that lined the walls were mainly bare, though some had empty cardboard boxes on them. Peeling labels still clung to a few of the boxes: Pinon Candles; Owl Prisms; Mica Wind Chimes; Honeydew Candles; Canyon de C Place Mats; Shot Glasses; Large Prisms.

"What was a prism, lover?" Krysty asked, wiping sweat from her forehead.

"No idea. Seen the word on sights for long-range blasters. Guess it must have meant something different back then."

"Look here. The front of this closet's broken in. Some kinda store behind it." She was on her knees, rummaging around. Ryan moved closer to watch her. "No. Just a lot of old boxes and stuff... Wait. Something smooth in here. Got it. Oh, Gaia!"

Krysty held up a round crystal ball, rubbing the dust off it. It was a little larger than the clenched fist of a grown man, shining in the shadows of the old store. Ryan whistled at what the crystal contained.

It was the severed head of an adult prairie rattler, jaws gaping as though it were about to strike. The flat eyes stared blankly out of the clear glass.

They took it outside where the brilliant sun danced off the polished surface. Doc and Lori were on the far side of the street, and Ryan called them over.

The girl was fascinated by it. "Can I be having it, Doc, please? If Ryan and Krysty doesn't want it? Can I?"

"Too heavy, child," Doc replied, taking the ball as if it were a religious totem. "By the three Kennedys! This brings back memories of such places. It's beautiful, is it not? When I was here back...in my first days here...there was a saloon up near Chinle. The barkeep had a large glass bell jar on the counter with a live rattler in there. Big son of a bitch, if you'll pardon my French, friends."

"Didn't know that was French, Doc," Lori said, puzzled.

"Figure of speech, my dear. Anyway, this man offered a five-dollar bet that you couldn't lay your hand on the outside of this jar and hold it there, eyes open, watching the snake. It would always strike at the hand. But you never knew when. It might be five seconds, might be five minutes. When it did, the speed and venom was so scary that you just *had* to take your hand off the glass. Couldn't help yourself. Guy made a lot of dough that way from greenhorn suckers. Suckers like me, if I tell the truth."

To Lori's sadness, he pitched the crystal ball down into one of the numerous gulches running off the street.

Krysty and Ryan continued up their side, peering through cracked windows that were smothered in spiderwebs. The planks on one of the stoops disintegrated under the girl's weight, and her leg plunged in to the knee. An army of vicious red ants came boiling out of the darkness, and Ryan heaved Krysty clear, while she stamped her foot to shake off the insects.

"Fall into that and you could have a hard time," she said, not quite managing to keep her voice from trembling.

A sign painted on the glass of the front window revealed what the next building had once been. It read: Ole Zeke's Rock Shop. All Welcome.

The lock on the front door had been smashed in and dangled, rust-red, from a broken iron staple. The place looked as if it had been deliberately wrecked. The tables were overturned and the glass display cases on the back wall were splintered. The floor was littered with piles of ordinary rocks, but if there had ever been anything of real worth it was long stolen. Krysty pushed with the toe of her boot at a heap of rectangular cards. Each one had a name, neatly printed with a firm italic hand.

"Uncle Tyas McCann knew rocks and stones and all their names," she said. "I recognize some of them. When I was a sprat I loved 'em. Uncle Tyas would recite them like they were the names of famous heroes." She bent and picked up the cards, reading them and then flicking them away to float in the dusty motes that drifted lazily along the spears of sunlight.

Ryan listened. He knew nothing of either gem-stones or heroes, but he admitted to himself that the names sounded good from Krysty's lips.

"Wolframite, dolomite, barite...that would have been a desert rose. Real pretty, pink shape. Fragile. I remember them. Chrysoprase...lovely name. Banded agate and chalcedony. Onyx, jasper, opals and car-nelian. Oh, I'd love to have come to this place when it was still filled with all... Turquoise and malachite."

A stray beam of hazy light bounced off something in the corner, near the bolted back door. Ryan's first reaction was to guess it was one of the shards of bro-ken glass. He walked across, boots crunching, and picked up a small, smooth stone.

"Nice," he said, wiping it on his jacket. It was roughly circular, polished and gleaming black.

"Obsidian," said Krysty.

"Yeah."

She took it from him, feeling the hard smoothness of the small stone. "Know what they used to call these in the old days?"

"No."

"Apache tears."

NEAR THE TOP END of the main street, there was an adobe house, better preserved than any of the wooden shacks. A wrought-iron shingle swung there, as neat as when it had been hung more than a century past: Portrait Photographs. Old Style Pix.

"Hey, come see double stupes," Jak shouted to the others.

J.B. was there first, fedora tugged low over his eyes against the harsh sun. Ryan and Krysty were joined by Doc and Lori. The old man was looking fatigued by the extreme heat, leaning on the girl's arm for support on the steep, rutted slope. The gray cat was parading up and down on the windowsill, back arched, purring in a loud dissonant rasp.

"Look in here," Jak said. "Must be craze-muties, clothes like them."

The door to the store stood open, the entrance step piled high with driven sand. Ryan glanced inside and saw that the place had been stripped of furniture. The walls, however, were still covered with serried rows of pictures. They were all sizes, all tinted light brown, all showing stiffly posed people, wearing the kind of clothes that Ryan had only seen in vids set in the Old West days: Long dresses and parasols and stiff collars and tall hats.

Come and pose. Fifteen minutes only. Complete satisfaction guaranteed or your money back. Show your friends how you might have looked a hundred years ago. Try on anything that takes your fancy. Mayor or gunman. Women's Purity League or wh*re. You got the fantasy and we got the camera.

"Look at them." The Indian girl laughed, her face wreathed in the broadest of smiles. "So silly."

Doc came to the front of the group, shading his eyes with his hand. He stooped to look at a large framed picture that held pride of place in the middle of the photographer's window.

There was a young woman, seated in an ornate armchair with golden cherubs carved along its arms. Her hair was knotted back, and she wore a wide-brimmed hat with a trim of osprey feathers. Her dress was dark velvet and pinched at the waist. A cameo brooch clipped the blouse together at her slender white throat.

A tall man stood behind her, one hand upon her shoulder, smiling down at her with an unaffected look of pride and love. His hair was parted down the middle and pomaded back. A luxuriant mustache curled around his lips. The frock coat was light gray, with darker piping around the lapels. A heavy gold chain drooped across his stomach, carrying a seal and a Masonic emblem. A little hideaway Derringer .22 was tucked discreetly into the top of his striped pants, showing its pearl butt.

He held a stovepipe hat in his beringed right hand.

"Never seen nothing more triple-stupe," Jak cackled, holding his bandaged ribs. "Nobody never looked like that."

Doc turned away, face stricken as if he had just witnessed the moment of his own death. "God help me, friends," he whispered. "That is . . . could be . . . It is like my dearest Emily and myself."

Tears began to flow and he walked off, back ramrod-stiff. Lori looked at Jak as if she were going to spit in his face. Then she spun on her heel and dashed after Doc, spurs tinkling in the stillness of the ghost town.

"What was...?" Jak began, his face slack with shock. "Just joke 'bout..."

"Those people, kid," Ryan said. "They're wearing the kind of clothes Doc and his wife wore when he was alive in the 1890s before those bastards trawled him. It just made him recall things he'd want to forget."

"I didn't think...I'll go say sorry an' tell Doc how..."

"Later, Jak," Krysty said. "Later."

It took a couple of hours for Ryan, helped by the Armorer, to recce the whole of Sometime Never, concentrating on the trails in and out. There were several places ideal for an ambush.

"We'll send word for a peace council here. They'll look for a trap, but we'll hit 'em on the way in. I can come back and pick the best place a coupla days before the meet."

J.B. nodded his agreement. "Sounds good."

"Reckon this General Yellowhair'll guess it's a trick?"

"Bound to, Ryan. Sneaky sec leader like that isn't able to think straight anymore."

Ryan looked around the scattered shacks, most of them in the last stages of decrepitude. "Must have been a good place to live. Once."

"Most places were," J.B. said, wiping sweat from his hands on the leg of his pants.

IT WAS GETTING TIME to head back. The cavalry didn't patrol toward Sometime Never very often, knowing the Apache kept away from the gulch. But it was as well to ride safely into Drowned Squaw Canyon before dusk crept over the desert.

From where he stood, Ryan was able to look clear down the steep valley. Jak was sitting on a porch with Steps Lightly Moon, stroking the cat. Doc and Lori were sitting together by a tumbled heap of timber that had once been called The Crazy Shack. J.B. was pitching pebbles at a metal sign, thirty yards away across the street, rattling it with nine shots out of ten.

He couldn't see Krysty and guessed she was still exploring some of the fascinating relics of the ghost ville.

His own eye had been caught by a stone-walled shack near the adobe photo store, but on the opposite side of the street. Loops of rusting barbed wire were festooned around it, and a sign fashioned out of the bottoms of green bottles, stuck in clay, read Hillbilly Heaven.

Ryan climbed cautiously up the slippery slope of loose stones, past a couple of handmade signs, both fallen and faded. He tried to make out the wording, but all he could read was a warning to keep out of the patch of land around the cabin.

Far below he heard Jak's reedy, cackling laughter and Doc's booming bass. It was obvious that the falling out between the old man and the teenager had been resolved.

Unusually the door to the hut was made from sheet steel, fixed in a sturdy wooden frame. Metal shutters covered the windows.

Ryan strolled around the curious building, puzzled at the security, more puzzled that it didn't seem to have been breached at all. Yet the state of the main bolts and hinges showed that a determined child could have pushed its way in.

Krysty's voice made him start. "What have you found, lover?"

"You shouldn't creep around like that. Get yourself chilled one of these days."

"Hillbilly Heaven," she read. "What's that mean? And how come it's still shut up tight as a duck's ass?"

"You shouldn't talk dirty." He grinned. "I figure this has to be the shack that the Apaches talked about. The lone crazy who liked some old country singer lived here at the end. The man they say haunts the ville."

"The ghost-town ghost, you mean? Could be. If it's bolted up and locked from inside, then it looks like—"

"The ghost's still there. Let's see."

He braced himself, then kicked out, his combat boot shattering the main lock. The door swung open, revealing a dusty box of utter darkness, blacker than the wing feathers of a raven.

Krysty pushed by him, pausing on the threshold and pulling a face. "Ugh. Something bad in here, lover. Long gone death."

"I'll break off a couple of the shutters to give us some light. Don't go in. It might be boobied."

"Yeah," she replied absently, still sniffing the arid air.

Ryan went outside and wrenched away two of the shutters, the metal giving a loud groaning sound of protest.

He heard a yell from Steps Lightly Moon, far below him down the gulch, but he took no notice, eager to follow Krysty inside.

The girl was poised by an inner door, surrounded by swirling motes of dust, the bursts of sunlight giving her a halo, setting her hair ablaze with rich crimson. She looked staggeringly beautiful, and Ryan felt a wave of love sweep over him.

She pushed open the door. Ryan heard the click of a contact breaking and an odd whirring noise. Out of the corner of his eye he caught the glint of metal, a huge ax with a curved edge, swinging toward Krysty's skull.

He started to move....

Chapter Twenty

RYAN'S SHOULDER CAUGHT Krysty just above the knees, projecting her across the far room like a gren from a launcher. She landed on her side, coming up with her blaster in her hand, the silvered finish glowing with light in the dimness.

"Why the . . . ?" she began, voice cracking in her anger. Words failed her as she looked behind Ryan and saw the swinging pendulum of the huge ax blade, hissing through the air. It reached its apogee, hung frozen for a moment, then plunged into its lethal arc once more.

"I guess . . ." She holstered the 9 mm pistol, then stood to brush herself down. She offered a hand to Ryan, who was still lying on the floor. "Thanks, lover."

"Crazy bastard didn't want nobody creeping in on him," he said, examining the mechanism of the booby, which had a simple switch trigger, and a waxed fishing line coiled on a spring under tension. A second switch released the ax head. He touched it with his index finger, finding it still keen enough to slice through silk.

"He's still here, Ryan," Krysty said, pointing to the dust-muffled shape on the truckle bed against the far wall of the hut.

An antique disk player stood by the bed, and a table by the window held a dozen empty liquor bottles. A heavy Smith & Wesson automatic, loaded, was on top of some frail, curling magazines. All dated from the year 2000. Leaning against the leg of the bed was a stack of extremely old record albums, warped black vinyl. From the covers, the illustrations so faded they were almost transparent, Ryan saw that the records were all of the same artist, with several copies of the same album. The young man's name was Dwight Yoakam and his records had titles like "Hillbilly Deluxe" and "Guitars, Cadillacs, Etc."

"Hillbilly Heaven," Krysty said. "The name of his cabin. Must have been that loner the Mescalero talked about."

"Yeah." Ryan turned as he heard the others arriving outside the shack. Despite his injuries, Jak was first, with the fleet-footed girl panting behind him.

"Very bad medicine here," Steps Lightly Moon said. "Home of all the spirits who do evil in this place."

"There's your evil spirit." Ryan pointed to the leathery corpse. "A lonely old man who lived here and died here. That's all there is."

Dust had settled in the empty, sunken eye sockets and the mouth hung dryly open. The hands were coiled shut against the palms. The cotton dungarees had rotted away as the corpse decomposed, and the bones thrust through at knees and elbow.

"Let's go," Ryan said. The last to leave, he pulled the outer door shut behind him, wedging it with a large stone so the remains wouldn't be disturbed by coyotes or any of the other desert scavengers.

THE WAR COUNCIL THAT NIGHT took place in one of the wickiups, around a smoking fire. The sky had lowered around dusk, and deep purple chem clouds, streaked with chrome-yellow, brought a rising wind and pounding rain. For several minutes hailstones pounded the box canyon, bouncing off the boulders, and the temperature dropped twenty degrees in two minutes.

They all ate a fiery bean stew, helping themselves with old metal spoons, marked with the name "Holiday Inns." After they'd finished eating, Ryan and J.B. stayed behind while the others went to their own huts. Cuchillo stayed, as well as two of his most senior warriors: Many Winters and Stones in Face.

"You think it will work, Ryan Cawdor?"

"Fireblast, Cuchillo, how the fuck can I answer that? I've seen some of the best plans ever made fall apart just because someone chose the wrong moment to fart. How should I know?"

"But it is a good plan," Stones in Face said, fingers absently tracing the runic patterns of pockmarks that seamed his cheeks.

"Best we got."

Many Winters was not so convinced. "If Yellowhair catches the scent of betrayal, then he will escape the trap. He will be angered and will come and burn us from our home."

Cuchillo Oro sighed. "Old men fear life. If one never risks the danger of the hunt, then one will finally starve."

"It's right," Ryan said. "Look, we send the message to the fort saying we want peace. Not from me but from *your* people. Offer a meet in three days from now in Sometime Never. Say there'll only be Cuchillo and one other warrior. Ask for the General and one sec man to come. They'll try treachery. Bound to. But we get there first. Ambush the trails and hit 'em on the way in. They won't look for that."

"Which road in will they take?"

"Covered that," J.B. said, unable to conceal his mounting irritation. "Ryan goes in and checks out all the trails."

"Sure. The word goes tomorrow. Day after that I'll go in to the ghost town on my own and recce it thoroughly."

"I'll come with you," the Armorer said.

"And me," Cuchillo added. "This is our war."

"Fine," Ryan agreed. "Day after tomorrow, we all go up there and check it out."

By evening of the following day they knew for sure that the Seventh Cavalry had safely received the invitation to a meeting. It had been written, after some argument and disagreement, by Doc Tanner. The final draft was short and to the point.

The armed conflict between us is harmful to both. I suggest a meeting in the ruined ville of Sometime Never, at noon, three days from now. I, Cuchillo Oro, war chief of the Mescalero Apache

people, will be there with only one companion. If
you wish a negotiated settlement, come with one
other and we will talk. It is the only way for peace
with honor.

Three copies were made, each taken by a trusted
warrior to a point where the sec men's patrols were
known to ride. By evening one of them brought news
that the message, placed in a conspicuous red-painted
carton, had been picked up by a ten-man patrol of the
pony soldiers.

"Now we wait," Ryan said. "And we'll go recce
some more tomorrow morning."

The day had passed peaceably enough. The Anglos
were regarded as honored guests, and the women of
the Mescalero almost fought for the chance to bring
them food and drink, or to wash or mend any of their
clothes that were showing the strain of their ceaseless
traveling.

During the hot time of the early afternoon, when
many slept, Cuchillo Oro had come alone and asked
to speak with Ryan.

"Sure. Come in."

"Alone."

Krysty raised an eyebrow at Ryan, who shrugged his
shoulders and walked out of the cool, shady wickiup
into the dazzling heat of the long canyon.

"Here. By the water. We can talk."

The Apache children were shooed away by their
mothers as Golden Knife and his dangerous one-eyed
Anglo friend sat at the edge of the deep pool beneath
the cliff.

"I wish to know where you come from. And how you travel. I have sent out scouts, and they have backtracked your feet beyond where we saw you."

"How far back?"

"Past chilled lion."

Ryan repeated the question. "How far back d'you track us?"

"To the rancheria of hot death. You came from there."

"The redoubt? Yeah, we did."

"There is only death there. A great illness lives within, a spirit that slays all. Why did it not chill all of you?"

Ryan nodded. "You're right. The rad count was pushing at the top end of the scale, but we didn't stay long."

Cuchillo Oro had drawn the great golden dagger, absently pricking a pattern of small holes in the moist earth by his soft leather boots. "I say again, Ryan Cawdor. Where d'you come from?"

Ryan rapidly rehearsed a variety of lies, testing them, and finding them all wanting. It was one of those rare occasions when the best story was actually the true one.

"It's a long story, Chief. Goes like this...."

IT TOOK A LONG TIME to explain about the redoubts and the mat-trans gateways within some of them. Ryan realized that Cuchillo Oro was torn between belief and suspicion, wanting to believe the magical tale of being able to travel from one end of the Death-lands to the other in the blinking of an eye.

"Life in Drowned Squaw Canyon is harsh, my brother," he said. "Times I would like to get away."

Ryan considered mentioning that he believed some gateway chambers could also be used for chron-jumps. Doc was living proof that this was so. But he hadn't seen any evidence of them being safe to try and he figured that they would only confuse the Mescalero chief even more.

"There's good and bad about the gateways," Ryan admitted. "But there's some lost or pulverized to dust or drowned under the seas when the nukings came."

"And you travel far and fast? Just the six of you? It must be a fine life for a warrior...and for his women."

Ryan suspected that Cuchillo Oro was leading up to something, maybe even asking if he could join them. There was no doubt that the Apache was a brave and skillful fighting man. And there'd been times that Ryan had wished desperately for more strength in a firefight. Yet there was the doubt remaining. The Mescalero came from a totally different culture. Better a close-knit team of six than a rabble of sixty.

In the end, Cuchillo Oro reined himself in just short of actually asking the question. So Ryan didn't need to answer it.

HE AND KRYSTY MADE slow, gentle love to each other during the evening, and a second time around three in the morning. Ryan was tugged from sleep by the feather-light touch of fingers on his body, insistently searching, finding.

Warm lips nibbled at him, drawing the inevitable response. His body tensed, his fingers locked in Krysty's sentient hair, feeling it rustling about his hands, caressing his skin.

"Nice," he said.

"Mmm," Krysty agreed. "Sure you don't want me to come tomorrow for the recce?"

"Sure. Me, J.B. and Cuchillo. Fewer the better. We won't be gone long."

"Too long."

They lay together, hand touching hand, hip touching hip, for a quarter of an hour or so. Ryan was mentally picturing Sometime Never, with all the winding trails around it, coming in from top and bottom of the derelict main street, trying to make it clear in his mind where it would be best to hit the sec men.

"Nickel for your thinking, lover," Krysty whispered at his side.

"Thinking it was time that we did some more love-making."

DAWN CAME UP WITH A sulfurous yellow glow. It had begun to get warmer around five, with an unpleasant, humid heat. The clouds stretched, unbroken, from edge to edge of the canyon. The three horses that were brought out were spooked, eyes rolling, whinnying their unease.

"When the ponies scent trouble, then the wise man is careful," said the skeletal figure of the shaman, who materialized wrapped in a filthy buffalo robe. His mirrored glasses hid his sunken eyes.

"I'll remember that, Man Whose Eyes See More,"
J.B. said, hunching himself lower into the collar of his
brown shirt.

Cuchillo frowned as he joined the two white men.
"It is not a good day, brothers. Should we wait and do
this on the morrow?"

"Tomorrow's too late." Ryan swung up into the
saddle. He'd left the G-12 behind in the wickiup, carrying only the SIG-Sauer P-226 on his hip.

The sky was so low it seemed to press down on the
shoulders of the three men as they cantered slowly toward the ghost town. There was no conversation between them.

Ryan felt depressed. The possibility of failure lay
flat and sour in his mind. This General who had appeared like a night demon out of nowhere... The way
the Mescalero talked about him, he *had* to be something out of the ordinary.

He scratched the stubble on his chin, trying to visu-
alize the tall figure with the bizarre mane of golden
hair. Ryan was certain-sure he'd seen the man before.

"Where?" he muttered to himself.

Anywhere in Deathlands. There were enough renegade killers stalking the hot spots. But there was
something special about this one. Ryan spit, clearing
his mouth of dust. It was no good. The memory was
stubborn, insisting on staying where it was.

ON THE PREVIOUS VISIT, Sometime Never had appeared attractive, a quaint relic of the long-gone past.

Now, it looked sinister. The tumbled shacks seemed filled with shadows, threatening.

"It going to rain?" J.B. asked, as they tethered their horses to an old hitching post at the bottom of the street.

Cuchillo hesitated. "When the sky is yellow, it is well to keep your animals close to the rancheria. It may be a storm of wind."

"Best get this done fast, then," Ryan said. "Fast, but careful. I'll go up the far end and over the ridge beyond Hillbilly Heaven. J.B., take the western side and Cuchillo the east. How's that sound to you? Okay, then, let's go. If there's any trouble, fire a shot. Others come running."

The wind was rising, from the north. It brought fine dust to blind Ryan's eye, filling his throat with the bitter taste of nitrate. It rustled through the banks of mesquite, loud enough to hide the approach of any kind of animal or reptile. Ryan stepped cautiously, head turning, sticking to the main trail. He'd passed the stores and shacks he'd investigated with Krysty the previous day, not bothering to check them out again. That wasn't what he was there for.

J.B. and Cuchillo Oro had vanished behind him, going to recce their quadrants.

Ryan paused near the top of the trail, only a few yards below the crest of the ridge. The old hermit's cabin was to his right as he swung around. He looked back down the street and across the baked land of New Mexico toward the maze of mesas and arroyos that concealed the rancheria of the Mescalero.

Because of the noise of the wind, Ryan never heard the sec man who'd crept up behind him, never saw the club that smashed across the back of his skull like a bolt of lightning. He plunged into a deep lake of sticky blackness.

Chapter Twenty-One

For a couple of minutes after he recovered a kind of consciousness Ryan Cawdor thought that he'd been blinded. Then he realized he'd been strung over the back of a horse, wrists tied brutally tight and linked to a length of whipcord knotted around his ankles. Blood had trickled down from the cut on his head and run into his eye, sealing it under a patch of congealing gore.

Every step of the animal sent a stabbing pain through his skull. His shoulders and ribs ached, and he felt as if the sec men had given him a good kicking before binding him and throwing him on the horse like a sack of flour.

His mouth was filled with dirt. He probed cautiously with his tongue, checking that none of his teeth had been damaged. One felt loose in the gums, but none were missing.

What really hurt was that he'd made the classic mistake of overconfidence. He'd underestimated the cunning of the General, and now he was likely to pay the highest price in the marketplace of death.

Since they hadn't simply killed him on the spot, Ryan figured that he was being taken back to the cavalry's fort for questioning. Having been second-guessed by Yellowhair, Ryan knew he didn't have much to look forward to. It was obvious, now, that the sec man had suspected a trap the moment he got the message with the peace invitation and had sent out a patrol to ambush the potential ambushers. Ryan wondered what had happened to J.B. and Cuchillo Oro. Since he couldn't see a damned thing, it was possible that they were hog-tied right alongside of him.

Gradually, as his head cleared, he was able to pick out voices around him, over the jingling of harness and the clattering of hooves on stone.

The jolting made him feel sick, and he battled to clear his mind of the pain and nausea. The horse wasn't saddled, which meant a pack animal. Which meant, in turn, that they'd come prepared to take a prisoner. Or several prisoners.

Unexpectedly the shaking cleared the scabbed blood from his right eye. For a moment he was dazzled by the brightness of the sunlight, and he had to squeeze his eye shut to try to blink the dust out of it.

"Fucker's woken, Sarge," a voice bellowed from his left.

"Put him to sleep again, Rourke," another voice replied.

"Leave him be. General said keep him from being spoiled, and sure that's what we'll be doing. Or I'll have the skin off any man does One-Eye any grievous hurt."

With a great effort of will, Ryan was able to lift his head, neck muscles straining, and saw that he was the only prisoner of the mounted patrol. There were

around a dozen sec men, in dark blue uniforms pow-
dered with pale dust, all with Springfield carbines
bucketed at their saddles. From his taut, agonizing
position, Ryan couldn't make out much more of the
men. And it wasn't worth the effort of trying to see.
They were obviously going back to their own ville.

He slumped forward again, trying to relax against
the tightness of his bondage and the jolting of the
horse.

"GENERAL LIKES TO HEAR singing, me merry buc-
kos, and we wouldn't want to be letting the General
down, now, would we?"

Ryan realized that he'd slipped into an uneasy half-
world that lay between sleeping and unconsciousness.

The voice, coming from the big sergeant, brought
him back to the real world of biting discomfort. He
coughed and spit, fighting to clear his nose and throat
of the raw dust.

"One and two and three..." bellowed the sec man's
voice, and the patrol began to sing. It was a ragged
sound, barely carrying the tune, the words curiously
old-fashioned.

Instead of Spa, we'll drink down ale,
And pay the reckoning on the nail.
No man for debt shall go to jail,
From Garryowen to glory.

Long years ago Ryan remembered that he'd seen an
old westie vid about General Custer, riding bravely to
perdition at the Little Big Horn, long yellow hair

streaming in the studio wind. The tune brought the memory back. It was the marching song of the Seventh Cavalry, "Garryowen."

Viewing the world upside down, Ryan saw massive wooden gates swinging open and a flag blowing above some buildings, which were made from hewn logs and adobe. The flag was blue, bearing crossed sabers and the golden number seven. The singing swelled to a roaring climax and then stopped.

"Platoon, halt!" came the shouted command from the sec man at the head. "Right face."

The horse that carried him was tugged around and then the morning was filled with a sudden near-silence, broken only by the occasional snuffling or the restless movement of hooves, or the jingling of a bridle as one of the animals tossed its head against the flies.

"Patrol returned safely from Sometime Never, General. Mission completely successful."

"Well, done, Sergeant. Take the prisoner inside. I'll see him shortly."

Ryan was on the blind side and couldn't see the speaker, but he knew it had to be the man the Apaches called Yellowhair. Yet again, despite the danger and discomfort of his position, Ryan tried to rack his memory for that voice. A low, calm, chilling voice. A voice that raised the short hairs at his nape. But the memory refused to become unburied, and all that Ryan sensed was that the memory was a bad one.

"WALK, YOU BASTARD Indian-lover," cursed one of the sec men, a tall, overweight trooper whose belly hung over the broad leather belt. He carried an old knife scar over the left eye that gave the impression he was winking at you. He and a shorter man had cut Ryan off the back of the horse, leaving his wrists tied in front of him. With the circulation cut off for three or four hours, Ryan stumbled and would have fallen to the raked earth of the parade ground if it hadn't been for the sec man with the three stripes on his arm. He'd caught Ryan and held him upright.

"Now, now, you don't want to go falling about and hurting yourself. There'll be plenty of time for that after you've had a nice talk with the General, won't there?"

Once he was upright Ryan had immediately started to try to get his bearings. Cuchillo had talked a little about the newly built fort, but his description was necessarily vague. None of the people had ever been into the fort and lived to tell of it.

The compound was rectangular, the long sides about a hundred and twenty paces, and the short about eighty. There was a wall of spiked logs surrounding the parade ground, around eighteen feet high. Two barrackslike blocks ran down one side, and Ryan could also see some stables. A glowing fire and the ringing of iron on iron showed him the blacksmith's forge, and a single-floored adobe-walled building, with another flag flying over it, was probably the headquarters of the fortified ville.

There was no time to take in anything else. Ryan was grabbed painfully by the upper arms and hustled across the square. He had a moment to see that the threatening yellow sky had cleared, and the sun was shining from a bowl of unspoiled blue.

Just as he entered the main building, Ryan heard the roar of an engine and glimpsed a dune wag with huge tires driving out past the forge.

It was the first sign of anything approaching modern life that he'd seen for days.

The distant rumbling of a powerful generator was almost drowned by the humming of an air-conditioning plant just inside the main doorway. The cool air struck Ryan like the touch of a whip, refreshing after the sullen heat outside.

Pushed and jostled, all he could do was snatch an impression of the building: offices and living quarters, with guns on walls; barred doors; and two sets of guards to pass. He was shoved through a double sec door and found himself inside a jail—but a jail that obviously doubled as a torture chamber. A smoldering fire in a metal brazier had several long implements resting in the coals, long rods, some with curved or hooked ends, and handles wrapped in rags to protect the user from the heat. There were several whips in a rack, and a long shelf held all manner of knives and scalpels, pincers and hammers, tools for the giving of pain, in so many differing ways. It was like the workshop of some demented and sadistic psychotic.

Another pair of guards had appeared, both holding old cap-and-ball Navy Colts. But Ryan's expert eye spotted that they weren't the decrepit antiques they should have been. These were more modern replicas, handled by men who looked like they knew their trade.

"General says against the wall, there. Cut his hands. We'll cover him."

One of the sec men pushed Ryan against the adobe wall, near a set of iron rings, placed at differing heights. "Keep still."

"You got a lot of guts," Ryan said. "Four of you. Don't take any chances, will you?"

The looping right hit him under the ribs, knocking every atom of breath from his body. He doubled over, gagging, dropping to his knees.

The sec man lifted his dusty riding boot to slam it into the helpless man's body.

"Leave him, Lance," shouted one of the troopers with a blaster.

"You heard him!"

"And you heard the General. Go out to the ghost town and pick up anyone there. Special to pick up the tall bastard with only one eye."

"We got him. Didn't say nothing about him breaking a finger or two."

Ryan regained his breath slowly. He lifted his head and looked at the sec man called Lance, making sure he'd recognize him if the chance ever came to chill him. He was heavy-built, with swarthy skin and a thin mustache.

"You want to damage the goods, then go ahead, but wait till the rest of us have gotten clear. You seen the General when he gets mad. Remember Carl Onas? Cut the General's stallion when he was grooming him. And drunk an' all. General filled his mouth with bits of razor steel. Tied some cloth around his face and had it tightened. Bits o' bloody metal pushed clean through his cheeks and tongue. Couldn't never speak after that."

"I know," Lance said sullenly.

"That was for a little mark on his horse. Nuke-death! Think what the General'd do if you spoiled this double-chilled bastard."

"Yeah, sure. Sure. Let's get him tied proper and leave him."

The steel cuffs had sliding locks that gripped tight and grew even tighter if you pulled against them. One had been placed around each wrist, holding his arms out at an angle. But they had left his feet free. Ryan badly wanted a drink, and his temples pounded like trip-hammers.

Otherwise, he didn't feel in bad shape.

There were no windows in the cell, and the sec men had dimmed the lights before leaving him. He could see across the room by the light of the embers that glowed brightly in the brazier.

Ryan had felt his life imperiled many times in his thirty-odd years of living. There was no point in giving up until your heart had stopped beating and your vision had dimmed for the last time. But he found it difficult to have much hope. If this General Yellow-hair was the swift and evil bastard that he seemed, then he was hardly likely to set Ryan free.

But there was a hope. Though the invitation to peace talks had veiled a trap, the sec men couldn't know that. They'd sprung their own ambush too soon. It was just possible that Ryan had been captured to be used as an emissary to the Mescalero for the General's own peace proposals.

What screamed against that hopeful view was the conversation by the troopers. Yellowhair had planned the raid purely to get hold of Ryan Cawdor.

"Why?" Ryan said aloud. "Why does he want me so bad?"

He only had to wait a little less than an hour to learn the appalling answer.

THE WALLS OF THE DUNGEON were thick, and Ryan could hear nothing of the life going on all around him. Once he caught the clear golden notes of a bugle, sounding what he guessed was probably a call to eat the noon meal.

The guard changed shortly after. A sliding panel in the door moved across, and Ryan could see the gleam of light in the passage beyond. Someone said something, and there was a guffaw of rasping laughter. Then the panel closed again.

The only other sound was the gentle shifting of the slow-burning ashes, tumbling in on one another. Ryan found that his eye kept returning to the small ruby glow of the fire. In the hands of an expert torturer, such as the monstrous Cort Strasser from Mocsin ville, a very little fire could give an appalling amount of suffering.

The door opened very slowly and very quietly, on well-oiled hinges. The spreading rectangle of light grew broader, filling with the lean silhouette of a man, then shrinking again to blackness. The tumblers in the lock clicked shut.

"You are a most welcome visitor to Fort Security, Ryan Cawdor."

It was worse than the punch to the guts. If they knew his name, then there had to be a traitor in Drowned Squaw Canyon. Nobody else in the Southwest would have recognized him. Unless it was some wandering mercie, hiring out himself and his blaster, who might have met Ryan when he rode with the Trader.

"I've waited some time to see you again."

Not a traitor. Someone from one of a thousand bloody yesterdays.

The voice was dry and taut, like old parchment, and there was the hint of an impediment, as though the man had suffered some sort of injury to his jaw or palate. The prison room muffled the voice, distorting it.

"You have nothing to say, Ryan Cawdor? Your one eye still works?" A sudden hint of doubt crept into the voice. "My gallant troopers have not harmed you? If they have then I'll... No, I see you are not hurt. Except, perhaps, your pride. You thought the General would fall like a ripe apricot into a maid's hand! Triple-stupe, Ryan Cawdor!"

Ryan kept silent. The more Yellowhair talked, the more might be learned. Ryan's night vision had been impaired by the light from the passage, when the door was opened. Now it was returning.

The General was extremely tall, the top of the flowing hair scraping at the low ceiling of the cell. The light was too dim for Ryan to make out the face, but it seemed to be gaunt and almost skeletal, with a heavy mustache blurring its details.

"Still dumb, Ryan?"

The man moved closer. "What if I was to pluck out that other eye? What then?"

"Better men than you tried that threat, Yellowhair. They're dead, and I'm still seeing."

"Good, good." Gloved hands clapped softly together.

"Why don't you go shag a dead mutie sheep, Yellowhair!" Ryan taunted.

"No, Ryan. If I shag anyone, then it might well be you."

The threat was delivered in the same dry, calm voice, and was infinitely more frightening for that.

"But time is wasting. You still don't know me, do you? No, of course you don't. Let me take off this foolish wig.... There. Now I turn up the light and..."

It was the nightmare figure of Cort Strasser.

All hope vanished.

Chapter Twenty-Two

BACK AT THE RANCHERIA Man Whose Eyes See More was drinking clear spring water from an old cup. He staggered suddenly, as though a high-velocity bullet had smashed into his brain. The mug dropped from his limp fingers and burst into a thousand jagged shards, the liquid splashing into the dry earth and vanishing in a dozen heartbeats.

At the same moment, Krysty ran from the shadowed interior of the wickiup, hair trailing in a stream of fire. Her mouth hung open in a soundless cry of despair, and her green eyes were turned toward the abandoned ghost town in the hills.

The shaman's eyes locked with the girl's, and he nodded very slowly. Then he knelt to pick up the sharp pieces of broken pottery.

"I THOUGHT YOU MUST HAVE DIED—hoped you'd died—back there in Mocsin."

Cort Strasser perched himself on the edge of the table, pushing away some ivory-handled tools with obscenely curved steel blades. Now, in the light, Ryan couldn't understand why his memory had been so treacherous. The former sec boss from Mocsin had changed little since their last meeting. The skin was still taut across the planed bones of the high, thin skull, a sickly color, like rain-sodden straw. Strasser was nearly bald; only a wispy fringe of dark hair circled his head, just above the narrow ears.

With the exception of the full, curling mustache, everything about Strasser was thin. The eyes, black as jet, were like deep razor cuts. The nose was hooked like a vulture's beak, and the mouth seemed etched with dark acid. In the gaunt face, it was the mouth that had changed the most.

The upper lip was crooked and swollen, the jaw not seeming to connect properly. As the sec leader grinned wolfishly at his victim, it was obvious that he had lost teeth and some of those that remained were jagged.

Strasser noticed the way Ryan was studying his face. "You know me now?"

"Sure. A piece of mutie shit like you sticks in the mind like dog crap on a man's boots."

"Good. Good, Ryan. I have followed your name for months. Paid informers to keep track on you."

"Yeah?"

The long, angular skull nodded slowly. "Indeed, I have. But...one of the matters that we must talk together about is where you've been. I've heard word of you from all over Deathlands. Unless there is another one-eyed crazy with some strange companions...unless there is, then you have moved fast and far."

"Can't rightly understand you, Strasser. Seems like there's something wrong with your mouth."

The light in the cell was strong enough for Ryan to see the flush of anger on the thin cheeks.

The sec man forced a narrow smile. "I'll soon tell you what I'm going to do to you, Ryan, my old, old friend."

"Can't wait." Ryan tried to bluff it out, but he could hear it, at the back of his voice, the hollow fear that comes to all men when they face the grim certainty of a harsh passing.

"I hear of you among the swampies. I hear of you in the wastes of snow to the far north. Then you are wriggling with the worms that live in your roots. A ville in the Shens. But all in such a short time, Ryan? How? Or are they lies? Where have you been since last we met?"

"Here and there."

"There is some trick you know about, something that is linked to the past. I've followed you, Ryan. Followed the stink of your running. Tracked the slime you leave behind you. And there is always a wall at the end of the trail. You are there and then—" he snapped his bony fingers together "—then you're gone again."

"Now I'm here. How come you got away from Mocsin? Thought you might- have stayed on as baron."

"I'd wanted that. I was about to chill that stinking tub of guts, Jordan Teague. I was sec boss for him. Then you come riding in with the Trader, and it all goes up in fire, the whole ville wiped out like snow on a griddle."

"Always did have a way with words, Strasser."

"You got that old prick away. Doc. And the mutie girl with red hair. And that little bastard with eyeglasses, Dix. You all still together?"

"Just the four of us." There was no real reason to lie to Strasser, but if he didn't know about Lori or Jak, then there wasn't any point in telling him.

"You know, I couldn't believe my eyes when I spotted you on that ridge. Thought you'd been delivered to me. The answer to my prayers. Then those sons of bitches come on their ponies and save you. Now, here you are."

"How come you're General Yellowhair, Strasser? Animal like you, running at the head of a pack of other animals?"

Strasser stood and walked around the room, slightly stooped beneath the low ceiling. "Had me some small difficulty in Kansas. The local baron had more blasters than I'd figured, so I chilled his wife, sister and all his mewling daughters and lit out south and west. Came across these good ol' boys sporting around the old museum. Read up some. General George Armstrong Custer. Yellow wig. Wasted one or two who thought they should run the show. Now I run it. Easy as that. Just as fucking easy as that."

"Now what?"

"You mean with you and me?"

"What do you plan to do, now you run this? You're the bastard baron of nothing, Strasser. Just a handful of dry, red dust."

"Go a few days east, Ryan, and there's some serious power and jack. I got me nearly half a hundred sec men who do what I tell 'em. This cavalry crap works, Ryan. Would you believe it, but it fucking well works?"

Strasser threw back his head and laughed, an eerie, howling noise that sounded like a rabid wolf. The obsidian chips of his eyes closed in ecstasy, and he hugged himself with the long, thin arms.

Ryan eased his wrists against the crushing steel of the cuffs.

"What about the Apaches?"

"Little red bastards? Been doing some work on old maps they got in the museum that show water runs in this part. In another few days I'll find where their water supply comes from. I know they got a canyon hole-up, someplace, and I got me some paraquat additives from the redoubt yonder. Pour it in, goodbye to the little red fuckers. Neat, huh, Ryan?"

"Then you and your sec army moves out and grabs a bigger piece of action. Yeah, Strasser, I figure I get it."

There was the distant sound of a bugle outside, the notes rising and falling.

Strasser heard it and stopped pacing the chamber. "Meeting of sec officers, Ryan, my old, old comrade. We have a patrol going out this evening to try to track down the canyon where the Apache live. I must give them their orders. But I shall return later. This is a moment that I've anticipated for such a long time, Ryan. I don't want to spoil it by being in too much of a hurry. Later we can talk some more. You talk, and I'll listen. Then you can tell me how to get to the Indian rancheria and all about that old imbecile, Doc. There's something 'bout him that I'd . . . Later."

The hugely tall and lean figure paused, adjusted the flowing blond wig, so that the golden locks tumbled over his shoulders. "I won't leave you alone. Got an old reel-to-reel audio recorder. Temperamental, but I use it for a kind of memory of folks I've had in here for a talk. I'll play you the last one. He was an Apache."

The machine, layered in dust, stood on a low shelf beyond the brazier. It had twin spools of tape, and a thick, primitive wire running to a socket, connecting it with the generator supply to the fort.

It took a great deal of poking and fiddling before Strasser could bring the aged machine to crackling life. He turned up the volume control, listening with his head cocked to the loud hissing.

"There," he said, approaching Ryan. The feral skull stooped, and the sec boss inhaled deeply, face inches from Ryan. "Ahh... The stench of mortal fear. How much I love it. The one thing that I love more, my dear Ryan, is the taste of other people's agony."

The door opened and closed behind Strasser, and Ryan was once more alone.

J.B. AND CUCHILLO ORO had returned to the rancheria, with Ryan's horse trotting behind them.

Krysty, Doc and the others were waiting for them near the neck of the canyon. The girl called out first. "They got him. They've taken Ryan, haven't they? Tell us."

The Armorer slid wearily from the saddle, handing the reins to a young boy wearing a leather breechclout.

"Yeah, Krysty. How d'you know? You see it?"

"Yeah. It was like a mainline hit of the best golden jolt the world ever knew, like a fist clenching inside my skull, like having my brain scooped out and replaced with ice. Yeah, J.B. I *saw* it."

J.B. knew that Krysty carried a strain of mutie blood in her. Not just the hair, or her unusually sharp sight and hearing. Krysty could sometimes "see," but not like a doomie who saw only the bad future. It was as if she could feel when something was happening, or was going to happen.

Doc was trembling. "Krysty said she felt something, around three, four hours ago. And the shaman said the same. He said he closed his eyes and saw an eagle falling down to the earth, and it had been slain by a shadow. That's what he said. That the eagle had been vanquished by a dark, enveloping shadow."

Cuchillo also seemed near to exhaustion. "I knew that it was not a good day. The yellow sky was a bad warning to us. But he said we must go."

"What happened? Sec men? Yellowhair? Let's go help." Jak was looking around for a pony, quite ready to set off immediately to rescue Ryan.

"No, Eyes of Wolf," said the Mescalero war chief. "First must come words. And much care."

"Trail showed a lot of horses, all shod in iron," J.B. said. "Must have second-guessed us. Smarter than we thought. Waiting at top of rise. Soon as they got him, they split. Never even looked for us. First we knew was the noise of galloping, and by the time we'd gotten ourselves up the main street, they were a cloud of dust heading toward their fortress."

"Is Ryan dead?" Lori asked.

"I see him waiting by the gate to the land of dark spirits," said Man Whose Eyes See More, looming over everyone, his mirrored glasses reflecting the bright sun.

"We don't need all that spirit shit," J.B. said angrily. "If Yellowhair's got him, then any double-stupe knows he'll kill him. What matters is when. And if we can get to mebbe save him. That's *all* that matters."

Krysty walked away from the others, finding a quiet corner near the still pool. Cuchillo had announced that he would hold a council after the evening meal had been served by the women, and that all of the Anglos would attend it, as well as all of the older warriors of the people.

J.B. had gone with Jak, Doc and Lori to rest in their wickiup. Krysty had sensed the feeling of bleak failure that hung over the entire camp. If General Yellowhair could capture Ryan as effortlessly as that, then what hope could there be for any of them?

She felt close to tears.

OVER THE MONTHS since he'd first met her, Ryan had been trying to learn some of Krysty's techniques for self-control, ways that she had been taught to take herself out of her own body at times of great danger or pain. Though he was becoming better at it, he still couldn't shut off the outside world in the way that his lover could. The crackling, indistinct sounds of Cort Strasser at his play seemed to grind on and on, into his mind, filling it with a dark horror.

The voice of the Apache being questioned by Strasser was mainly inaudible. Ryan guessed that the man had been gagged by Strasser for much of the time. The snatches from the whining old recorder were more than enough to feed Ryan's anticipation of what was to come.

The running commentary was provided by Cort Strasser himself.

"Good strong body, young man. Muscles like iron. But soft here..." Laughter and a muffled groan of distress on the tape. "Hurts, doesn't it? Yet such gentle pressure, really. And if I get this a tad hotter and then push it as far as it'll go... Can you hear the steam as it hisses? Now, a long, shallow cut along the line...elbow, where we can hook this under the tendon and scrape...shaving the bone."

There came the sound of splashing water and Strasser laughing to himself. "So many guests fall asleep when they should be talking to me. Now you're awake again, and so am I. Very awake, Indian. If I place this wedge in your mouth...so much easier now the teeth and tongue are out of the way, and screw this to make it wider. Wider. There."

Ryan heard a vile, choking sound that told its own story. Strasser's cruelty had been a legend clear across Deathlands.

What was particularly horrific was that the sec boss wasn't actually making any effort at all to interrogate his prisoner. He wasn't bothering to ask him where the entrance was to the rancheria's canyon, or how many fighting warriors were in the band of Cuchillo Oro. All that interested him was the further levels of torture for its own bloody sake.

The tape machine seemed to be losing power, the voice slurring. It wasn't possible to catch any sound from the tortured Mescalero. Ryan guessed that he must have finally, and mercifully, succumbed to his injuries.

"Sleeping?" came Strasser's gentle, flat tones. "You didn't answer any of my questions. Perhaps you're trying to trick me. Let's... poke this and cut along and then reach and pinch the... No? Then you must be dead. Yeah, why not? Useless alive, you red-skinned bastard. Find a use for you now..."

There was a sigh of contentment. With a sharp click the tape machine switched itself off, and the room was suddenly awash with welcome silence.

IN THE SHADOWED CANYON, Krysty sat alone, refusing the offers of food, fighting to clear her mind and link it with Ryan. She used every arcane skill that Sonja Wroth had taught her daughter. She knew that Ryan thought he had recognized the tall, skinny leader of the sec men. And she, too, thought... But the memory was blocked.

"Thin, with thin eyes. Tall and triple-bad. Someone that maybe I know as..."

Suddenly, with the violence of a chem storm, Krysty remembered.

"Gaia! It's Cort Strasser!"

Chapter Twenty-Three

"CORT STRASSER!" Doc Tanner began to tremble, licking his lips nervously. "That cacodemon! No, Krysty, it surely cannot be he?"

She had joined the others around the bright fire, telling them her dreadful suspicions about their enemy.

"It all makes sense, Doc."

"He died back in Mocsin. Surely the man died! It is more than a soul can bear to think Strasser still breathes the same air. No. I can't..." He waved his gnarled hands helplessly. Lori patted the old man on the arm, trying to comfort him. Krysty thought that Doc had aged fifteen years in the past five minutes. Recalling the way that the former police chief of Mocsin had used Doc Tanner for his plaything, it wasn't surprising that Doc was so deeply shocked at the news.

"You can't be certain," J.B. said, pensively drawing on one of the Apache pipes as it was passed around.

"Oh, I'm sure enough, J.B.," she replied. "It all fits. Strasser on the run after Mocsin was burned out. Ryan had hurt him bad, remember. He runs south and west, and finishes here. He finds the renegades that

Cuchillo talked about and takes them over. When he learns about the legend of General Custer he becomes the General. Times fit.''

"He was the right build," Doc muttered. "Skinny as a stock whip."

"And the way he went for Ryan. Only Ryan. Not you or Cuchillo," Krysty insisted.

"This Strasser, mean bastard you spoke 'bout?" Jak asked, leaning forward, his hair tinted a voracious pink in the light of the fire.

"Yeah, that's him," J.B. said, turning to face Krysty again. "But are you *sure*? Sure that it's him?"

The girl nodded. "I saw him in my mind, like a homicidal animal. That dead skin and dead voice. And he's got…" Her voice tailed off into silence, and she buried her head in her hands. Her crimson hair curled protectively around her face.

Cuchillo drove his golden cinqueda deep into the earth between his feet, clear up to the hilt. His face showed his anger and his frustration.

"Ryan Cawdor is a friend of the people. He is an Anglo, but he is a brother to us. For him to be taken as prisoner by Yellowhair brings nothing but shame to the Mescalero. If he dies, then we are without honor."

"And Ryan is without life," Lori added. "Which seems badder to me."

"But we can do nothing. They have guns and the fortress. If we attack they will cut us down like corn before the scythe."

"And they have blaster with many mouths that spits fire and lead very quickly," Stones in Face said.

"Gatling?" J.B. asked interestedly. "Bastard can jam on you, but while it works... Yeah, they could do some good work against your warriors on horseback, Cuchillo."

"We are not able to come at them in any other way. The place where old clothes and blasters are kept is under the hang of a mesa."

"Couldn't we try and squeak in?" Jak asked. "At night, mebbe?"

J.B. sucked on his front teeth. "Strasser knows me. Knows Doc. Knows Krysty."

"Cort Strasser knows me, and I know Cort Strasser," Doc agreed. "A man who smiles and is a devil. A hellhound that will not turn. A wolf in wolf's clothing. Eyes as smooth and hard and black as Apache tears. The knife in the groin, the cold in the night, the shark beneath the polished surface of the limpid ocean. By the three Kennedys! Strasser is the walking death!"

With a cry of anguish, Doc rose clumsily to his feet and stumbled away toward the wickiup, followed by an anxious Lori.

Jak broke the silence. "Strasser don't know me. Never met me. Didn't see in firefight."

"So what?" J.B. asked. "You going to go and spring Ryan on your own?"

"Why not?"

"Come on, kid—"

"Don't call me..."

The Armorer held up both hands, palms out, offering his apology. "Sorry, but come on, Jak. They got four or five dozen sec men, well trained. You figure you got a chance?''

"You figure got better one?" the boy retorted, eyes blazing.

The Armorer didn't reply, all watching him, waiting for him to speak. Cuchillo spoke, ending the silence. "Eyes of Wolf speaks with the tongue that is straight."

The albino looked around at the others. "Any got better idea? No? Then I go."

"Then we'd best give some time to talking this one through, Jak," the Armorer suggested, the dancing flames reflected off his glasses.

"Sure. How get there. How get in. How get out. How get back. Easy."

The Mescalero veterans all smiled appreciatively at the confidence of the young warrior.

Later that evening Krysty ticked off the points that Jak had raised. "Get there on a pony. We'll come as close as we can with you. Get in by pretending to be a mercie. A gun for hire. You got the balls to carry that one through. Last survivor from a train of land wags massacred by the Apache. Say you want to join up with the sec men."

Jak nodded at J.B.'s words. "Find Ryan. Free him. Steal horses."

Krysty finished it off. "And we'll be around to try and escort you back here, hold off any pursuit."

"When?" Doc asked. The old man had finally recovered his nerves and had joined the rest of the small group in their own low hut.

"Tomorrow," Jak insisted. "Ryan mebbe chilled now. Sorry, Krysty, but true. If too late try and get out. Must go soonest."

"Boy talks like a bothersome telegram." Doc sighed. "Incidentally, young fellow-my-lad, you better watch out for Mr. Strasser and his not so pleasant tricks."

"What tricks, Doc?"

"Man's a damnable ass-bandit, Jak. Just don't drop the soap in the showers when Cort Strasser's anywhere close."

From the boy's expression, Krysty realized that Jak hadn't any idea what Doc was trying to say.

"Jak," she said.

"Yeah."

"Doc's telling you that Strasser's a double-perve. He likes boys."

"Why didn't say so, Doc?" Jak grinned. "I'll chill Strasser if I can."

"In Deathlands let it ne'er be said that I slew a sleeping man," Doc muttered, shaking his head and looking very puzzled.

Lori led him away to their end of the wickiup, taking him behind the blanket, pausing to throw a dazzling smile over her shoulder.

J.B. sighed. "Times it seems Doc's on the road back to us. And times it's like he's lost his field manual to living."

Krysty nodded in agreement. "But when he's good he's very good, J.B., isn't he?"

"Yeah. Listen. I gotta strip and clean my blasters. Early start again tomorrow."

"Sure. I'm tired. Doubt I'll sleep easy without Ryan, but you got to try. Wake me in good time if I'm not up."

"Sure." J.B. went to his own section of the hut.

"Got to see 'bout things," Jak mumbled, heading for the door.

"What about having your bandages changed? Isn't Man Whose Eyes See More going to do that for you, Jak?"

"No. Got to..." But the words trailed away and Krysty couldn't hear what he said.

"What?"

"Steps Lightly Moon'll do 'em."

"The bandages, Jak?"

"Yeah. Why not?"

"Come on, don't snap at me like that. I only asked you."

"Sorry, Krysty. Know bad feel 'bout Ryan. Me too. But you know I've never...kind of...and she's real nice to me."

She watched, fascinated, wondering whether the white-faced teenager was capable of blushing. But his cheeks remained as muted as alabaster.

"Jak. Just don't get hurt. And don't hurt Steps Lightly Moon, either."

"Wouldn't."

"In the next few days we'll know which way the knife landed. Point or hilt. Point and we're likely all chilled. Hilt and we'll likely move on, somewhere else. Where does that leave you and the girl, Jak? Think about it."

"Can't live on what might happen, Krysty," he said, slipping out through the door.

She wondered whether Ryan still lived.

Chapter Twenty-Four

STRASSER WASN'T TAKING any chances with his prisoner.

He didn't reappear himself, but after a few hours the cell door opened again. No less than six sec men came jostling in, all with handguns, Colt Navy replicas from the late 1990s.

"General says you gotta be fed," said one of them, with the twin stripes of a corporal on his sleeve.

Ryan felt the tiniest rise in his spirits. If Strasser was giving him food then he wasn't likely to begin the butchering process for a while yet. And time was life.

While the troopers ranged themselves around the cell, with one on each side of the heavy sec door, the corporal sidled toward the manacled prisoner. There was a bunch of keys hanging on a hook to the left of the entrance, and he used one of them to snap open the cuffs.

"Blink out of place and you get chilled, Indian-lover," he said. Ryan pulled a face, turning away from the man's rank, stinking breath.

One of the sec men backed into the corridor and came in with a tray, which held a battered metal bowl and a drinking mug. He put it down in front of Ryan and moved away.

"Eat it," the senior sec man ordered, pointing at the tray with the barrel of his Colt.

"What is it?" Ryan asked, sniffing at the brown sludge in the bowl, noticing that the spoon they'd given him was of soft plastic. Strasser being careful again, he thought.

"Don't mind what it is, you bastard. Just eat it like you're fucking told."

"Six blasters at your shoulder makes even a prickless little bastard like you into a hero, doesn't it?" Ryan sneered, aware that feeling was flowing into his hands and arms now that the cuffs were off.

The troopers glanced at one another, waiting to see what the noncom did. A vein began to throb over his right eye, across the temple. He swallowed hard before saying anything.

"I seen big talkers like you, Cawdor, you one-eyed filth. Them Indians all come here filled with piss and importance." He shook a menacing finger at Ryan. "You can say what you like now. General's busy for the night. But he'll come see you on the morrow, Cawdor. I seen big men, strong men, crawling on this floor here, weeping like babies. Blood pouring from empty eyes, their own guts tangled around them. Weeping and begging. Your time'll come, Cawdor, and it'll be me here watching you at your lousy ending."

"You still didn't tell me what this crap is." Ryan held up the bowl threateningly, as if he might throw it at them. He smiled grimly as they all winced away from the threat.

"Beans," said a runty leather-faced man with a dropped shoulder.

"Always beans, stranger," a second man added.

"Fried beans. Boiled beans. Beans over easy. Beans well done. Beans medium rare."

"Forgot something," another of the watchful sec men put in.

"What's that?"

"You forgot the fucking beans."

For a moment the hostility seemed to have been forgotten, but the corporal restored it, shouting at the laughing troopers.

"Stop the flap-trapping! Grindly, General wants him chained. Neck collar, and link it to that wall ring."

At least Ryan was able to sit down. His feet and hands were left free, but the heavy iron collar bit into the skin of his throat. After the sec men had left him, Ryan tugged a few times at the chain, testing its strength, realizing that it was utterly immovable.

The bunch of keys dangled on the hook across the room, taunting him with their nearness.

The beans tasted terrible, and the water was brackish, but he finished it all, knowing the value of keeping his strength up.

The chain was cinched too short for him to be able to stretch out and sleep on the pile of straw in any kind of comfort, but he found a position where he could doze.

Normally Ryan Cawdor managed to sleep without any dreams that he could remember, but that night in

Fort Security was different. Twice he woke sweating, jerked from sleep by horrific nightmares.

In the first he was sitting by a deep, still pool of water that was similar to the lake that backed up Drowned Squaw Canyon. The sky was a velvet purple with soundless slashes of pink and silver chemlightning torn across it.

Tall saguaro lined the edge of the pool, their long spines decorated with the corpses of little reptiles and birds. Somewhere in the distance Ryan could hear mocking laughter that went on and on.

Krysty Wroth was swimming in the pool, naked, floating on her back a few yards out from where he sat. In the dream Ryan stood up, and he saw that the water was clear as any crystal. He could see his lover as she swam, deep down, over the sandy floor of the lake. And he could also see the fish that were moving toward her.

Thin as sword blades, with shimmering iridescent scales that gleamed turquoise, blue and green, they swam with a peculiar, undulating movement, more like snakes than fish. Their mouths were long, lips peeled back off triple rows of saw-edged teeth. The biggest of the fish was about four feet in length.

Ryan waved and yelled, but his mouth felt as if it were filled with cotton. Krysty still twined and waved to him, oblivious to the menace that was approaching her.

He was about to plunge into the pool when he stopped and touched the surface with his hand. It was as hard as glass, and hot. So hot that the skin on his fingers puckered and blistered.

The creatures closed on Krysty, and Ryan saw blood clouding the water. But she continued to swim and frolic under the lake, still smiling up at him as the saurian fishes tore great strips and chunks of living flesh from her body.

That was the first time during the long, restless night that Ryan Cawdor woke to a deep, guttural cry in the jail cell, realizing that the noise was torn from his own throat.

His second dream was different.

He was driving, peering through the ob-slit at the front of a heavily armored war wag, lumbering along endless roads that stretched out ahead of him. The barren and gray landscape totally lacked features.

Nobody else was in the vehicle with him. Every now and again, Ryan saw someone standing at the side of the highway, patiently waiting. The face and the body were shrouded in a dusty brown sacking robe that hung loosely about the figure. None of them made a move as he drove past, and they were utterly unrecognizable.

And yet he seemed to know them.

Out of the side viewers Ryan would occasionally glimpse something moving, always on the periphery of his vision. It seemed to be a loping animal that ran, sometimes on its hind legs and sometimes on all fours. It was a dull brown, blending into the flat landscape. In the dreariness it was inexpressibly menacing.

There was a rectangular wire grille in front of the steering wheel on the war wag and at intervals a tinny voice came out of the speaker.

"Without a judge there is no jury," it said.

"All play and no work makes Ryan a dead jerk."

"No man for debt shall go to jail."

"You are born into a grave."

Ryan tried to ignore the voice, fighting to control the wag on a road that was becoming more and more uneven. The figures came closer and more frequently, and the animal vanished from the horizon.

Past a dip in the highway, a single figure stood directly in front of him, only fifty yards or so from the fender of the war wag. Ryan jammed on the brakes, yet nothing happened.

The veiled person held up a hand, the cloth revealing sere skin, the nails on the bent fingers cracked like horn. Ryan realized that he knew this hidden person. The war wag drove remorselessly onward. The brakes had failed.

At the last second, before the crushing impact, the figure lifted its other hand and began to strip the veil off its face.

Once more Ryan yelled out in his sleep and ripped himself awake, shivering in the cell, his mind blanked of what the face had been beneath the rotting material of the shroud.

JAK WONDERED WHETHER the bandages around his broken ribs had somehow become much tighter. It was odd that he was finding it so difficult to draw a clear breath.

Steps Lightly Moon had led him away from the wickiup of the other Anglos, picking her way between the scattered stones that lined the floor of the canyon, leaving the sinking fires behind her.

"There is a wickiup against the cliff," she said to Jak, who ghosted along in her footsteps. "Where girls go before a practice of the way of becoming a woman."

"Yeah," the albino boy said, puzzled.

"It is deserted now, Eyes of Wolf. There has not been such a way for six moons. The last time it was for me. When I ceased to be a girl and was given my woman's name."

The adobe hut was almost invisible in the darkness, lurking against the towering wall of the cliffs like some slumbering animal, the windows seeming blackened eye sockets.

"Come inside, Eyes of Wolf."

The girl fiddled with something in a niche by the door, and a little clay lamp flickered into a pallid glow. Jak saw well in the darkness and could make out a table, two seats and a mound of sweet-smelling dried grass near the ashes of the fireplace.

"Nobody will disturb us here," she said, sitting down in a rustle of movement, beckoning to him to join her.

Jak, somewhere in his fourteenth year, was finding that his breathing was becoming more and more constricted as he sat beside the dark-haired girl.

"Tomorrow will be a good day," she said to him, smiling up into his face.

"Good day t'die. That what Cuchillo says?"

"My father says that you are the bravest white man he has ever seen. To ride in and fight the General on your own, slay him and then return to us with your friend One Eye Chills."

"Not going to fight General. Try get in and get out with Ryan."

The girl sighed. "Such bravery, Eyes of Wolf. My father says that it would be an honor to welcome such a man into the people, though you are not of the people."

Jak sat down carefully, trying to avoid straining his ribs. The mystical healing power of the tall shaman was going well, and he already felt hugely better. But there was still discomfort that verged on pain. The boy was no horseman, and he was dreading the ride over the broiling desert to enter the fortress ville of the sec men. Particularly, as J.B. had pointed out, since he'd have to remove all the strapping. His story wouldn't support that kind of medical treatment.

Though he was only fourteen years old, Jak Lauren was a skilled practitioner in the ways of death. There'd been an old man down in Louisiana who'd told him that "killing is like everything else. It has to be learned and then practiced."

Jak had taken that advice to heart.

But as he sat in the scented grass next to the slim girl, his mind was flooded with a mixture of doubt, fear and anticipation. He'd never done "it." Never. Friends younger than him had either done it with willing girls from the ville, or saved up jack to go with local gaudy whores. But not Jak.

Now it seemed as if they were going to do it. Steps Lightly Moon was going to allow him to make love to her.

"Will you kiss me, Eyes of Wolf?" she whispered. "It would give me much happiness."

He leaned over her, the tumbling flood of pure white hair hiding them both beneath its curtain. Jak moved hesitantly, his lips brushing the smooth warm skin of her cheek, finding her mouth. He gasped in a breath as the girl's tongue darted between his lips. Clumsily he reached around her back, gripping her to him.

"Do it softly, Eyes of Wolf."

JAK WAS OVERWHELMED. He'd finally done it—done it properly and done it well, if the moans and sighs of the girl were anything to go by.

After the second time they'd made love, Steps Lightly Moon had unwound the length of bandages from Jak's damaged ribs. There were smears of purple bruising across the dead-white chest and stomach, but most of the swelling had gone down. And the boy had recovered most of his former agility.

When he finally woke he could see the shimmering glow of first light through the deep-cut window holes. Steps Lightly Moon was asleep at his side, one arm across her eyes, the handwoven blanket just below her firm breasts. The boy felt himself becoming aroused again, but he turned away, reaching for his clothes, knowing that he had another, greater obligation.

Jak could already catch the faint scent of frying meat from across the canyon. The older women would have prepared a breakfast for him and for those who'd accompany him on the first stage of his perilous journey to the sec men's fort.

He pulled on the familiar leather-and-canvas jacket in camouflage colors of gray, green and brown, taking care not to cut himself on any of the shards of razor blades that he had carefully sewn into the material. Jak's ponderous handgun, the massive satin-finish .357 Magnum, went into its holster on his hip, and he checked that the leaf-bladed throwing knives were in their hidden sheaths. The combat boots went on last.

He hesitated, brushing a hand through his white mane of hair. He looked down at the sleeping girl, wondering if he should wake her before he left. He licked his lips and sighed. Going to the fireplace and picking up a broken branch that had a charred end, the boy painstakingly wrote a message on the wall near the door, where Steps Lightly Moon would see it when she woke.

"See you when I get back. I love you like you love me." He was going to sign it "Jak," but on a second thought he wrote "Eyes of Wolf."

And then he left her.

Chapter Twenty-Five

"I AM NOT A MAN GIVEN to hasty decisions, Ryan Cawdor."

Food had been brought, the ubiquitous mess of stodgy beans, with some indeterminate meat, badly fried, and some reasonable corn bread. The mug contained some freeze-dried coffee that Ryan guessed must have come from the sealed redoubt. It was a long time since he'd drunk anything so good.

Cort Strasser had come looming into the cell, yellow hair streaming across his shoulders. He carried a dark blue slouch hat ornamented with gold braid.

"I don't give a flying fuck about you, Strasser. What you do or what you think."

"Big words again, Ryan Cawdor. I can snuff out your life between finger and thumb, or I can keep you alive for days, mute, halt, in perpetual darkness, in your own filth."

"You can only do it once."

"But you will die," the lean man said, unable to hide his disbelief.

"We all do, Strasser."

The wig came off, revealing the bald scalp beneath. The sec boss of Fort Security leaned against the table, flicking at the dust with his gauntlets. Ryan noticed that he was now wearing a side arm, a 9 mm Stechkin blaster with a powerful laser nightsight attached.

"Hot morning, Ryan."

"Yeah."

What was going on inside the man's elongated skull? The slit eyes gave nothing away. Yesterday afternoon, after he realized who his captor was, Ryan had genuinely expected that he would be dead before the turning of the moon. Indeed, death was the very best he could have hoped for.

But now?

A sidewinder was a model of directness compared to the subterranean maze of Cort Strasser's perverted mind. If he was going to keep Ryan alive a while longer, then he had a good reason.

Strasser moved from the table to stand directly in front of Ryan, taking care to keep just beyond the reach of a flailing boot.

"You're wondering why, aren't you?" he asked.

"Why you haven't chilled me already?"

"Yes."

"Sure."

"Want to know why?"

"Fireblast! Can't we cut out the games, Strasser? You've got a reason. A reason that you hope might benefit you and your plans. So why not save us both some time and tell what it is? Then I can have a good laugh, and we can take it on from there. How about that?"

"I have read much. Anyplace I find an old book or mag or a vid to view... I know that in pulps the hero of darkness often asks the hero of light to join him.

Never happens. Not in the fics, it doesn't. But what of real life, Ryan?"

"You... you drugged me, Strasser. Fucked my hearing so I'd hear weird things. Like you asking me to join you."

Strasser's parchment face stretched into something close to a smile. "Grin in the jaws of death, eh, Ryan Cawdor?" With no warning and no change of expression he kicked out, the toe of his polished combat boot thunking into the helpless man's thigh. Ryan groaned and dragged his leg clear.

Strasser carried on as though nothing had happened. "Don't disappoint me. Don't be a stupe when I know you aren't. Don't try to jolt-mouth me, specially not in front of the troopers, or you get hurt. Hurt bad, Ryan. This is good advice I'm giving you, like mother's milk. So listen to me, and listen real good."

"I'm listening, Strasser."

"You scarred me, Ryan. Ruined years of work and planning. Stole things I wanted. Not many men do that. I don't have a single enemy, Ryan, but for you. Not one."

"No enemies, Strasser?" Ryan said disbelievingly. "Not one?"

"Alive, Ryan. Man like me needs another man the same. Don't say anything smart-ass, or I'll chill you now. Come in with me and take a half share for you and the other three. Persuade them to join me and ride with me."

If he'd had any doubts before, Ryan knew than Cort Strasser was sublimely, totally insane; mad beyond the craziness of any ordinary lunatic. His dreams of conquest had tipped over the abyss what little sanity had remained.

But the knowledge offered a peephole of light for Ryan if he stepped cautiously like a man walking on explosive eggs.

"I'm listening to you, Strasser."

The face split, making the lopsided jaw look even more bizarre. "Then come around Fort Security with me, Ryan. And we can talk some more."

JAK'S RIBS WERE ON FIRE. The jolting of the nimble little pinto pony had undone much of the shaman's good work. Every time he tried for a deep breath, jagged pain lanced through his body. It felt as if someone was rubbing the ends of two broken bottles together inside his chest. Twice he'd had to dismount to vomit. The second time the horse nearly broke away from him, but he just managed to hang on to the bridle.

Flurries of wind kept swirling around him, bringing a pillar of red-gray dust that made him cough. He had borrowed a cotton kerchief from one of the warriors, which he knotted over his mouth and nose.

At the last moment J.B. had suggested that it might be better to leave the big Magnum behind.

"Kid like you...blaster like that. If you're going to get in without too much fuss, then leave the handgun behind."

As he rode slowly along, following the detailed instructions of Cuchillo Oro, the boy found that his mind kept turning to Steps Lightly Moon and the pleasure she had given him.

The memory cheered Jak, and he kicked his pony's flanks, moving toward the fort with a renewed sense of purpose.

STRASSER DIDN'T TAKE any chances. Despite his protestations that he wanted Ryan to become his friend, he kept him securely cuffed, both at ankles and wrists.

Coming out of the dim light of the prison block, Ryan blinked in the dazzling sunlight.

The flagpole carried the fluttering pennon of the Seventh Cavalry. It was a truly amazing sight. If he hadn't known better, Ryan could easily have been convinced that a chron-jump had been made successfully, and that he was back in the late 1800s. Only the dune wag and Strasser's Russian blaster gave the game away.

"Bastards like this would have ruined everything," the sec boss said. "If I hadn't come along and showed them the right way, they'd probably have burned down the redoubt and the museum by now, and gotten themselves chilled over some Mescalero torture fire in the bargain. I showed 'em different."

"What's that?" Ryan asked, pointing at a large blaster set between two cart wheels. It seemed to have several barrels.

"Gatling gun," Strasser answered. "General Custer had one when he went up into the Black Hills of Dakota, the sacred lands of the Sioux. Didn't do him a lot of good. It's like a machine gun. Got too hot and jammed a lot. Looks good for show."

As he glanced around the fortified building, Ryan felt the sullen swell of despair. Even if, by some miracle, he avoided being chilled by Strasser, he didn't see any hope of the undisciplined Apaches being able to defeat the sec men. Fort Security was too powerful and the General too shrewd...unless they could somehow be lured out from behind the thick walls into the neutral killing ground of the desert....

JAK SAW THE MOUNTED PATROL before it saw him. He'd stopped among a jumble of rounded orange boulders to take a couple of mouthfuls of precious water from the canteen and eat a strip of jerked meat.

During the rising heat of the morning, the boy had seen innumerable dust devils, whirling clouds of wind-borne sand that danced across the land and collapsed in on themselves as suddenly as they'd appeared. But this column of dust was different: larger and higher, moving steadily toward him along a trail that Cuchillo Oro had shown him on a rough map. A trail that he knew led to the fort.

He didn't bother to get up and mount the horse again. At their present speed he figured that the sec men would reach him in something under a half hour.

Jak wasn't in that much of a hurry. He leaned back, shading his sensitive eyes against the sun, and waited.

"SERGEANT MCLAGLEN."

"Yes, General?"

The big raw-faced noncom snapped off a cracking salute. His face creased in a genial smile, but it was a smile that failed totally to get anywhere near the arctic-blue eyes.

"Showing Mr. Cawdor here around our home. It's possible that he might be joining us."

"Is that so, General?"

"Do I hear a note of doubt, Sergeant?"

"Course not, General. You order it, then begob but it's as though you wrote in on a marble tablet."

"McLaglen here was number two in a big sec unit for a ville out east. Folks come on a sailer from Europe, didn't they, Sergeant?"

"They did, General. Bad hots over there. Took 'em near two months in a leaking barrel."

"McLaglen had to leave his ville suddenly, didn't you, Sergeant?"

"Them bastards would have strung me up by the balls, General. You know why."

"Tell Mr. Cawdor."

The big man shuffled his boots in the raked sand of the parade ground. "Sure and I wish you'd not make me, General."

"Tell him," Strasser said, his voice like the silken caress of a whore's whip.

"Just that I had to punish a couple of men that stepped out of the line. Didn't expect them to get chilled."

Ryan was only half listening, using the time to look around the place, trying to find a weakness. But there wasn't one. Cort Strasser was too good at his chosen profession.

"I think most men would have thought their chances of survival were slim, Ryan," Strasser smiled. "Go on, Sergeant."

"I was about staking the bastards on some rocks by the sea." He paused. "Well, I suppose they were more in the sea, as you might say."

"They drowned," Ryan finished flatly, not wanting to get into this murderous game playing that Strasser had begun.

Sergeant McLaglen threw his head back and bellowed with laughter, showing a mouth filled with rotten teeth, sprinkled with a few aging plas-dents. "Sure and that's what they all think, isn't it, General? No, it wasn't the Lantic got to 'em, though they was a mite wet and cold from it. I'd clean forgot that there was some mutie king crabs on that stretch of the coast. Clean forgot, I had."

A picture flashed into Ryan's mind.

When he was a young boy he'd gone out on a hunting trip with his father, the Baron Titus, and his brothers, Morgan and Harvey. Ryan would have only been about four years of age. They'd gone in wags from the ville in the Shens, heading eastward until they reached the rolling gray waters of the Lantic. For reasons that Ryan couldn't recall, he'd been left alone on a stretch of dismal shingle, while the others went off in search of something or other.

And the crabs had come for him.

If he closed his eye, Ryan could still see them, could hear the noise of the scaly shells as they skittered over the wet stones. There'd been a mist drifting in from the water, veiling both ends of the beach, leaving him utterly isolated and alone.

The creatures looked as though they'd been around for all eternity, scuttling about the great feet of the meat-eating dinosaurs at the time that rocks melted and the oceans steamed. Their spiked tails left furrows in the pebbles, and they were moving toward Ryan as fast as a walking man. The nearest of them was four feet across the top of the carapace, seven feet to the tip of its tail. But it was followed by a mutie monster, fully fifteen feet across and nearly thirty feet to the end of the menacing tail.

Ryan had screamed for help, his voice vanishing in the fog, swallowed by the endless tumbling of the breakers. He'd run, his little legs scampering, slipping and falling in the treacherous hollows of the long beach. All he'd had to defend himself with was a dagger, a pretty toy, with a maroon hilt, taped with a light blue ribbon. The blade was no longer than six inches.

The safety of some low cliffs, easily climbed, beckoned the toddler, but the huge leader of the king crabs was closing on him, so near he could hear the harsh sound of its breathing. If he'd fallen then the creature would have overwhelmed him.

Only yards from safety, the young boy had turned, tiny knife in his chubby fist. He watched the approach of the nightmare horror, his feet planted apart for balance, falling by some primitive instinct into the classic knife fighter's crouch, knife held point up.

The thing was on him, hardly hesitating, seeing no threat in its puny opponent. Instead of backing away,

Ryan dived in, jumping over the top of the thing, cutting down at the boggling eye.

Desperately wounded and half-blind, the crab shuddered to a stop, seeking its prey. But Ryan was quicker. Dancing around it, he stabbed through the other eye, feeling its clammy ichor spurting over his fingers and wrist, clear to the elbow.

The boy had escaped easily after that, watching while the other crabs turned on the helpless giant and devoured it.

The memory was so powerful that Ryan almost forgot where he was. Strasser's voice tugged him back into the present.

"And the crabs began at their feet and worked their way up, did they not, Sergeant?"

"Indeed they did, General. One of the bastards had his head, chest and left arm remaining. The other was just a head, rolling around in the surf like a large pink rock."

Once again there came the bellow of raucous laughter from the noncom.

Strasser smiled indulgently as though one of his pet hounds had just performed a clever trick.

McLaglen's merriment stopped as quickly as it had begun, and he stared belligerently at Ryan Cawdor. "Seems like he don't think it's funny, General. Mebbe he's not the man for the Seventh. Mebbe he ought to prove to us that he's not just a one-eyed piece of spare baggage."

Ryan had been challenged often enough in his life to know that this wasn't a joke anymore. And he knew

enough about Cort Strasser to feel confident that this
had all been engineered.

"Sergeant's right, Ryan. New man here might have
to face up to a challenge. Who d'you suggest, Sergeant?"

"Trooper Rourke's gentle as a newborn lamb,
General. Mebbe Mr. Cawdor might care to come
'cross with him, d'you think?"

Ryan saw the logic behind the madness. If he beat
the sec man, who he guessed was the best they had at
hand-to-hand, then it would establish him if he ac-
cepted Strasser's offer. If he lost, then a good beating
would give some pleasure to Strasser.

"Do I get to take the chains off?" he asked.

"Of course. All fair and aboveboard, isn't it, Sergeant?"

"Sure it is, General. Why, I believe that's Trooper
Rourke over there. We should settle this real soon."

"Yeah," Ryan agreed. "Why don't we do the show
right here and now?"

He recognized the sec man. Rourke was the tall,
scar-faced thug, three inches over six feet and twenty
pounds over the three hundred mark.

"Call him..." Strasser began, but a shout from the
main guard post, on the tower at the side of the entrance gate, stopped him.

"Patrol coming in!"

"Shouldn't be in until tonight," the sec boss said,
eyes narrowing.

"Got a prisoner!"

"Looks like we better wait for the maul, Ryan. I
could be busy. Sergeant McLaglen here can show you

around the Seventh Cavalry museum, over by the lip of that mesa.''

Now they could all hear the sound of the returning patrol, the distant beat of hooves and the sound of voices, raised in the marching song of the Seventh.

The massive gates swung slowly open and Ryan watched the line of horsemen canter in.

At their center, on a small pinto pony, was the unmistakable figure of Jak Lauren.

''Fireblast,'' Ryan whispered to himself.

Chapter Twenty-Six

"Men like Ryan Cawdor live close to the edge. They pass their lives dancing with the widow-maker, flirting with the old bitch. Then they break free of her embrace before she sets her teeth into their throats. Young Jak's the same breed. So's John Barrymore Dix. I would guess Krysty Wroth comes from the same breed, but not me. Not Lori."

Doc was sitting, awkwardly cross-legged, by the dying embers of a cooking fire.

The rancheria was quiet; nearly all the Apaches stayed in their wickiups. Everyone knew that the one-eyed Anglo had been taken by Yellowhair and that young Eyes of Wolf had offered himself as a sacrifice to try to get into the fortress of the pony soldiers. There was nothing to do now but sit and wait.

Cuchillo Oro had sent out a half dozen of his young warriors to keep watch from a long, flat butte overlooking the desert that ran toward the fort. If anything happened they'd gallop to the rancheria and report it. Or if Jak or Ryan—or both—made a break for it, they might be able to help with covering fire.

But nobody expected anything to happen until the next day.

Maybe the day after that.

And maybe never.

J.B. had retired to strip and clean his arsenal, complaining that the fine dust of New Mexico was ruining the delicate mechanism of his blasters.

Krysty had left the fires to go to sit near the pool under the scarred cliffs. Since Ryan had been captured she'd said very little, seeming locked into her own private fears.

Doc and Lori had remained outside in the evening warmth, the girl leaning against the old man for comfort. Doc hadn't eaten much of the chili-and-beans stew, complaining that it gave him gas. But Lori had polished off his bowl as well as her own, asking for seconds. There had been a movement in the gray shadows, and Steps Lightly Moon had come shyly to join them.

Her question about what might happen had prompted Doc to launch into his diatribe about dancing with the widow-maker.

"I shouldn't go on like that, little girl," he said apologetically. "By the three Kennedys, but this waiting is irksome. You wouldn't have anything that I could ease my dry throat with, would you, my dear lady? I'd be obliged."

Steps Lightly Moon rose with the ease of a young fawn, reappearing with an earthenware mug and three beakers. She poured out refreshing drafts of the juice of the mesquite bean.

Lori smacked her lips appreciatively. "Drink very good. Thank you so much."

For several long seconds they sat in silence, until the Mescalero girl spoke.

"Will Eyes of Wolf survive?"

"Does a bear…" Doc began, changing his mind just in time. "Course he will."

"My heart is his heart," Steps Lightly Moon said, eyes downcast.

"He's real young." Lori shook her head disapprovingly. "Much youngest for you."

"And you aren't too youngest…I mean, young, for me, my honey bear?" Doc asked, kissing the blond teenager on the cheek.

"That be different, you old galoot," Lori replied crossly.

"Galoot! I didn't teach you that, did I? Upon my soul, I fear that I did. There can hardly be a living soul in all Deathlands that would use such a word."

"My father tells me you have traveled far. He says that after this… If it has been a good day for the pony soldiers to visit the shadow lands of their ancestors, my father says that you will all move on from here." She paused. "All of you?"

Doc hesitated. "There are two kinds of folk, Steps Lightly Moon. There's the kind like a flower, or like one of those big cactus plants. And there are those like the wind. I think you know what kind of a person Jak Lauren is."

"Yes, I know. But there is time and there is hope. Is there not?"

Doc smiled, showing his peculiarly strong teeth. "Child," he said, "there's always hope."

THE SIGHT OF THE YOUNG albino boy, riding in the middle of the cavalry patrol, gave Ryan one of the worst moments of his life. He had a great deal of affection and respect for Jak. To see him now, taken prisoner, was a bitter disappointment.

For a moment the thought surged into his mind to shout and encourage the boy to keep his chin up. The white hair was stained with orange dust, matted with sweat. Jak rode slumped in the saddle, holding his shoulders in a peculiar hunched, tight way. Ryan guessed that his damaged ribs were causing him trouble on the horse. The red eyes glanced up and around the parade ground, passing Strasser, flicking for the smallest splinter of time across Ryan's face, moving incuriously on to the rest of the buildings and uniformed sec men. Jak showed no sign of recognition.

Ryan swallowed hard, coughing and spitting in the sand as though some of the billowing dust had got in his throat, in order to cover his surprise at seeing Jak, seeing the way Jak reacted when he saw him standing there!

If the kid was deliberately pretending not to know him, then he'd come in as part of a setup. Of course! Strasser knew Doc, Krysty and J.B., so it had to be either Lori or Jak. Which meant it had to be Jak.

"What a most bizarre-looking young man," Strasser said. "They call them albinos, with that white coloring and hair."

"Yeah," Ryan said.

The lanky corporal in charge of the returning patrol shouted out the command for them to halt and wheel to face the General. He saluted Strasser.

"Who's that?"

"Kid says his name's Jak Lauren, General, last survivor off of a wag train the far side of Shay Canyon. Had a run-in with Gold Knife and his murdering 'paches. Come looking for us after he stole a horse off one of the bastards. Killed him for it. Wants to join up here at Fort Security."

Strasser licked his lips with a long, leathery tongue, half turning to stare at Ryan. "You wouldn't know the young boy, I suppose, Ryan? No, of course not. Hardly think one skinny kid can be the rescue column, can it? No, of course not." He turned back to the noncom. "Get our guest washed and cleaned and uniformed, Corporal. Then bring him to us after the noon meal. Wait. Want a full briefing of all of you. Every noncom. Want to talk 'bout the Apaches. I'll see the boy after that. Sergeant McLaglen?"

"Yo, General?"

"Take Ryan to the museum. Might interest him. Have the maul later. I'll tell you when. And...and look after him carefully, Sergeant. No 'falling down stairs,' or I'll have you flogged with my special whip."

With a bleak smile toward Ryan, Strasser marched toward his own quarters. The patrol was dismissed, and Jak was led away by a pair of sec men. He never even looked back at Ryan. The sergeant clapped Ryan on the shoulder.

"Ready, my bucko?"

"What's special about the General's special whip, huh?"

The bluff face, rank with honesty and good fellowship, turned toward him. "Cross him and you find out, friend. The General's special whip has little slivers of broken glass, woven into the plaits of wire. One blow opens you like a fist in silk. Five and it's the infirmary. Ten and you'll likely die."

"Thanks, Sergeant," Ryan said, shuffling after the big man toward the rear entrance of Fort Security and the museum that lay behind it.

Many of the rooms had been grossly vandalized, something that Ryan guessed had happened before the arrival of Cort Strasser in New Mexico. Most of the damage had been cleared and swept up, but there was still broken glass on some exhibits and many of the dioramas had been damaged.

The dangling sign said proudly: The National Museum of the United States Cavalry—Past, Present and Future.

"Rockfall brought down half the bastard mountain on top of the Present and the Future," McLaglen told him. "Not that they had too much future, back in them days. Blessed Mary knows that things isn't good now, but I'm about telling you that they must have been worse when the skies darkened."

"Guess so," Ryan agreed. "So there's only the past left. That's why you've only got the rep-blasters here?"

"Sure, and that's right. Springfield carbines, 1873. Shoots a single .45 round, and if you're inside a barn with the doors shut you got a chance of hittin' it. And the side arms are all Colt Navys. General made us dump any blasters we had 'fore he came. His Stechkin's the only modern gun in the place."

"Springfield and the Colt are good blasters if you use 'em right."

"Sure. Against the Mescalero we're in good shape. But if we come against another ville . . ."

"Mind if I look around?" Ryan asked.

"Sure. Bores the ass off of me, it does. There's only this one way in and out, so don't get clever. Wouldn't want you hurt 'fore Rourke gets to grips with you."

A COUPLE OF TROOPERS lounged against the wall of the washroom, keeping a careful eye on Jak as he rotated under the shower.

"Pale piece of chicken meat, ain't he?" the skinny one of the pair cackled.

"Tender, though," the other smirked, unashamedly rubbing his hand against the swelling at the front of his dark blue breeches.

Jak didn't say anything, contenting himself with trying to relax under the warm stream of water, feeling the pain easing from his broken ribs.

"Gotten a bad knock on your side, there, boy. Been fighting a cougar?"

"Yeah."

"Don't talk much, do he?"

"Like 'em that way."

"Keep their mouths shut."

"Not all the time. Need their mouth open some of the time."

"Then you close it."

Jak ignored the ribald laughter, making no effort to hide himself from the prying eyes, knowing that it would only give them more ammunition for their filthy comments.

"Mouth shut an' legs open."

"Mebbe the General's going to want first go at this one?"

As long as they kept talking, Jak knew he didn't have anything to worry about.

ON HIS OWN, WITH ONLY the hobbling effects of the chains and manacles to hinder him, Ryan was free to walk where he wanted around the single-story, rambling building. Gazing on row upon row of uniformed dummies, many in broken cases, quickly became boring. As he wandered by he read out an occasional card, describing what the battered figures wore. All of them were from the period between about 1860 and 1890. The later sections were buried under the collapsing walls of the great mesa above Fort Security.

Brigadier General George Cook. The best Indian-fighter in history, seen here wearing his own sky-blue version of the cavalry overcoat, lined in crimson and with a collar made from the pelt of a wolf shot by the general himself.

"He would, wouldn't he?" Ryan muttered, biting his lip as he tried to use the time to figure out what Jak was in the fortress for. Was he there to bring a message? Or to recce the place? On his own, he certainly wasn't there to try to spring Ryan.

There was a list of some of the main engagements of the Indian Wars of the period, with a capsule account of each. Ryan glanced through them, passing the minutes, aware that before he could get to speak to Jak he was going to have to fight Trooper Rourke, and play out his part in the small drama directed for him by Cort Strasser.

"Pyramid Lake, Nevada. Apache Pass, Arizona. Canyon de Chelly, 1864. Adobe Walls." Ryan remembered that name. Something about a warrior being knocked off his horse by a Sharps rifle at a range of a mile.

"Don't spend all day there, my bucko!" came the warning bellow from Sergeant McLaglen. "Won't save you from Bully Rourke's care."

The dioramas showed scenes from some of the famous firefights described on the walls. Little figures—only a couple of inches high—posed stiffly on plastic hillsides among faded trees and tinsel streams, with tiny puffs of cotton representing powder smoke. Some had fallen over, showing greater losses than had originally been intended. Indians with miniature feathers whooped silently up the coulees of the models.

On one of the them stood brave Custer. General Yellowhair, in a perfectly modeled buckskin jacket, a pistol in each stumpy fist. At some time in the past century a fat spider had managed to get into the case and had woven its fragile web across the golden straw that represented the slopes above the Little Big Horn River. Now it lay dead, a dried husk, halfway between the trapped general and the equally trapped defense site of Reno and Benteen.

"Sand Creek, the Haybox Fight, Washita, Slim Buttes, Palo Duro Canyon, Rosebud, Bear Creek, Wounded Knee." Doc had told him something once about Wounded Knee, linking it with Sand Creek. Massacres, he'd called them. Massacres.

All of them seemed to be victories for the whites, except for the Custer defeat. But Ryan noticed one other exception. Not listed under Battles or Campaigns or Victories. It was just called the Fetterman Disaster.

Ryan stooped to read the faded card, finding a sketchy account of how some soldiers had been lured out of the Bozeman Trail Post of Fort Phil Kearney, by Sioux, Cheyenne and Arapaho. "Treacherously ambushed in a most cowardly manner and butchered by overwhelming force. Slain to the last man, horse and dog. The bodies of the brave Captain William J. Fetterman and eight of the cavalry's boldest, hideously mutilated."

Ryan glanced at the little plan of the action and a description of what had led up to the disaster, shaking his head at the thought that the brave Captain Fetterman might have guessed he was being suckered into an obvious trap.

But if the bait was tempting enough and caution had been buried beneath a fiery charge, then even the wiliest fighter might get cold-cocked into riding, grinning, into an ambush.

It was a thought to hold.

"Sure and you'd better come out of there, 'fore I come and drag you out."

"Coming, Sergeant," he replied.

The museum was a depressing place. Worse than many abandoned redoubts, it had nothing in it of life. Monuments to death and to the oppression of one people by another. If this was what Strasser was seeking to re-create, then Ryan was on the side of the Mescalero, though it was probably too late now to recover from being caught.

On the way back to the entrance he walked along a line of photographs of famous Indian leaders and fighters, staring blank-eyed into the lens of the white man's camera. He knew from old books that some of the Indians feared that the cameras would steal their spirits. The theft had been far, far worse than that: Yellow Wolf; Little Cloud; Victorio; Kicking Bear; Young Man Whose Enemies Are Even Afraid of His Horses; Sitting Bull; Kicking Wolf; Geronimo; Gall; Red Cloud; Quanah Parker; Cuchillo Oro—not the war chief who waited back at the rancheria in the canyon, but his famous forebear. Ryan peered at the tinted picture, rubbing at it with his fingers, smearing the film of dust. He was just able to make out the gleaming blur that was the great golden knife that the Cuchillo he knew now wore at his belt.

Many things had changed, but many of them still remained the same.

Chapter Twenty-Seven

STRASSER WAS NOWHERE to be seen when Ryan and Sergeant McLaglen walked through the broken swing doors of the United States Cavalry Museum. Someone was working hard over at the forge, a hammer singing a merry song on iron. Sparks flew from the bellows, rising into the warm, late-morning air. Ryan stopped and took a deep breath, savoring the scent of hot metal, horses and sunshine.

"Interesting in there?" the tall noncom asked, tugging at the slouch hat with the gilt crossed swords on its front.

"Lot of dummies. Lot of models. Words and pictures. Battles lost and won. Massacres, disasters and firefights. I saw rooms filled with losers but not many winners."

McLaglen snorted. "Best watch it, mister. Or I'll give Rourke the say-so to rip the muscles off of your bones. General's made us proud of what we done."

Ryan could hardly believe his ears. Was Cort Strasser that good? Good enough to take a murderous rabble of mercenaries and hired guns and make them wear uniforms? And then make them proud of their fictitious past?

"And that Sand Creek..."

"What about it?"

"Sure and it wasn't the cavalry, mister."

"Then who...?"

"Colorado volunteers! Vigilantes, they were. Not regulars."

"That make a difference?"

"Damned right it does. Listen, mister, I got to say that you don't seem a bad sort. Like my grampa used to say, I like the cut of your jib."

Ryan had never heard the expression before, but he nodded to the noncom. The sudden approach of friendliness didn't surprise him all that much. His guess was that the sec man had sized him up and seen the possibility that maybe, just maybe, Ryan might beat Rourke. Someone like McLaglen wouldn't miss a trick when it came to trying to get on the side that was winning.

The troopers had established a rough ring in front of the forge, setting up posts and stringing ropes between them. Ryan glanced back at the main buildings of Fort Security, hoping to spot Jak, but the windows remained empty.

Rourke was already waiting for him, sitting on a small three-legged stool in one corner of the fighting area, with a brace of his cronies to second him. Apart from the stool, the other corner was empty.

"Want me to back you, mister?" the sergeant asked, pushing a way through the silent crowd.

"Yeah. Better than nothing, I guess."

There was a momentary delay while McLaglen looked for the keys to release Ryan from the chains. Once he was free he rubbed at his arms, bending and straightening the knees, feeling circulation flowing again.

Rourke had stripped to the waist, wearing only his dark blue breeches tucked into the high leather boots. Checking him over carefully, Ryan noticed that the sec man still kept the stubby cavalry spurs on the heels of the boots.

"Big, ain't he?" McLaglen said.

"Fat's the word," Ryan replied. "Carrying more spare weight around his gut than a farrowing hog."

"Mean son of a bitch, though. Use his weight on you. Try and pin you. Mebbe use the spurs. That's the way he fights. Killed a young boy from Ohio only a month ago like that. Tore him up real bad. Lad bled to death."

"Why d'you tell me all this? You want me to chill the bastard for you? That it?"

"He wins, then he's harder to order around. Might challenge me one day. But the General wants him to win. Not chill you, mister. Get the bucko to rough you up some. So I got a bet each way. Kind of bet that I really like."

"Come on, One-Eye!" Rourke yelled from the other side of the ring, which unleashed a burst of shouts in his support from the watching crowd. "Got a yeller belly, have yer?"

Ryan considered making a joke about the size of the sec man's wobbling guts, but he decided that silence was the best reply to the hectoring. He simply continued to ready himself, checking the feel of the ground and where the sunlight fell.

"Any rules, McLaglen?" he asked.

"Try and leave the ring without being thrown or kicked out, and they'll put you back. I'll stop it if Rourke's got you ready to buy the farm. Same if you manage to beat him. General won't want any killing 'tween you."

"Any other rules?"

"Yeah. Do him 'fore he does you."

JAK WAS FEELING BETTER. The shower had eased the pain of the long ride across the desert, and his broken ribs had simmered down to a dull ache. The sec men who'd been ogling him had finally stopped when they saw the pale boy wasn't going to rise to their baiting. He'd been given a full uniform to wear, which fitted him reasonably well, though the pants seemed to have been made for someone a size or two smaller around the hips.

The troopers escorted him to the main admin block of buildings. They showed him into a room that held a table and a couple of chairs as well as a wide bunk bed covered in a handmade Amish quilt and a long couch against one wall, upholstered in dark blue leather. The window looked across the parade ground, but the drapes were pulled most of the way across it.

Jak could make out some sort of gathering beyond the flagpole, but he couldn't see or hear what was going on.

"Food's on the way, kid," one of the sec men informed him. "Eat well and keep your strength up. Ready for when the General comes calling on you. Y'all hear me, now?"

"Don't he look real purty in them breeches?" the other cavalryman said softly. "Snug around that firm young ass. Why, I swear I could take a—"

"Shut that mouth of yourn," his friend snapped, pointing with his finger behind them to the other rooms in the building. "*He* don't take to that kind of... You double-stupe bastard!"

They'd left Jak alone, shutting the door behind them, but he didn't catch the clicking of any kind of a sec lock.

The food was brought in on an elegant, polished beechwood tray, served on real china plates with gleaming cutlery and a genuine glass.

The sec man put the tray down on the table, winked at Jak and flounced out again. The albino boy noticed that his breeches also looked uncomfortably on the tight side.

Jak hadn't eaten that kind of food for a long time. Once, back in Louisiana, they'd found a store out in the suburbs with its own nuke-solar generator still running, and it had been filled with sealed packs of amazing food. Jak's gang had broken into them and mixed them in large copper pans over bottled gas cookers, not knowing what a lot of them were.

This meal was excellent. There was a tureen of vegetable soup, with peas, small chunks of reconstituted potato and turnip and some fragments of meat that Jak deduced were ham. He noticed that all of the crockery and the knives, forks and spoons carried the neat crest of crossed sabers and the letters US, with the number "7" on them.

Another covered dish contained several slices of chicken or turkey, with cranberry jelly, as well as creamed, dried potatoes and some irradiated vegetables in side bowls. Jak helped himself, his mouth filling with saliva at the scent and taste of the food. For a moment his mind wandered back to the rancheria at Drowned Squaw Canyon, to his friends who were waiting for him and to Steps Lightly Moon. He laid down his fork for a dozen heartbeats. The whole balance of his life had shifted forever in the past day or so. Now he'd finally made love to a girl; there would never again be a first time for him. The Mescalero chief's daughter said that she loved him. Whatever that might mean.

And maybe he also loved her.

Whatever that might mean.

The last part of the meal was a kind of pastry with some cream stuff on top and some red fruit that Jak guessed were strawberries. They didn't taste like much to him.

Before leaving, the sec man had poured a glass of a dark crimson liquid that was thick and sticky. Jak sipped at it, feeling a fiery warmth spreading through his body.

It had been good food, but his mind was not locking onto the problem of how he might make contact with Ryan and find some way of getting them both out.

There was shouting from outside the window and Jak rose from the table, wiping his mouth with a damask dinner napkin. He tugged the drape back, the material dry and frail between his fingers. The crowd of sec men out on the parade ground had grown, and they were now ringing something around, something that was clearly exciting them. But Jak had no way of even guessing what it might be.

Behind him he heard the door open and he began to turn, conscious yet again of how uncomfortably snug was the fit of the dark blue trooper's breeches.

THERE ARE TWO SCHOOLS of thought about hand-to-hand fighting, particularly when you're up against someone who tops you by inches and outweighs you by more than one hundred pounds.

"Get inside. Close in and stay tight and use speed and skill."

"Keep away. Stay out of reach and move in and out quickly."

Ryan had never actually subscribed to either theory. He went along with what the Trader used to say about close combat.

"Do what's right, and do it hard and do it fast. That's all."

McLaglen had patted Ryan on the shoulder. He had chosen to strip like the sec man, keeping on his combat boots and his pants. It was a hot day, and it would help to be sweating and slippery.

"Quiet down!" the noncom bellowed. "Grudge fight between Rourke here and Ryan Cawdor. No rules, no stoppages. Man down and can't get up loses."

"Man down, can't get up... is fucking dead!" roared the massive trooper, getting a cheer of encouragement from his fellows.

"Start on my word. Stop when I tell you. And I mean that about stopping, Rourke, my bucko. General's orders."

"Sure thing, Sergeant." The big man grinned, licking his blubbery lips.

"Then . . . get ready. Fight!"

JAK TURNED, SEEING that Cort Strasser was in the room, just as Krysty and Doc had described him. He wore a long yellow wig, framing a face of petrified cruelty. The boy was immediately struck by the thin skull, narrow eyes and hooked nose. His lips were like twin furrows hacked across the stretched skin. His full mustache spilled down both sides of his jaw, partly hiding the scars of what looked like a severe beating.

He was wearing a long duster coat in beige linen, belted at the waist. The polished toes of riding boots protruded from under the hem.

"So, you want to come and join us here at Fort Security, do you, young man?"

"Yeah. Do."

"You will call me General like everyone else here. Do you understand, Jak?"

"Yeah, General. Understand."

Strasser sat down on the couch, smiling pleasantly at Jak. "You look very well after your ordeal. I believe you have injured your ribs."

"Yeah, General."

"Does that make it difficult for you to move? Let me be fucking specific, Trooper Lauren. Does it stop you from bending over?"

AS MAULS GO, THE ONE between Ryan and Trooper Rourke wasn't much to talk about. It only lasted a minute or so, and the end was so abrupt that half the sec men watching didn't even realize that it was over.

The ring was small enough for Rourke to think he could swamp the one-eyed man with his own bulk, corner him and wrestle him to the dirt. It had worked several times before.

It should have worked again.

It didn't.

As the fat man shuffled toward him, arms spread, Ryan stood his ground for a moment, watching him. Then he began to back away, but he seemed to catch the heel of his boots in the raked earth and he stumbled over. There was a great whoop of delight from the watching crowd, and Rourke rushed in, diving on top of the sprawled figure.

But Ryan wasn't there anymore. He wriggled to his left, feeling the ground shake as the sec man landed at his side. Before Rourke could move, Ryan was up on his feet, kicking the trooper with a cold, savage accuracy. The point of the toe cracked open the delicate elbow joint, into shards of bone and rags of torn cartilage.

Rourke shrieked in agony, crabbing his way to the farther corner of the ring, helping hands reaching through to tug him to his feet. The left arm dangled uselessly at his side, and the slobbering grin of anticipation had vanished. A look of sweating terror had taken over.

"Come on, fat boy," Ryan whispered in the sudden stillness.

Rourke was surrounded by sec men. Magically, a knife appeared in his right hand, passed from behind. A short-bladed hideaway knife, with a handmade, taped hilt.

"Hey!" Sergeant McLaglen shouted, without any real attempt at interference.

"Don't matter," Ryan called over his shoulder, beckoning to Rourke. "I told you to come on, fat boy. Come on!"

"Fucking Indian-lover bastard," Rourke screamed, coming in at Ryan again, the tip of the knife making jerking darts toward his opponent.

Ryan waited, perfectly balanced on the balls of his feet, relaxed and ready. He feinted toward the knife with his left hand, swiveling like a dancer, kicking at the sec man's knees. Rourke dodged him, realizing too late that the kick had also been a feint.

Ryan swung all the way around in a complete circle, shifting feet, altering the direction of the real kick, following through like an old football player on a faded vid, going for a fifty-five-yard field goal.

Because of Rourke's size, the spread of flesh on his thighs protected him from the killing power of the kick. But Ryan's boot still crunched hard enough into the sec man's groin to fold him over as if his appendix had ruptured.

There was a sour whoosh of breath from the open mouth, and the knife fell from the trooper's fingers. "Get 'em going, keep 'em going," had been Trader's instructions. Without a split second's hesitation, Ryan crouched and brought up the heel of his right hand, with devastating force, against the injured man's nose.

He felt the impact clear to his shoulder, hearing the familiar splintering of bone.

Rourke went down like a steer under the poleax. His eyes were wide open, but only the bloodshot whites were showing to the bright sky. His legs kicked and twitched, fingers scraping at the sand of the parade ground, the nails breaking in the earth.

A thin worm of crimson crept from between the thick lips.

"He's broken his nose," someone said, voice high with surprise.

"No, he hasn't," McLaglen said resignedly, climbing into the ring, his pistol drawn. "He's fucking killed him."

STRASSER ROSE, UNCOILING himself from the sofa, going to peer out of the window. Both he and Jak had heard the raucous cheering fall into an instant, shocked silence.

"I hear the sound of death," Strasser said. "I do fear that Trooper Rourke has proved better than I thought. Or Ryan Cawdor has proved too old and slow."

Jak's heart missed a beat, and it seemed as though someone had sucked the air from the room.

"Trooper, I had best go and view the remains of my old friend. We can talk later and by then your ribs might be rather better." He paused at the door. "I hope, my white-haired young man, for your sake, that you are well enough for ... what I have in mind."

As the door closed, Jak picked up the pitcher of water and poured himself a drink, finding that his hand was trembling.

Chapter Twenty-Eight

VOMIT COVERED MUCH OF Ryan's muscular chest, dappling the naked groin, trickling over his legs to form a stinking puddle around his bare feet.

Cort Strasser had been coldly furious at the ease with which Ryan had butchered his tame bully.

McLaglen had winced under the withering attack from his commanding officer, stammering and shuffling his feet, trying to explain that he'd warned Ryan not to chill the trooper. But it had all happened too quickly for him to be able to do anything.

The General ordered Ryan to be stripped and then chained, standing, in the farther of the two sec cells. McLaglen wiped the sweat off his forehead once they were out of Strasser's office, glowering at the prisoner.

"You've done yourself, now, me bucko. And you fucking nearly did for me, sure you did."

"I don't fight for fun. Man wants to take me on, then I'll try and chill him. That can of grease had it coming."

McLaglen had left him, having obeyed the order from the General to make sure the fire in the brazier was burning brightly and the various torture implements were glowing white-hot.

When Strasser had come in, Ryan had heard the command to lock the dungeon from the outside. The General wore his wig, strands of it sticking to the beads of perspiration on his forehead. He wore a long coat, loosely belted at the waist. As he strode up and down, Ryan could see that the sec boss was naked beneath it.

"I won't waste words on you, Ryan Cawdor," he said. "Talk costs nothing. Action can cost everything. Everything. I warned you what would happen if you crossed me. I was fucking triple-stupe to ever think you might work with me. Triple-stupe. So, I can start and take some pleasure."

Ryan had lived long enough to be sure that this wasn't the main course. Though he was securely chained to the adobe wall, he still had some degree of movement. And for some really serious punitive torture, you needed the victim to be very still. Ryan had seen some experts, had even suffered at their hands, and he had witnessed the amount of delicate skill that they all used. A needle or a scalpel in clumsy fingers can easily do either too little harm, or too much.

This was all for starters. To relieve Strasser's feelings and let Ryan know that there would be much, much more to come.

Strasser didn't actually use any of the heated metal probes, pincers and knives on his prisoner. He took them out of the brazier, holding them carefully by the rags wrapped around the handles, and he waved them close to Ryan's face, making sure he could safely flinch from the ruby glow. The parchment skin stretched in a narrow smile as one of the implements, curved like a corkscrew, neared Ryan's good eye, bringing sweat to his face.

"Hot, isn't it, Ryan Cawdor? So hot that only an inch or so nearer and the radiation of the fire would sear out your vision. But I don't want that. Oh, no, not at all. Want you to see everything that goes on here. Right to the last."

Mostly the sec boss had contented himself with using his strong fingers.

Pinching and tweaking, leaving neat rows of swollen, purple bruises across the tanned flesh. Taking his pleasure from all the tender parts of Ryan's body. Beneath the arm and behind the elbows and knees. Along the insides of the thighs and at the back of the ears. Ryan nearly passed out when the sec boss took each nipple between thumb and finger, squeezing hard, harder, leaving them throbbing with pain, surrounded by white, puffed skin.

"Now this," Strasser whispered, cupping Ryan's genitals in the palm of his right hand, tightening the pressure a little, grinning wolfishly as Ryan raised himself on the tips of his toes to try and avoid the inevitable suffering.

The obscenity was Strasser's obvious and visible arousal at the pain he was causing Ryan. His breath came faster and his skinny tongue danced over the chapped lips. His fingers tightened convulsively, making Ryan gasp, bringing a weird giggle from the sec boss.

"Just beginning, my dear friend," he whispered. "I have a new companion, with the most dazzling snow-white hair and eyes like those glowing coals there. I think I shall go to him, perhaps bring him to watch. Perhaps..." The fingers squeezed and loosened, bringing the sour taste of bile floating into Ryan's throat. "Perhaps little Jakky might want to share the funning. Perhaps he *might*."

At the last word the sec boss's skeletal body gave a great involuntary shudder, and he gripped Ryan's balls so ferociously that his prisoner slumped unconscious in the chains.

By the time the darkness lifted, the sec door was firmly shut and the cell was empty again.

KRYSTY STARTED AWAKE, eyes darting around the wickiup, past the yellow lights of the small earthenware lamps. The blankets that separated the long room into sections hung motionless. With her mutie hearing she could detect the regular sound of J.B.'s steady breathing, Lori's breath, lighter and more shallow, and the sonorous snoring of Doc, rasping like a file through cedarwood.

"Gaia!" It had been like a fist, groping feverishly inside her head, plucking her awake, sweat trickling cold down her spine. Her burning hair coiled tightly and protectively around her skull.

It was Ryan.

Ryan was in bad trouble and needed help. Jak hadn't been able to get to him, which probably meant the albino kid was already chilled.

"Earth Mother, help me," she prayed. "Show me what we have to do. Should we go to the ville and attack it? Or is this the parting of the ways? Tell me, Earth Mother, I beg you."

The curtain at her side twitched back, and the Armorer stood there, fully dressed, even to the jaunty fedora. The wire-rimmed glasses glittered in the poor light, hiding J.B.'s eyes.

"Heard you, Krysty," he said quietly. The blaster in his hand slid noiselessly back into its holster. "You got something on Ryan?"

"Yeah. Bad. He's in pain. Can't tell more than that, J.B., but it's gone wrong."

He nodded. "Looks like Jak could have gotten trouble. Wasn't a good plan, but it was the damned best one we had."

"What do we do now?"

"We go talk to Cuchillo Oro."

JAK WAS SLEEPING in his neat room, only a few steps along the passage from the quarters of Cort Strasser. He'd finally managed to drift off, after a light meal of soup and fresh corn bread. The boy's brain had been racing, running over what he'd seen and heard during the day at Fort Security.

From what the orderly had told him, he now knew that Ryan was in the deepest shit, that he'd killed a sec man in a fight and the General was already torturing him.

The place was run tighter than a rat's ass. If he got to Ryan, he had to spring him from the sec cell, then get the main gates opened and buy enough of a start for a mounted patrol to lose them out in the desert. That was all.

A knife slash of golden light appeared on the far wall of the boy's room, sufficient to bring him fully awake. The strip widened, then disappeared as a man's shadow blocked it out. Jak kept still, all his senses alert. It was the smell that told him who it was, before his eyes picked out the long shape, black in the blackness. The scent was dried sweat, laced with fear and madness.

"You 'wake, boy?"

"Yeah. Yeah, General."

"Get yourself up and dressed. Full uniform, trooper. Quick as you can."

"What is it, General?"

The laugh chilled the fourteen-year-old. It was like a creaking gate in a midnight cemetery.

"You and I will... We'll do some things. That's what we'll do. We'll both do some things. Get dressed!"

RYAN HAD COME AROUND, his body sore all over, a dull ache pincering his groin. But he knew that what Strasser had done to him thus far was only a childish, spiteful beginning. Nothing had been done that wouldn't stop hurting in a few hours. Apart from some superficial bruising, it would be completely over in a day.

He also knew that Strasser would come back. And keep coming back until time and light and dark and day and night all ceased to have any relevance to him. Ideally, Ryan wanted one single chance at the sec boss. A moment to tear the grinning mask of flesh off the long, warped skull. If he died with Strasser that wouldn't be so bad.

With that thought, Ryan suddenly realized that he understood the Apache concept of there being a good day for a man to die.

Outside in the passage, he heard the sounds of boot heels, someone muttering orders and a guard marching briskly away.

The door opened once more. Opened for the last time.

EARLIER, JAK HAD BEEN DISGUSTED by some pix that Strasser had shown him. He had sat next to the boy on the bed, one hand on his thigh, describing what each picture showed, who the prisoner had been, whether it had been male or female. Often, the torture had reached such an advanced stage that it wasn't possible to tell, particularly when the area between the legs was simply a mess of clotted blood.

The gloating delight in suffering recalled only too vividly for the boy the way that his own father had died at the hands of the monstrous Baron Tourment, among the swampies.

One of the instant pix had stuck in the boy's memory. Strasser had told him that it was a young boy from the Mescalero rancheria, who'd strayed too far on a hunting trip and had been picked up by a roving cavalry patrol.

The General had tightened his grip on Jak's leg, inching it higher, as he'd panted out the disgusting details of the torture of the little Apache boy.

There had been a close-up of the victim's right hand, pinioned with a broad leather strap. Strasser had been particularly proud to point out where the whiteness of bone showed through in several places, boasting of his own skill in whittling away the flesh and sinew. It had taken all of Jak's self-control to avoid trying to kill the sec boss.

The General had ushered Jak along the corridor from his room, past his own quarters, to where a trooper stood guard outside the pair of cells. One had its door, with a sophisticated lock, standing partly open, the keys in place. The other door was firmly locked. Strasser ordered the sec man off duty, telling him there would be no need to return until he received further orders. The man saluted smartly and marched off.

Jak felt Strasser's hand caress him briefly through the tight material stretched over his buttocks. "Now we won't need to worry at all 'bout our being interrupted, Trooper Lauren. We got us all of the night to do...whatever we want."

The key turned in the lock and the door began to open.

THE ABSURDLY TALL SHAMAN, Man Whose Eyes See More, sat across the freshly built fire from the Anglos. He wore a vest of flowered brocade, the scarlet cravat a brilliant splash of color at his throat. The mirrored glasses reflected the leaping flames from the dried branches. Cuchillo sat next to him, his daughter at his shoulder, and a half dozen of his older warriors ranged alongside him.

"You share the power of seeing, Fire Hair Woman," the shaman said. "I have read the signs. I loosed a snake and it tried only to destroy itself in my fire. One Eye Chills is in great danger. And Eyes of Wolf has not been able to aid him.''

Many Winters croaked something in the guttural Apache tongue, which Cuchillo translated for the others. ''He says that your friends have chosen their own path of knowledge and they must now hunt it alone. He says to try and help them is to destroy us all.''

Doc opened his mouth, but J.B. held up a hand. ''He's right, Doc. No way we can take out the fort. Best we can do is mebbe ride out after dawn. Take a look at things. If they're gone, then they're gone.'' He turned to Krysty. ''Sorry, but that's the way it has to be. Throw more corpses on Ryan's body if you try anything else.''

She nodded slowly, knowing that the Armorer spoke the truth. But that knowledge didn't stop the tears from gathering. ''Then we'd best get ready for dawn,'' was all she said.

CORT STRASSER TURNED to the boy, the skin across the high cheekbones seeming so stretched that it might tear like calico. ''You and me, Trooper Lauren, are going to finish it this night. I've decided that Ryan Cawdor's race is run.'' He pushed open the door of the cell.

Chapter Twenty-Nine

THE CANYON WAS FLOODED with the opalescent glow of early dawn. The cliffs that rose sheer above the still pool of water were daubed with bright splashes of red and orange, reflected in the mirrored surface below.

The women, having been roused in the darkness, prepared food, while the young boys got horses ready for everyone in the recce party. The warriors who would have gone out to relieve the night's watchers joined Cuchillo Oro, some of the elders of the tribe and the Anglos.

There was an atmosphere of nervous tension in the rancheria. Everyone knew that things had rushed to a sudden moment of urgency. The fire-haired woman and their own shaman both felt that something crucial was happening.

Everyone checked his blaster, holstering it against the perpetual sand. Krysty was rubbing grease into her silvered Heckler & Koch P7A-13 when a shadow fell across her. She looked up and saw the tall figure of the war chief.

"Cuchillo?"

"I want to speak silently with you, Fire Hair Woman. I mean, Krysty."

"Silently?"

"So nobody hears us."

"You mean privately, don't you? Yeah, go ahead. Nobody can hear."

"You will not tell anyone?"

Not apart from any of the group, she thought. "No, course not. This is 'tween you and me, Cuchillo Oro."

He knelt at her side, glancing around to make sure none of his people was within earshot of them. "If all is lost, you will go from here?"

"Yes. Nothing to keep me."

Cuchillo nodded. "I understand that. Man Whose Eyes See More thinks that Ryan and Jak are both in great danger. Perhaps already in the land of spirits."

"I know that. That's what we aim to try and find out."

"My daughter will weep if Eyes of Wolf does not return to us. It is the way of women of the people to cut off a finger if their warrior does not return. My daughter does not hold to the old ways. But her heart will weep tears of ice."

Krysty put her blaster away, standing up, the heels of her boots giving her enough height to match the Mescalero. "Where's this getting us, Cuchillo Oro? Speak plain."

"Ryan said that if...if he did not come back...then when you went you might take me with you. And Steps Lightly Moon, as well."

"Ah," the girl said, "I see."

"What is the answer?" the chief asked, unable to conceal his concern.

"Why not stay here?"

"With my people?"

"Yeah."

"Because I have talked with Ryan about where you have been. And what you see. I am a great warrior. In any fight I would help you, and there would be much honor for me."

Krysty looked at the Apache, trying to get the feel of the man, seeing pride and anger and a deal of raw courage. She wondered if that mix would be the right one for him to join her and the others in their journeys.

"You do not reply?" he said.

"I don't have the answer, Cuchillo. I'm not saying it's impossible, but we're a team. Ryan's the leader. Got to be his word."

"But he is dead and...!" There was a flaring of rage behind the bronze face and the dark eyes, swiftly controlled and driven back beneath the ground. "I should not have spoken with those words. We will talk of this later."

"Sure."

RYAN STOOD AND WATCHED as the door of the torture cell began to swing open.

Jak peered around the stooped figure of Cort Strasser, seeing Ryan, barely able to stand upright with the tight chains, his body marked with dozens of small bruises.

"Now." Strasser leered.

Jak didn't hesitate, didn't stop to think through the possible consequences of his action. He simply stiffened the fingers of his right hand and drove a savage, punching blow into the General's back to the right of the spine, over the kidneys. Strasser gasped, staggering against the frame of the door. To Jak's amazement and horror, the sec boss didn't go down, despite having absorbed an attack that would have taken most men out of the action.

"So..." Strasser grated, fingers tightening into claws as he fought to draw breath.

"Again, Jak," Ryan called, knowing the phenomenal strength and power of Strasser, knowing that the dice had been thrown and there was no going back for either of them.

The boy didn't need the advice.

He tried for the knee to the groin, but Strasser was too tall and too fast, blocking it with a turn of the thigh. The General reached out for Jak's throat, but the boy was quicker. He snatched the little finger on the right hand and jerked it back with a dry snap.

"Fucking bastard!" The sec boss grunted, pulling away in a pained reflex action.

Although the absurdly tight breeches hampered him, Jak stamped down hard on Strasser's right foot, feeling the jolt as the heel smashed home. The tall man staggered again, trying to back away from the ferocity of the albino's attack. But Jak was after him, long white hair whirling about his face.

Years of practice had hardened Jak's fingers and hands, and he chopped at the General's left thigh, deadening it, slowing Strasser down.

It was time to put him down. Jak bent the first two fingers of his right hand at the lower joint, bracing them against his palm. He struck upward with a crippling blow that landed under Strasser's ribs, driving deep into the solar plexus. Against a weaker opponent it would, quite literally, have been the killer punch. Even with someone like the General it paralyzed his breathing, sending him to his knees. Jak slapped him hard against the side of the face, which knocked the man to the dirt floor.

As a precaution he kicked him twice, the toe of the polished cavalry boot thudding home at the side of the angular head.

"You got him?" Ryan asked anxiously. He could hear the sounds of the fight, but couldn't see out into the corridor.

"Course. Wait."

Jak took Strasser by his feet and pulled him roughly into the other cell, leaving him in a tumbled heap on the earth. In the poor light it was difficult to see whether the sec boss was still breathing. Jak didn't care much either way.

He slammed the heavy sec door, turning the keys in the lock. On an afterthought the boy opened the obslit and threw the keys inside, knowing that a door like that could only be opened from the outside. It would slow things down a little.

Time now was life or death. One of the sec men might come through at any moment, and once the alarm was raised, living was going to be measured in a few beats of the heart.

Jak sprinted through into the cell where Ryan was chained, grabbed the keys off the wall and unlocked the manacles.

Ryan showed an uncharacteristic sign of weakness, falling for a moment to his knees. He rubbed at his wrists before straightening, patting the boy on the shoulder. "Fireblast! Good to see you. Have you chilled the evil fucker?"

"Don't think so."

Ryan took a handful of blood-crusted rags off the table and tried to wipe himself clean. "No? Where'd you put him? I'll send him to buy the farm right here and now. Give me more pleasure than... What's wrong, Jak?"

The boy slapped himself on the forehead. "Triple-stupe!"

"Why?"

"Locked him in cell next along."

"Then give me the key and—"

"Strasser's out cold. So pushed keys into cell. Make it hard get him out."

"Oh, for...!" Ryan whistled through his teeth. "Okay, it's done. But I'd have given a year off of my life to see that streak of dirt dead in my hands."

"Sorry, Ryan."

"Don't apologize, kid. It's a sign of weakness. You did good. Saved my skin. Now all we have to do is get out of here." For the first time he noticed what the albino boy was wearing. "Anyone ever tell you those pants are too tight, kid?"

"Yeah, Ryan. And don't call me kid."

It only took a few minutes for Jak and Ryan to find their own clothes. The albino took a pair of the Navy Colts, making sure they were fully loaded. Ryan recovered his own SIG-Sauer P-226 from a shelf in Strasser's office. Ryan noticed the sec boss had hung a Russian sniper's rifle on the wall, like one that he'd

once seen up in the icy lands that had been called
Alaska. It was a Samozaridnyia Vintovka Dragunova
with a PSO-1 telescopic sight.

"Can I take blaster?" Jak asked, seeing the long
gun.

"Slow us down. We hit 'em close, or we don't hit
'em at all. Let's get out of here before someone comes
along."

Jak led the way out of the side door to the main
block, and walked straight into a patrolling sentry,
knocking the sec man off balance.

"What the . . . ? You're the kid come in yesterday.
One the General . . . Hey!"

He held the Springfield carbine in his right fist and
grabbed at Jak's camouflage jacket, pulling his hand
back with a yelp of dismay. He stared unbelievingly at
the streams of blood, black in the moonlight, seeping
from the deep cuts in his fingers. The fragments of
razor steel in the boy's coat had done their job.

Before the man could get over the initial shock, Jak
had drawn one of his slim-bladed throwing knives.
Gripping it by the tapered, weighted hilt, he thrust it
as hard as he could into the angle between throat and
jaw. He felt the trooper's stubble on the back of his
hand as the knife penetrated deeply.

There was very little blood.

"Catch blaster," Jak hissed, holding the slumped
figure of the dying sentry.

Ryan snatched the Springfield as it dropped toward
the planking of the narrow porch, offering it to Jak.

"Which way?" the boy asked, lowering the corpse
gently.

"Main gate there's got two guards. Could try and take them out. There's another door out back, under the mesa, near the Cavalry Museum. Either we get a good start, or we blow the whole ville here. Can't do that. Could kill all the horses."

Jak shook his head, hair dancing like a mane of fiber optics. "Make too much noise."

"There's a dune wag. Saw it near the smith's forge."

"Let's go."

Chapter Thirty

It was virtually impossible for any potential enemy to attack Fort Security from the rear, unless they came up over the mesa. But there was a narrow trail that wound out between the main doors of the museum and the back wall of the fortress. Apart from the sentry whom Jak had taken out, Ryan could only see the two patrolling troopers on either side of the front gates. Jak's eyesight in the brightness of noon was poor, but in the gloom he could see excellently.

"No others," he whispered. "Wag's there. By forge. Cover me."

Ryan followed him across, running light-footed over the sand, only the faintest sound breaking the stillness of the night. The wag was in a poor state of repair, with the faint stencil, USCM, barely visible on its battered flank. The fat tires were worn smooth and some of the gleaming solar panels had disappeared. Ryan had driven similar vehicles and knew that the nearer they'd been built to the year 2000, the better they were likely to be. Up till then the use of solar power had been limited and inefficient. The range on this dune wag was unlikely to be better than thirty miles without some sort of recharging.

The rear entrance was only secured by a pair of large bolts and Jak eased them both down, pushing the gates apart on greased hinges.

Ryan glanced at the instrument panel of the wag, checking that he knew what he was going to do before he risked starting it up. It was the usual button ignition with tiller steering and independent four-wheel drive and braking. Six forward gears and one reverse. He beckoned to the boy to climb aboard, motioning him into the wide back seat.

"If anyone sees us, start shooting. If you don't hit any of 'em, it'll keep their heads down. Slow 'em down from coming after us."

He reached out and pressed the start button.

THREE TIMES ON THE winding trail out of the canyon J.B. had to call to Krysty to slow down.

"Spur on like that and the poor beast won't have a run left in him, if you need it."

"And a galloping man raises more dust than a walking army," Cuchillo Oro added.

"Damned homespun wisdom," Doc muttered, lumping along on a rawboned bay mare, his straggly hair blowing in the light breeze.

"How much furthest?" Lori asked, trying to pick grit out of her eye.

"Another hour or so," Steps Lightly Moon replied, wheeling her pony alongside the tall blond girl.

"Think we'll know any more?" J.B. asked.

It was the shaman who answered. "A man might believe he sees everything, and discover that he actually sees nothing."

Doc grunted.

NOTHING HAPPENED WHEN Ryan pushed the starter button.

He tried it again. There wasn't the least flicker of movement.

"Sec lock?" Jak whispered.

"Could be. Fireblast! Anyone comes around the corner there they'll take us colder than a well-digger's ass. Mebbe the gearshift's got . . . Yeah."

There was a small switch that he flicked down, reaching again for the starter.

The engine was almost soundless, a faint whirring sound and a gentle vibration, ticking over in the dune wag. Jak patted Ryan on the shoulder.

"Just keep looking," the older man said, cautiously engaging first gear. He eased the pedal and released the hand brake.

The large wheels began to roll. Ryan kept one hand on the steering tiller, holding the pistol in his other one. The wind tugged at the gates, making them blow across, half-shut. Simultaneously, shouts erupted from the main building; lights flicked on.

"They found Strasser," Jak hissed, readying himself to vault out and hold the gates.

But the breeze relented, allowing the gates to swing open again. Ryan gunned the engine, knowing that it would only be a matter of seconds before their escape was detected.

A siren began to sound as they drove out of the fortress, the noise like an amplified bugle. More lights came on, including big floods all around the parade ground. Ryan heard more shouting and then the crack of a firearm, followed by the much louder noise of Jak's carbine.

"Fucking single-shot!" the boy cursed, struggling to reload the primed .45 cartridge.

The engine was now racing as Ryan pushed it up through the gears, fighting to hold it as it careered past the front of the museum, onto a trail that snaked down the slope along the western flank of Fort Security, the log walls only feet away from them.

A head appeared over the rampart, silhouetted against the bright spotlights. Ryan snapped off a shot, seeing the man disappear in a spray of bone and brains.

"Yeah," Jak shouted.

"Get down. Can't hope to do anything with that Springfield. There'll be some lead flying real soon, now," Ryan called to the boy.

Dawn came early out in the desert. Ryan could already see the pale lightening of the sky to the far east, over toward Drowned Squaw Canyon. He'd noticed on the journey to the sec ville that the track was rough and rutted. Even with the big wheels of the dune wag, he couldn't hope to make any real speed. Not without the risk of rolling the buggy.

He wondered how long it would be before Strasser got the troopers organized enough to send out a realistic pursuit force. His guess was that the sec boss would be so maddened at the escape that he would throw everything after them, regardless of the risk. For some reason, Ryan suddenly recalled the items in the Cavalry Museum on the Fetterman massacre. The soldiers had been carried away with the thrill of pursuing what they thought was an easy target and had run blind-eyed into the jaws of the trap, victims of the cunning of High Back Bone of the Miniconjou and Red Cloud of the Sioux.

That had been a good day.

As Fort Security boiled into furious life behind them, Ryan thought more about the story of the Fetterman massacre.

STRASSER WAS CARRIED ALONG in a haze of white anger. He struck out indiscriminately at anyone who got in his path. The fact that such a puling boy had beaten him, sprung Ryan from his cell . . .

Sergeant McLaglen narrowly avoided being punched to the ground when he came rushing to the General's quarters for orders. His first shock was seeing the sec boss without the mane of yellow hair. The scraped skull with its fringe of sparse black hair made him blink in amazement.

"Don't stand like a fucking frog with a needle in its belly! I want every man in the fort mounted and ready to leave in fifteen . . . no, in ten minutes. Gatling gun, everything."

"They got the dune wag, General."

"I know that, you bastard stupe! But it's been giving us trouble for weeks. Won't take them far. Get moving and get ready."

The tall man moved stiffly, holding his stomach as though he had a chronic attack of indigestion. There was a large bruise just behind the left ear, and a worm of brown blood was smeared across the sharp planes of his cheeks.

McLaglen stood rooted to the floor of the office, fascinated by the intensity of madness that glittered in the deep-set eyes of the General.

"You got five seconds to be obeying my order, Sergeant. Then I gut-shoot you and find someone else who can do like they're told."

McLaglen snapped to attention. "Sure and I'm gone, General."

RYAN'S GUESSTIMATE WAS that they'd only made about five miles before the dune wag died on them. There wasn't any warning. No spluttering or coughing. It simply cut out, rolling quickly to a halt on an upgrade.

"Want look at engine?" Jak asked, hopping out of the back seat.

"No time. I reckon that Strasser'll turn out every sec man in the place after us. Best bet's that he'll be right here in less than a half hour."

STRASSER, WIG BACK IN PLACE, immaculately uniformed, held up a gloved hand at the sight of the abandoned buggy. He checked his wrist chron. "Thirty-five minutes from Fort Security, Sergeant. Can't be far behind them. Tracks are easy to follow."

The dawn wind had fallen away as the day began to brighten, and the tracks of the two fugitives stood out like splashes of blood on a white satin bed sheet.

Strasser stood in the stirrups, peering over the neck of the stallion. McLaglen heeled his own horse nearer, realizing that the General was in better spirits. He was singing quietly to himself. McLaglen felt more scared than he had when the General had been in a devouring rage.

"We push on, General?"

"Fucking right we do."

The sergeant eyed the low ridge of a line of buttes a couple of miles ahead of them, with a weaving nest of trails through their center. "You don't mebbe think it could be a trap, General?"

The smile broadened. "I think I hate nothing more than a coward, Sergeant." The gloved fist fell to the butt of the Stechkin pistol. "That's what I think about it."

McLaglen nodded, frightened to speak in case his voice vanished in a squeak of fear.

The cloud of dust from the cavalry patrol of nearly fifty men rose in a gentle spiral, circling in the desert air, warning Ryan and Jak that their pursuers were gaining fast. The thought of the long-range Russian sniper's rifle he'd seen in Strasser's room was worrying Ryan. Already the sec men had closed to within a little more than a mile of them. On horseback, over rough terrain, they'd run them down in less than a half hour. The ridge was invitingly close, but there was only more desert on the other side. There was no possibility at all of their reaching the safety of the rancheria before Strasser caught up with them or before they were within easy range of the blaster.

"THERE!" SHOUTED one of the troopers, a mutie from somewhere up in the high plains who found it hard to see a hand in front of his own face, but who could count the feathers on a bird's wing at a mile.

Strasser reined in at the yell, following the man's pointing finger. He sat gazing out across the barren wilderness for several seconds before he located the two tiny specks that were moving toward the lower slopes of the buttes.

"Hit 'em with the rifle, General!" McLaglen shouted.

"No, Sergeant. I want to see their faces. Watch 'em and smell 'em and taste 'em. See their eyes when they see death grinning at 'em."

"They'll be over the rise, yonder, General."

"So will we, Sergeant. Sooner the better. Bugler! Sound the charge."

JAK FELL AGAIN, rolling against a pile of loose stones, crying out with the shock of pain in his injured ribs. As Ryan stumbled back to help the boy, they both heard the clear golden notes of the cavalry bugle, letting them know that the hunters had seen their prey.

"Does that mean what think means?" Jak panted, hair now filthy and tangled across his scrawny shoulders.

"Yeah. Only hope's to make the crest of the butte. Hold them off for a while from there."

"Fifty of them. We only got carbine and ten rounds. Three handguns. Won't take long. Can ride right over us, Ryan."

"No." He hauled the boy up, holding him with an arm around the shoulders. "Nobody's that fucking happy to get themselves chilled. They'll stop when we open fire on them."

"Then what?"

"Shoot off all our ammo and chill as many of the bastards as we can. Mebbe even take Strasser off the earth."

"Then what?" Jak repeated, gasping for breath with the effort of striving for the top of the steep slope.

"Then, when it's all done, I put one through the back of your head and kiss the barrel of the SIG-Sauer. Leave them dead meat."

"I'll go with that, Ryan," the boy said, managing a pale ghost of a grin.

"NEARLY AT THE TOP," Sergeant McLaglen shouted, spurring his horse to the side of the General.

"Get them first! Be just like Custer at the Little Big Horn. Won't quite make it to the top!"

Strasser was wrong about that, as well.

The terrain was more difficult and the patrol had to slow, giving Ryan time to help drag the albino over the rim, rolling several feet down the far side before he could draw breath and open his eye.

"Hello, lover," Krysty said.

Chapter Thirty-One

THE DEFENDERS OF THE RIDGE had enough firepower to make the cavalry turn back in some disarray. At least six of the sec men went down under the sudden hail of lead, but the rest were able to take cover in a snaking arroyo that ran parallel to the line of buttes.

Ryan left Jak in the comforting arms of Steps Lightly Moon, who wept with joy at seeing the boy still alive. J.B. clasped Ryan by the hand, showing his delight with the favor of one of his rare smiles. Doc also shook hands, while Lori kissed him on the cheek. Krysty kissed him, long, hard and slow, on the lips. The shaman nodded, the sunlight flashing off the glasses, and Cuchillo Oro drew the golden cinqueda and hurled it spinning into the air, catching it by its jeweled hilt.

"Tell us how..." Krysty began, but Ryan stopped her with a shake of the head.

"No time. This is it. The chance to take them all. One chance." Over the side of the ridge they all heard the sudden explosive chatter of the Gatling gun, the noise stopping almost as quickly as it had begun. J.B. grinned again.

"Bastard's jammed," he said. "Go on, Ryan. Tell us the plan."

DESPITE HIS RAVENING ANGER, Strasser still held enough shreds of sense to know that he would never drive his sec men up that hill into the teeth of rifle fire from the defenders. For the time being he had to wait, contenting himself with sending gallopers out to both sides of the long ridge, to warn him if his prey tried to slide away. The buttes ran too far for him to be able to surround Ryan and the others.

The skirmishing line covered most of the one long side, with his men hidden behind the tumbled boulders. The shooting was irregular, with neither force wanting to take the risk of offering targets to the enemy. It was past noon before there was any change in the status quo.

One of the cavalry gallopers came bursting up to Strasser in a cloud of dust, shouting that the hostiles were withdrawing. Simultaneously Ryan and Jak showed themselves on the crest of the butte, pouring in a burst of lead at the sec men below.

The General threw himself to the ground, wincing as splinters of bullet and rock screamed all around him. "How many fuckers gone?"

"Dozen or so, General. Two white women with 'em. One redhead, one yeller. Can't be many left up there."

All the sec men heard Ryan Cawdor's voice. "You're chicken shit, General. Hide behind your double-stupe scum! You got no belly for a firefight!"

Strasser reached for his Russian-made rifle, easing it around the corner of his cover. But there was no sign of anyone on the ridge.

"What do we do, General?" Sergeant McLaglen called, anxiously.

"We wait, until I say to move."

"Sure thing, General. Sure thing."

THERE WAS RYAN, Jak—his ribs restrapped by the shaman—J.B. and four of the oldest of the Mescalero warriors, including Many Winters. Cuchillo had led the others back to the canyon to put the most important part of Ryan's plan into operation.

The immensely tall wise man of the tribe, clutching a decorated Sharps rifle, also insisted on remaining behind with Ryan's group.

"Will they attack?" he asked Ryan.

"Can't tell. We gotta hold 'em here another hour or so, then break for the rancheria and lead 'em after us."

Man Whose Eyes See More shook his head slowly. "Yellowhair, General, Strasser, Longhair. He is the night."

"And I'm the day," Ryan replied, squinting down the slope at the hiding sec men.

"No."

"No?"

The shaman touched him gently on the arm. "You are the night as well, One Eye Chills."

"Then what's the difference between me and Cort Strasser?"

The Apache pondered the question for several seconds. "One night a little child might walk fearlessly through a darkling wood. On another night an armed man will tremble with terror on an open plain, swept with confusion. That is the difference between Strasser and yourself.''

"They're moving, Ryan," J.B. called. "Guess Strasser thinks he's waited long enough. Looks like he's…yeah, he's going to split them and come around both sides."

"Fireblast! We need a half hour more. How the big fire can we slow the bastards down?''

"I will do it," Many Winters said in his creaking English.

The shaman turned to the old man and said something in the Apache tongue, something that sounded like a question. The warrior turned his lined face up to Man Whose Eyes See More, looking past him, into an infinite distance. He said something and then moved away.

"Don't tell me," Ryan said. "He said that it was a good day for him to die."

"Yes. You are learning our language fast, One Eye Chills."

"No. I'm learning something about Indians."

Many Winters was helped onto his pony by Jak, who handed him the coup stick, a pole, ten feet long, decorated with bands of color and with the feathers of eagles. Each mark, Ryan knew, indicated some past honor.

The old man took the battered Winchester rifle from its bucket by the saddle, throwing it to the earth. He drew a broad-bladed knife from its deerskin sheath and dropped it on top of the blaster.

"What?" Jak said.

"The honor comes from riding against the blue coats without any weapon," the shaman answered.

"Bastards'll chill him," the boy said in an anguished voice.

"That seems to be the idea," Ryan replied. "Man knows when it's his moment to join the spirits of his ancestors. For Many Winters, the moment's right now." He paused. "And it should puzzle the bastards down there. Mebbe buy us the few minutes we need. Get ready to pull out the moment the old man buys the farm."

"WOULD YOU LOOK at that, General?" McLaglen called.

"What?"

"Yonder. Coming over—"

Strasser interrupted the gaping noncom. "I see him, Sergeant."

His long hair braided, holding the feathered coup stick, Many Winters kicked his heels into the flanks of his pony and began to move slowly down the sloping face of the butte, toward the watching sec men.

As he advanced, without any weapon, the old man began to chant his death song.

Ryan and the other remaining men on the ridge readied themselves for the final withdrawal toward the rancheria.

Many Winters was halfway toward the sec men, and still no shots had been fired.

"What's he singing about?" J.B. asked Man Whose Eyes See More.

"About honor," the shaman replied. "He tells the pony soldiers that he is pleased to meet with them. That they will bring him honor by allowing him to end his days with them. He hopes to be able to touch many of them with his coup stick. That is all."

"It's enough," Ryan said quietly.

Down on the flat desert, Cort Strasser called for someone to pass him his Samozaridnyia Vintovka Dragunova rifle, then steadied the long gun on a convenient boulder, centering the cross hairs of the sight on the chest of the advancing Indian. His right index finger tightened on the trigger.

But he still didn't fire.

Many Winters was more than three-quarters down the hillside, still chanting in a frail, quavering voice, his eyes turned blindly toward the sun.

"Chill him, General," one of the soldiers shouted, beginning to lose his nerve at the steady approach of the crazed Mescalero.

Strasser's concentration slipped for a moment. When he looked again, the Apache had vanished for a moment into a dip in the trail, though he could still hear the droning voice.

He lowered the rifle, cursing under his breath. The biting anger for the way the whitehead kid and Ryan had fooled him was still close to fever heat. Just as he'd been about to slam the buffalo horns of his pincering trap, this stinking old fart with his whining voice had come doddering along to distract everyone's attention.

Many Winters appeared for a moment between two pinnacles of weathered stone. Hastily Strasser lifted the rifle and snapped off a shot, seeing the puff of red dust as the bullet missed the Apache by a good yard. The chanting continued as though nothing had happened. And more time passed.

Ryan was peering down. "Any moment now," he said. "Many Winters'll come out from behind cover and then Strasser'll pick him off easy as squashing a bug on your hand."

"That blaster's got a real distinctive noise to it," the Armorer said. "Know it if I get to hear it anywhere."

The Dragunova barked once more.

The white-haired Mescalero threw his arms wide, the coup stick flying high in the air, feathers whirling. The chant ended abruptly, choked as the 7.62 mm rimmed bullet tore out the front of the warrior's throat, sending him kicking off the pony's back in a welter of tumbled blood.

There was a cheer from the watching sec men. "Good shooting, General," Sergeant McLaglen called.

"Fucking awful," Strasser muttered, knowing that he should have opened fire much sooner and chilled the old man minutes ago. "Mount up and let's get after those bastards!" he yelled, the order repeated by the noncom.

By the time they reached the flanks of the butte, Ryan and the others were already dust, a mile or more away from them.

McLaglen waited for the word from the General, but Strasser simply stood in the stirrups, shading his eyes against the lowering sun, watching the snaking pillar of orange dust.

"General?"

"Yeah?"

"We going to follow them?"

The man turned with a terrifying smile hooked on his thin lips. "Follow them? Course we follow them, Sergeant. We follow Ryan Cawdor into the jaws of the grave."

IT WAS A DESPERATE SCRAMBLE. The three surviving Mescalero warriors led the way, whooping and kicking their heels into the slats of their animals. J.B. struggled next, barely keeping them in sight through the weaving trails of the narrow canyons. Ryan and Man Whose Eyes See More rode together, falling behind, trying to keep alongside Jak, who was suffering once more from his injuries.

Twice Ryan risked a glance over his shoulder, seeing that the swirling sign of the pursuers' dust was closing in fast. Now he cursed himself for not insisting that the boy went on with the others. They were still some distance from the hidden mouth of the box canyon and the sec men were drawing nearer.

After what seemed an eternity, Ryan glimpsed the narrow opening to Drowned Squaw Canyon. The cavalry patrol was less than three hundred yards behind them.

The die was cast.

Killing time had come.

Chapter Thirty-Two

THE LIGHT WAS FADING FAST, great banks of menacing purple chem clouds gathering all across the western horizon. Almost as if it were greeting their arrival in the canyon, there was an echoing peal of thunder, the pressure of the sound squeezing between the high cliffs.

The rancheria looked normal. Not far off the fifty or so wickiups were scattered about the base of the half-mile-wide canyon. Cooking fires gleamed brightly, and there was the strong scent of chili stew cooking in the iron caldrons. Ryan followed the ponies of the rest of his group, noticing the stacks of barrels of cooking oil piled high against the one wall, not far from the wickiup that had been the home of the Anglos.

Everything was precisely as it would have been on any one of ten thousand other evenings at the Mescalero rancheria.

STRASSER HAD DRAWN the brass-hilted cavalry saber, waving it over his head as he led the mad dash through the narrow entrance to the box canyon, past walls of rock that clamped in on the riders, less than a dozen feet across. He whooped exultantly, the sound almost drowned in a rumble of distant thunder.

"It's their fucking ville!" he screamed to Sergeant McLaglen, who was almost at his stirrup.

There were low huts, each with a small fire glowing in the half-light. The sec boss's nostrils brimmed with the smell of spicy cooking. Out of the corner of his eye he spotted a pile of kegs of oil, near the cliff.

Everything was precisely as it would have been on any one of ten thousand other evenings at the Mescalero rancheria.

Except that there was nobody there.

No men relaxing by their homes, smoking a last pipe before eating their evening meals.

No women bustling about with the cooking, scurrying to ready the children for their beds.

No children running and leaping and screaming, eager to hold off the moment when their mothers would catch up with them.

No horses feeding contentedly near the placid pool of water.

Nobody.

At the farthest end of the canyon floor there was a walled depression, where Cuchillo Oro had told Ryan their ancestors used to keep and breed cattle. The old corral was two hundred feet across, with high earth walls, backed by the cliffs above the mirrored lake. Ryan was the last one inside, leaping from his horse and letting it go. If the plan worked, he'd be able to recover it later. If the plan didn't work, then he wouldn't be doing any more riding. Not ever.

The three Apaches were at the earthworks, rifles at the ready, J.B. and Jak joining them, the boy walking with a pained stiffness.

"How far are they?" Ryan shouted.

"On top of us," the Armorer replied. "They haven't spotted the— Yeah, yeah, they have now."

Strasser wasn't the first one to notice. It was Sergeant McLaglen, spurring on at the flank of the blond-haired death's skull, who realized there was something badly wrong.

"Nobody!" he screamed, voice cracking with sudden gut-tearing fear. "Nobody! The bastards are gone! General! Halt for God's sake!"

The terror spread like a brushfire in a dry summer. All the sec men began to look around them, the blinding heat of the chase cooling as they saw there was no exit at the far end of the canyon, just the biting jaws at the entrance. Some men reined in immediately, while others tugged their animals to left and right. One fell, then another, horses crying high and thin. The flailing hooves kicked up a blinding dust that made it impossible for anyone to see what was happening.

Strasser's voice rose above the bedlam. "Take Cawdor! Find the one-eyed man and bring him to me! They can't have left the canyon. Find them and kill them!"

"Pour in some lead," Ryan called from their hiding place.

Even firing blind they couldn't fail to find targets. Men began to go down, yelling, clutching bullet wounds. More maimed animals fell, bringing down others.

Ryan heard the voice of the sergeant, bellowing above the chaos. "Withdraw! Get the fuck out of here.... Way we came in ... Way we came in!"

"No," Ryan said to himself.

Cuchillo—with Krysty, Doc and Lori—had marshaled his forces well, keeping everyone out of sight as the trap was baited. The Apache women and children were already more than a mile away, in a small canyon, guarded by a half dozen of the younger warriors. Every other man of the people who could carry a blaster was there, either climbing up the side trails to line the cliffs, or spilling from hiding to turn the narrow entrance to Drowned Squaw Canyon into a maelstrom of instant death.

It took several minutes for the dust to clear. In the confusion, several of the fires had been knocked over, setting light to three of the wickiups. Smoke began to billow around, making it hard to see just what was happening. Above the reek of cordite, the canyon was brimming with the flavor of chili stew.

Ryan held his own fire after the initial burst of shooting, wanting to conserve ammo as much as possible, readying himself to pick targets when they showed. But the clearing of the dust showed that he wasn't really needed.

The old Remingtons and Winchesters of the Apaches had done sterling work. Already better than half of the attacking cavalry patrol was dead or dying. Bodies lay sprawled everywhere, flung to the dirt. The sound of firing from the rim of the canyon and from down by the entrance was constant. The chem storm seemed to be flooding closer, seamed with silvery-purple slashes of lightning. But if there was any thunder roiling in the heart of the storm it was drowned by the noise of the killing field.

J.B. was at Ryan's elbow, peering cautiously over the top of the age-old wall of the corral. Jak was sitting, legs out in front of him, holding his arms wrapped around his chest. The shaman was stooped at his side, trying to help him, looking like a bizarre stick insect.

"We got 'em," the Armorer said, never a man to use four words when he could get by with just three.

"Looks like it. They won't break out. Entrance blocked with dead horses and men. Rest are running around like chickens with their heads gone."

One of the older warriors, still levering and firing enthusiastically, pointed out into the canyon, beyond the water, and shouted something in the Apache tongue.

"What's he say?" Ryan called to Man Whose Eyes See More.

"Fire! He sees a fire."

"There's dozens of fires around. Look, there." He showed J.B. where there was a flare of smoky, golden light under the far wall.

"Cooking oil's gone up, Ryan!"

"Fireblast! Look at that bastard smoke coming up from it."

"They can't get out. Unless they're like that man they said climbed the cliff above the lake."

"Wings on Feet," the shaman said, towering over them in the demonic light of the spreading blaze. "But that was legend."

"Heard Doc once say something about if the legend got bigger than the facts, then you stuck with the legend," Ryan said.

"I looked at that rock face," J.B. told them, "and nobody human could get up it. Even with the hounds of hell at your back."

The smoke was becoming thicker. The shooting persisted, but now the volleys were becoming more scattered. The distinctive crack of the Springfield carbines came less frequently as the sec men were butchered by the jubilant Apaches.

A couple of troopers, bareheaded, eyes wide in near panic, broke around the side of one of the burning wickiups and ran toward the old corral, each man holding a smoking Colt Navy blaster.

"Mine!" Ryan shouted, steadying himself, the SIG-Sauer clamped in his right hand. He braced himself, legs slightly apart, squeezing the trigger four times. Two spaced shots at each man. The range was a scant twenty yards. At that distance, using the excellent blaster, Ryan was able to put eight rounds from eight inside a circle of two inches across.

The leading sec man was hit a finger's width above the sternoclavicular joint, plumb in the middle of his chest. It stopped him in his tracks, frozen as the second round took him through the heart, smashing the spine on the way through, punching an exit hole the size of a baseball. The impact knocked him over in the dirt, his pistol flying in the air, eventually falling with a soft splash into the pool.

The second man saw his friend go down and made a late, doomed effort to dodge sideways, ducking for cover. Both bullets hit him in the lower part of his face. By a ballistic freak, they completely tore away the man's bottom jaw, sending it flapping to the earth, like a bizarre, crippled bird.

The trooper tumbled backward, head thrown up. Ryan had seen some dreadful sights in his life, but even he winced at the horror. The dying man's tongue flopped down, across his neck, writhing in his death agony. Exposed by the loss of the bottom jaw, it was a hideous length, gray-purple in color. It looked as if the sec man had swallowed a monstrous worm, but hadn't quite managed to get down the last fourteen inches of its tail.

"Fireblast!" Ryan leveled the blaster and fired a third round. The bullet punched through the cavalryman's forehead, putting him out of his suffering.

"Getting soft, friend," J.B. said. "Waste of a perfectly good round of ammo."

It wasn't much of a firefight. Cuchillo Oro had taken the time bought by Ryan and by Many Winters to place his warriors well, making sure they stayed in hiding, picking off the trapped pony soldiers where they scurried for shreds of cover.

Within fifteen minutes it was virtually over and done. A few, a very few, of the sec men had managed to find places to make a last stand, and there was still the sound of sporadic shooting. The smoke from the burning oil billowed everywhere, rank and thick, coiling all around the walls of the canyon. The sun had virtually disappeared, and the rancheria was in near darkness.

Ryan walked cautiously from the old corral, moving along the flank of the pool of water. The body of one of the sec men lay partway in the lake, the back of his head blown away by a large caliber bullet, the blood spreading languorously from the waving hair.

The smoke hung thickest at the box end of the canyon. It was virtually impossible to see the cliffs beyond the bloodied pool. Ryan tried to look up and see the top of the sheer rock face. For a frozen fragment of a second a gust of wind from the speeding storm tore a window in the smoke. Ryan blinked his good eye, unable to believe what he thought he'd seen.

J.B. caught the moment. "What is it?"

"Thought I saw..."

"What?"

"No. Can't be. Looked like the ghost of old Wings on Feet halfway up the cliff, hanging there like a spider." He shook his head. "No. Couldn't be. Trick of the shadows."

The Armorer wiped his glasses on his sleeve, pushing back the brim of the fedora and looking above the dark mirror of the pool. "No. Can't see a damned thing up there."

"Guess so. Come on. Let's go help pick up the pieces."

"CAN'T BE CERTAIN-SURE until dawn," the shaman said. "But it looks like General Yellowhair managed to fool us all."

Ryan punched his right fist hard into the palm of his left hand. "That's what I saw on the face of that bastard cliff. That was fucking Strasser."

"Might be hiding in one of the wickiups," Krysty suggested.

"No. My people have searched every place."

Ryan looked at Cuchillo. "So, he's gone?"

The war chief nodded slowly. "Only a demon of the night winds could have climbed that cliff to escape us."

"That's Cort Strasser," Doc agreed, his arm still tightly around Lori. "A man from the deepest circle of Hades."

"We do not think any other of the soldiers got away from us," Steps Lightly Moon said. The girl had immediately made for Jak when she and the other women were summoned back to the canyon.

The sun was long set, the floor of the rancheria sodden with darkness. Fires burned once more, and once again there was the rich smell of cooking. The bodies had been dragged out beyond the neck of the canyon, to be moved farther away when morning came.

And there were the prisoners.

Despite the overwhelming firepower of the defenders, six of the sec men had managed to hole up in a rocky corner, protected by an overhang, keeping a brisk fire against the Mescalero. But they finally ran out of ammo and were beaten to the earth. Sergeant McLaglen had been in charge and he had fought bravely with his saber, killing three warriors before they finally overcame him.

Now he and the other four survivors, one of his party having been killed in the final storming of their redoubt, had been taken prisoner and were bound and tied to stakes in front of the chief's wickiup.

In all, nine of the Mescalero had died during the great battle.

"They died with much honor," Cuchillo Oro said, a touch pompously. "They have saved us all. The people have won again. Never more shall Anglos threaten our way of living."

"Until next time," J.B. whispered.

Ryan was bone-weary.

All he wanted to do was get to bed and rest after the suffering and tension of the past couple of days. He'd eaten his fill of chili stew and beans, enjoying the pleasure of being again with his five friends. Man Whose Eyes See More joined them for a half hour, and Ryan realized how much he'd come to like the wry humor and natural wisdom of the shaman.

"Time for bed, folks," he said, reaching a hand down to help Krysty to her feet. The others followed suit, Jak gently disentangling himself from the fond arms of Cuchillo's daughter.

The boy caught Ryan's eye, beckoning him to the far side of the fire.

"What is it, Jak?"

"Just that Steps Lightly Moon and father kind of want come along."

"I know that."

The boy's hair was cleaned and neatly brushed back off the high, white forehead. "Yeah. He wants talk you."

"Now?"

"Yeah."

"All right, Jak. Listen, one other thing I gotta say."

"If it's 'thanks' then don't."

"Okay. It was, but I won't. But thanks all the same."

"You'd done same. Any of us would. That's why so close."

"Would you like Cuchillo and the girl to join us, Jak?"

"He's brave fighter. She's..."

The shaman had silently joined them. "I see Eyes of Wolf makes eyes of sheep," he joked.

"Boy wants advice."

The shaman smiled, eyes enigmatic behind the inevitable sunglasses. The storm had passed by the canyon, but they could still hear the occasional rumbling of distant thunder.

"He wishes to see tomorrow. And many more tomorrows. Every man wishes that at some time in his life. It becomes harder to see yesterday as you grow older, Jak."

"Me an' the—"

"The girl, Jak? It all comes to wanting and being able. A man could stand on top of those cliffs and want to fly safely to the earth. It's a good idea and would be wonderful if he was able to do it. But to leap because you *want* is not always the best idea."

"Then you think shouldn't—"

The shaman held up a skeletal hand. "I do not *tell* you, Jak. You must decide. Perhaps time will help you."

"Don't have a lot of time," Ryan said. "Guess we'll be moving on tomorrow or the day after. Our work's done."

"Like the wind." The shaman gently mocked him. "I know. There are times when to move on is much to be desired."

"Jak says Cuchillo wants to talk with me about joining us."

"He does."

"Do us a favor, Man Whose Eyes See More. Tell him I'm totally wasted. I'll speak to him in the morning."

"I'll tell him, Ryan. And sleep in peace, my friend."

Chapter Thirty-Three

THE SCREAMING WOKE HIM, a sound filled with shock and piercing pain, so dreadful that Ryan felt the skin tighten protectively around his balls. He opened his eye, looking first at the luminous wrist chron. It was a few minutes before one in the morning. Outside the wickiup he could see that the fires must have been built up. There was the orange brightness of soaring flames and skipping shadows moving past.

"Gaia!" Krysty exclaimed, sitting up. "What's going down?"

"Sounds like some chilling," J.B. said from behind the fragile partition of the faded blanket.

The scream was repeated, rising and rising, higher than seemed possible for any human voice. It scraped at the nerves of the listeners, stretching on and on.

"Upon my soul!" Doc whispered from the far end of the hut. "Some poor devil is in direst torment."

"Torture," Lori said, appearing by the door fully dressed. "Heard it starting and getting up to see what is gone on. The sec men."

Jak was last to rise, struggling with the greatest difficulty to pull on his camouflage jacket. "Who's...?" he began.

"Lori's right." Ryan tugged on his high, steel-capped combat boots and picked up the G-12 from the side of the bed. "You never forget a sound like that one."

THE WHOLE OF THE MESCALERO tribe was there, surrounding the banked fires. The walls of the canyon seemed to glow with the vivid colors of red and deep yellow, highlighting the flaws and faults in the rocks.

Above the lingering tastes of the evening's meal, they could all catch the elusive, unforgettable smell of burned flesh.

Jak was at Ryan's elbow as they walked down the gentle slope, past the area of blackened grass where the oil had been torched. "You going t' talk Cuchillo?"

"I don't know, Jak. You think it's a good idea taking them both along?"

"Think love her, Ryan."

"Mebbe, son, mebbe. Talk a little later. Let's find out what's..."

The words trailed away as the crowd opened up to give the honored visitors a good view of the people's celebration of their victory.

Cuchillo Oro had his golden knife in his hand, and he waved it above his head to welcome them. "Come, brothers and sisters. Join us in honoring our enemies. Come, son-to-be." He beckoned Jak to sit by him, next to Steps Lightly Moon.

Krysty grabbed Ryan by the arm. "Leave it, lover. Come back to the hut."

"Listen to her, One Eye Chills," said the tall shaman, a towering shadow a little to their right, away from the fires.

"No. Got to see. It might help make a decision on something."

The dazzling light of the fires and the movement of the crowd still obscured the center of the attention. The screaming hadn't come again, but there was a constant, muffled moaning and gurgling sound.

Doc was hesitating, with Lori on his arm. Ryan turned to the old man. "Take Lori and Krysty back to the wickiup, Doc. No reason for 'em to see this."

There was a nod of agreement and Doc led the two girls away from the fire, back into the shadows beneath the cliffs. Ryan, with Jak and J.B., stepped forward to join the Mescalero.

Cuchillo stood and embraced them all, hugging them and clapping them on the shoulders. Ryan could easily catch the rancid taste of stale alcohol on the chief's breath. There was a ragged cheer from the watching men and women.

"Our Anglo brothers honor us. As token of my love for them I give the golden knife of my great forefather, Cuchillo Oro, to Eyes of Wolf, that he may carry it all his days with us in honor."

"He'll ask for it back in the morning, when's he's sobered up," Man Whose Eyes See More whispered in Ryan's ear.

The albino hesitated, then reached out and took the beautiful, antique cinqueda, clasping his long pale fingers around the jewel-studded hilt, feeling the fine balance of the blade. He nodded his thanks to the chief.

Cuchillo laughed loudly, clapping his hands. "Carry on, my people." He turned to Ryan. "Come, One Eye Chills, and see how the enemies of the people come to pay their price. Two have already joined their spirits," Cuchillo continued, stumbling and spilling liquor from the earthenware jug in his hand. Ryan noticed that most of the tribe seemed to be thoroughly drunk. "The women were clumsy and did their work too fast. But the others will last longer."

What hung on the two farthest stakes bore little resemblance to human beings. Ryan could make out where the skulls were and where the limbs had been. But to the casual glance the corpses looked only like ragged carcasses of scorched meat, from some totally unidentifiable creatures.

Sergeant McLaglen was nearest to them, then came the last two of Cort Strasser's private cavalry. Each helpless man was surrounded by a dozen busy women, ranging in age from young girls to white-haired grandmothers; torturing was mainly women's work.

J.B. whistled softly through his teeth, speaking quietly to Ryan. "This fair turns my stomach. I'll be in the hut if you need me." He half turned, then came back, gripping Ryan's arm just above the elbow with fingers as tight as steel clamps. "Don't try to come between them on this. Look around. One wrong word and we're all dead. Or tied along those poor bastards. Let it be, Ryan. For tonight."

The Armorer spun on his heel and strode away from the fires. Some of the warriors jeered him, calling him a weak woman, but J.B. ignored them.

Ryan could feel that Jak was trembling. "Stay real careful, kid," he said, knowing that J.B.'s warning had been timely. Any attempt to interrupt the Apaches at their pleasure would probably result in their being instantly overwhelmed and butchered.

"Want go, Ryan," Jak said. "Throw up soon. This real bad. Worse than I've... Got to go."

The boy also swung around, darting quickly up the hill after the retreating figure of the little Armorer. The golden knife glittered in his belt. Steps Lightly Moon looked as if she wanted to go after him, but her father stopped her.

"Why do your friends leave?" he asked Ryan. "Do they wish to insult the people?"

"Of course not, Cuchillo Oro," Ryan replied. "They are very tired, and they do not wish to intrude on the sport of the people."

Breath stirred his ear and he barely caught the faint whisper of the shaman. "Wise answer, my brother. It keeps your heart within your body and your eyes in their sockets."

"But you will watch, One Eye Chills?"

"Of course, Cuchillo Oro. I am honored."

The chief laughed delightedly, patting his daughter on the cheek. "Go, Steps Lightly Moon. Show the old friend of your husband-to-be of your skill in giving honor to an enemy."

The girl giggled, dropping a hasty curtsy to her father and to Ryan. She drew a small flensing knife from her belt and ran to the nearest captive.

The next two hours passed for Ryan in a blur of revulsion.

The women had used the living flesh of the first sec man to demonstrate their skill at sewing and embroidering beads. As he had strained against the ropes, they had covered the skin of his chest, upper arms and thighs with intricate patterns, piercing his genitals hundreds of times with the small needles as they sewed on dozens of tiny colored plastic beads.

The trooper's tongue had been hacked off and his mouth filled with suffocating wads of cloth to muffle his screams. To stop him from trying to claw at the woman, they had simply cut off all his fingers and thumbs, cauterizing the bleeding stumps with burning twigs from the fire.

When one of them completed a particularly attractive piece of sewing all of the women would stop and praise it, giggling with delight. One of the older women kept rubbing her hands over the beads, tugging at them, causing the wretched prisoner the most exquisite agony.

Once there was no more flesh uncovered, Cuchillo Oro gave them his permission to kill the man. Ryan watched, face set like granite, as Steps Lightly Moon begged for the honor. Her father smiled benevolently.

She began to dance in front of the man, caressing her breasts through her dress, lifting it to show him her smooth, bronzed thighs, touching herself and smiling as she moved closer to him. Ryan fought to steady his own breathing as he saw the sec man, despite the horror of his own situation, begin to show visible signs of arousal. The pain as the sewn threads tightened was beyond imagination.

Steps Lightly Moon laughed out loud, the rest of the watching women cackling with her, mocking the doomed man. The girl drew her little knife again, lifting her hand to touch it to the wide, staring eyes of the cavalryman. She called to two of the women to come and hold his head steady while she probed with the point of the knife, lifting both eyes from their sockets. Ryan thought of the whispered warning of the shaman, feeling his gorge rising at the way the Apaches were taking such gloating pleasure in the destruction of a human being. Whatever the cause, it was too much.

Ryan felt the arm of Cuchillo Oro sprawl across his shoulders, and he barely won the battle not to pull away in revulsion.

"I would have made their suffering longer, my friend. Perhaps we keep the three-stripe man for that. We blind him and cut out his tongue. Cut off his ears and nose. Hack away his balls and cock but take care to stop him bleeding to death. Hamstring him by cutting tendons at knees and elbows. Then everyone in the tribe can use him for what they wish. He can be beast to carry and be whipped. Or target for children's arrows. We can use him for seat or for... for many other things. He can live for our laughter for many moons if we care for him."

Cuchillo's voice was drunkenly loud, and Ryan saw that Sergeant McLaglen had heard him. The noncom's body streamed with drying blood from dozens of small cuts, but apart from that he wasn't harmed. He wasn't even gagged. His eyes met Ryan's eye, filled with a mute appeal.

Ryan looked away.

Steps Lightly Moon had just won the praise of her father for finally killing the sec man she had been torturing. She had taken a barbed hunting arrow, inserting it, to the helpless sniggers of the women, between the trooper's spread thighs. She pushed it an inch or so higher, then twisted it and pulled it out. The man wrenched so hard at the ropes that for a moment it seemed he would break free. But the girl was quicker than the rest, ramming the long arrow its length into the man, clear to the flights. The white man shuddered once and died.

After innumerable humiliating and painful tortures, the second sec man was given a rapid and spectacular passing. The women made dozens upon dozens of narrow cuts, all over his body, each one sliced down to form a tiny pocket. From his forehead, over his cheeks and neck, across his chest and stomach, around his penis and buttocks, all the way to his ankles. Then, each cut was carefully filled with coarse grains of black powder from old rifle cartridges.

A wizened woman took a burning branch from the fire and handed it to Cuchillo Oro, who nearly dropped it. Recovering, he offered the torch to Ryan. "Send him to his maker below the earth, my brother."

"No thanks, Cuchillo Oro. You won the victory. You chill him."

It had been a close call, straining Ryan's buried vein of uncontrollable rage. For a moment his hand had reached for the torch, wanting to thrust it into the chief's face.

The Mescalero stood up, staggering a little, waving the torch to and fro to make it burn more brightly. He approached the bound man, who slumped in the ropes. The suffering and the terror had caused the sec man to lose control of both his bowels and his bladder.

"Nearly done, Harry, me bucko!" McLaglen yelled, struggling to turn his head.

The flaming branch was passed quickly across the surface of the trooper's body, igniting the pockets of black powder. Every inch of flesh exploded in glowing fire, the night filling with the overpowering stench of cordite and roasted meat. Blackened and smoking, the body of the sec man jerked convulsively, before it stopped and finally remained still.

There was a wave of cheering from the Indians, and Cuchillo passed a mug of fiery liquor to Ryan, urging him to drink. Fighting the desire to vomit, Ryan drained three mouthfuls, feeling the alcohol burn its way down his throat into his stomach.

"Now we drink more," Cuchillo shouted, holding out the mug for one of the women to refill.

"I'm gut-weary, Chief," Ryan said, standing up. "Gotta hit the bed."

"Sure, sure you have. Last of the pony soldiers'll be there tomorrow for some more laughing and all...and all that. Sleep well, my brother."

"Yeah, and you," Ryan muttered, picking his way between the Mescalero toward the wickiup. As he neared it he was suddenly aware of the shaman again at his elbow.

"You did well. There are times when it is harder to sit still than to stand and fight."

Ryan paused, looking up at the serious face of the wise man, trying to see the eyes behind the glasses. "Yeah. Wouldn't have saved those poor sons of bitches. And it'd have done for all of us."

"Yes. It is as well you seek to know that this has always been their way. Always the Apache has suffered at the hands of the others. Cruelty breeds cruelty, One Eye Chills."

"The name is Ryan Cawdor, and don't forget it. I know you speak the truth, Man Whose Eyes See More. But that sure as hell doesn't make me like it any more."

"No. May your night be good, my brother."

"Sure." He turned toward the shadowy entrance of the wickiup.

"Ryan."

"What?"

"I see your heart. Take care and move early and fast."

Ryan nodded slowly, trying to mask his surprise. "I'll do that. We won't meet again, my brother. I thank you for everything."

The shaman didn't reply, staring at Ryan for a moment, then moving silently down the hill. The last Ryan saw of him was the distant gleam of the torture fires reflected off the mirrored glasses.

Chapter Thirty-Four

THE DAWN WIND DROVE thin gray skeins of smoke around the bowl of the canyon from the embers of the cooking and torture fires of the long night. The canvas flap across the front of one of the wickiups fluttered, where it hadn't been properly laced shut by one of the drunken occupants.

Ryan led his five friends down the slope from their hut, toward the five stark torture stakes. Four of the five carried a corpse. The fifth one had the naked body of Sergeant Sean McLaglen tied tightly to it. His head was sunk on his chest, and the whole of his torso was covered with black threads of blood. Since Ryan had seen him, someone had smashed both of the sec man's knees, so that they were swollen and bloody, with sharp bone showing whitely through. A heavy picket iron had also been hammered into the wood, through the soft skin of McLaglen's genitals.

"He's gone," J.B. said.

"No, I think not. See. His chest is still rising and falling." Doc looked around in disgust. "By the three Kennedys, but the Lord Almighty should send a murrain upon this place. They are as bad as Strasser and his brood."

Though the old man kept his voice quiet, it was enough to drag the noncom back into a sort of consciousness. His mouth was filled with a crude hemp gag, but the eyes flickered open, turning to where Ryan and the other five stood, looking at him. They carried their blasters with them, as well as canteens of water and some dried food.

Krysty squeezed Ryan's hand. "You can't leave him, lover. You can't."

"Can't take with us," Jak whispered, face set like alabaster.

"It's true," Ryan agreed. "Not with his legs broke like that. And the man's near done."

"You said they threatened to keep him alive for weeks. Last night, when you told us all that happened here. You said what Cuchillo boasted they could do to their prisoner."

"Yeah, I know, Krysty. I know."

"Make a noise and we wake the camp. Only their drinking last night gives us a chance," J.B. said. "Fire a blaster and we're all chilled meat."

McLaglen was moving his head slowly from side to side, listening to their quiet words, blinking his eyes as if he were trying to send a message to Ryan.

"Take his gag out, Jak."

"But, Ryan, he'd killed us if he could," Lori protested.

"Do it, Jak," Ryan ordered. "Time's wasting. Just do it."

Fresh blood gushed out, following the removal of the tight coil of rope. The noncom breathed, deep and slow, several times, the sound rattling harshly in his chest. His mouth opened and closed, struggling for a faint, croaking word.

"What's he say?" Lori whispered.

"Water," Doc replied. "Poor wretch's asking for water."

Ryan uncorked his own canteen, holding it carefully to the man's bruised lips, watching him slurp a couple of mouthfuls.

"No more, Ryan," McLaglen wheezed. "Sure an' it'd be a terrible waste, seeing as how I'm done for."

"Can't take you."

"Wouldn't... Oh, that nail in me balls is... Wouldn't want you to, Ryan, my bucko. But you could do me the one favor, if you've a mind, that is."

"Have to be a knife," Ryan said quietly.

"Think that worries me?" McLaglen asked, managing a crooked, wry grin. "Just do it now. And me thanks to you. Do it, Ryan."

The hilt of the long panga was cool to Ryan's fingers as he drew it from the sheath. The light in the bottom of the canyon was growing stronger, and he knew that time wasn't on their side if they were to get away safely.

He didn't waste words on the stricken man, knowing that he had probably earned his chilling. But no man deserved the kind of chilling handed out by the women of the Mescalero.

The steel thunked into the side of McLaglen's throat, opening the big artery beneath the ear, releasing a gushing flood of bright blood that patterned and vanished into the dust. Ryan had deliberately tried to pull the blow, not wanting to sever McLaglen's head from his body, but the edge was keen and it jarred into the thoracic vertebrae. The man's mouth opened once more, and it looked as if he were trying to say something. But there was no sound, and in less than thirty seconds he was dead.

Ryan stooped and cleaned the blade in the warm ashes of one of the fires, wiping it on the earth. He resheathed it and turned to face his friends.

"That's the ending. Let's get the horses and quit this place."

But it wasn't quite the ending.

Nobody was stirring in the rancheria as they untied five animals from the picket line, not bothering to saddle them. They contented themselves with a rope bridle and a blanket thrown over each pony's back.

Ryan began to lead them between the wickiups, but stopped at a quiet word from Jak.

"What is it?"

"Something got to do. Something got I don't want keep."

"What?" Ryan asked, seeing the albino reach and draw something from the back of his belt, something that gleamed richly in the roseate light of the full dawn. "Ah, the gold knife."

"Don't want it," the boy insisted, seeing that Ryan was thinking of arguing with him. "Not now. Not ever."

Jak handed his bridle to J.B., taking the few steps that brought him to the edge of the deep pool beneath the sky-scraping cliffs. He held the cinqueda by the rough, gem-studded hilt, weighing it in his hand for a moment.

"Hell of a waste," the Armorer breathed.

"Man's got to do what a man's got to do," Doc said. "There are some things that a man can't ride around."

"Pearls of wisdom, Doc." Krysty smiled.

But all of them were watching Jak. He threw the knife, underhand, pitching it high into the air. For several beats of the heart the golden dagger seemed to hang suspended in the air, catching the sharp rays of the morning sun before it toppled down, plummeting into the lake with only the barest sound. The ripples had vanished before they reached the shore.

"Now we can go," Jak said.

As they passed the last of the wickiups, a tiny naked boy came toddling out, blinking and rubbing his eyes, staring up at the Anglos as they walked past him. Krysty stopped and blew him a kiss. He gave them a bubbling, shy smile and pattered back into the hut.

The companions had no more alarms, passing through the narrow jaws of the canyon. They skirted the pile of draggled corpses of the slaughtered sec men, disturbing some coyotes that were tearing at the bodies.

Now it was safe to mount their horses and begin the journey to the hidden redoubt and the gateway that would transport them from the baking deserts of New Mexico.

THERE WAS NO PURSUIT. When they eventually began the long climb toward the ruined blacktop and the concealed fortress, there was no giveaway column of dust to reveal vengeful Apaches on their trail.

The sun was high in a clear, cloudless sky, and the air was filled again with the mixed scents of sagebrush and mesquite. Across the far side of the valley, a half mile or more away, a bird of prey rose suddenly into the air, winging upward, as if something had disturbed it.

The contours of the winding road kept them out of sight of the plateau for most of the time, but they eventually emerged in front of the main gates into the redoubt. Ryan paused, slipping from the back of his horse, slapping it on the flanks and letting it go free. The others followed suit, stretching after the ride. Ryan made his way to the edge of the drop and looked out across the limitless expanse of the desert. At his lapel the tiny rad counter was beginning to cheep its warning to him, the counter well past the orange, shading into the red.

The eagle on the far side of the valley came floating toward where Ryan guessed it had a nest. But once again it veered sharply away, as if frightened by something. Or someone.

Ryan's one good eye was as sharp as that of any normal man, and it caught the glint of light on the cliffs opposite.

"Down! Now!" he yelled, grabbing Krysty by the wrist and tugging her to the rocky earth outside the redoubt.

The snap of the bullet smashed against the stone wall, kicking splinters over the group as they flattened themselves behind the cover. The boom of the blaster came a second or so later, the sound echoing from cliff to cliff, back and forth across the valley.

J.B. articulated what Ryan had already guessed. "Russian rifle. Recognize that noise."

"Samozaridnyia Vintovka Dragunova," Ryan said. "Course. That murderous son of a bitch Strasser got here first."

"He can't get in the redoubt," Krysty offered. "Once we get inside the gates we're safe. And they're covered from him by that outcrop."

It was true, Ryan realized, glancing behind them. Strasser hadn't wasted another shot from his sniper's rifle. He must have seen by now that he'd missed his one and only chance of killing Ryan. If they kept low they could get inside the redoubt without ever coming under his fire again.

They all crawled slowly to the doors, finally being able to stand while the entry code was punched in. Lori went inside first, followed by Krysty, then Doc and Jak. J.B. hesitated, waiting for Ryan.

"Coming?"

"Sure. Just wishing that I'd been able to chill that triple-crazy butcher."

"That was yesterday. There's plenty of tomorrows to come."

They both heard the voice, faint, carried to them on the light breeze. It was calling Ryan's name, over and over.

"Let's go in," J.B. urged. "Ignore him, Ryan. Come on."

"Yeah, you're right," he agreed. As he went inside the vast mausoleum of the redoubt the last sound he heard before the doors closed was Cort Strasser shouting his name. Again and again. The words merging until it became a single crazed howl of end-less red-eyed hatred.

They moved quickly through the hot spot that the redoubt had become, retracing their steps until they reached the door that led through to the main mat-trans chamber. Jak was in the lead and pushed at the handle.

The opening door revealed the gaping muzzle of a .50-caliber Sharps buffalo rifle, pointing in their direction.

"Greetings," said Man Whose Eyes See More.

Epilogue

THE SHAMAN WAS WEARING the same clothes that he'd been sporting when they first met him: the waistcoat of flowered brocade with the soft gleam of mother-of-pearl on the buttons; a striped shirt and a cravat of a brilliant scarlet that rivaled Krysty's hair; the silver claw stickpin with the jewel missing. The kerchief in the pocket of the vest was a pale cherry-red. The pants were frayed seersucker with one leg missing. His feet were bare and dusty.

The mirrored glasses reflected their faces, staring at the vastly tall shaman.

"How did ... ?" Ryan began.

"If you do not believe, then there is nothing I could say to you. If you do believe in the wisdom of other realities, then you would not need an explanation. I knew. I knew last night. I told you, Ryan, did I not?"

"Yeah. You did. And now you want to come with us?"

Man Whose Eyes See More smiled.

THE ARMORED GLASS WALLS of the gateway chamber were a vivid golden yellow. The group of friends ranged themselves around the floor, avoiding the metal disks.

Ryan stood by the main door control, ready to send them speeding on their next journey. He noticed that Jak looked tired and depressed, but there was nothing he could say to cheer him. Only time would do that.

"Ready?"

Krysty was sitting next to the shaman, who had drawn up his angular knees and rested his chin on them. She shuffled uncomfortably and reached behind her. She took something out of the back pocket of her pants and held it out to Man Whose Eyes See More.

It was the tiny, polished black stone that she'd found in the ghost town. Apache tears.

Ryan closed the gateway door.

Out of the ruins of civilization emerges...

DEATHLANDS

PILGRIMAGE TO HELL became a
harrowing journey high in the mountains. $3.95

RED HOLOCAUST brought the survivors
to the freakish wasteland in Alaska. $2.95

NEUTRON SOLSTICE followed the group
through the reeking swampland that was
once the Mississippi Basin. $2.95

CRATER LAKE introduces the survivors
to a crazed world more terrifying than their
own. $2.95

The DEATHLANDS saga—edge-of-the-seat
adventure not to be missed!

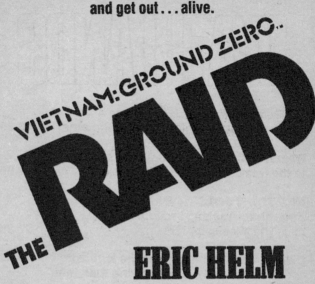

Mack Bolan's

by Dick Stivers

Action writhes in the reader's own streets
as Able Team's Carl "Ironman" Lyons,
Pol Blancanales and Gadgets Schwarz
make triple trouble in blazing war. Join
Dick Stivers's Able Team as it returns to
the United States to become the country's
finest tactical neutralization squad in an
era of urban terror and unbridled crime.

Able Team titles are available
wherever paperbacks are sold.

**GOLD
EAGLE**

AT-1

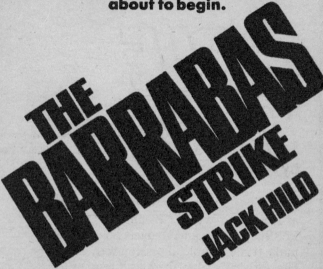